Children Around The World

The Multicultural Journey

By Jane Caballero-Hodges, Ph.D.

HUMANICS LEARNING
P.O.Box 7400
ATLANTA, GEORGIA 30357

1994 Revision by Susan Chamberlain
Illustration by Susan Chamberlain and Masako Masukawa

LIBRARY OF CONGRESS CATALOGING-IN-PUBLICATION DATA

Hodges-Caballero, Jane.
    Children around the world the multicultural journey/Jane Caballero,--Rev. ed.
      p.cm.
    Rev. ed. of : Chidlren around the world today. c 1983
    Discography ; p.
    Includes bibliographical references.
    Summary : Introduces various cultures and people from around the world
with native recipes, music, games, and activities.
ISBN 0-89334-033-2
    1. Manners and customs--Juvenile literature. 2. Intercultural education--Activity
programs.
(1. Manners and customs. 2. Cookery. 3. Handicraft.) I. Hodges-Caballero. Jane.
Children around the world. II. Title.
GT85.H63   1990
390--dc20

Contents

Foreword

Many of the attitudes children form about the peoples of other nations stay with them for life. It is important for parents and teachers to help children build positive attitudes toward those who live in other parts of the world.

Children Around the World has provided rich resources for broadening children's knowledge of people in many different countries: people who are like themselves in many ways, yet with differences that make the kaleidoscope of world cultures interesting.

The games, songs, dances, recipes, and other activities in this book will help children to see that children all over the world enjoy many of the same things. They have the same human emotions. Yet there are differences due to geography, religion, government, tradition, and other factors which should be appreciated and understood. The most important thing children can learn, however, is that no matter where people live, they have much in common with humanity as a whole and their destinies are linked with those of their fellow human beings. When we help dispel stereotyping and prejudices, as this book does, we help children discover that they have friends all over the world.

Alma W. David, Ed.D.
Professor Emeritus,
University of Miami
Coral Gables, Florida

Introduction

The understanding of a country or region requires not only a knowledge of the geographical location and size of a country but also an awareness of its cultural history, its economic condition and its relationship to other countries. A basic philosophy of this book is the belief that knowledge leads to an understanding and appreciation of each country and to respect for uniqueness in individuals. An equally important philosophy is the belief that no child is too young to begin to learn and appreciate the beauty and diversity of his world given the opportunity.

Each country has its own personality. That personality is reflected in the country's language, history, geography, dance, song, and foods. A child is deprived of a significant part of education if he is denied the opportunity to obtain knowledge and appreciation of other countries and cultures. This book is designed to aid the teacher in providing a multi-cultural approach to education.

With respect to each country, the format consists of background information, an activity page, a map to be used to locate and identify points of interest, and a flag which can be colored. The format for each country may also include a dance or song. Dances and songs are an integral part of the heritage of the countries. By learning a dance or song, the children actively participate in the learning process, enabling them to relate more fully to the people within that country that they are studying. For most countries we have also included a brief section that describes some popular foods and a few simple recipes which may be prepared in the classroom or at home. Ethnic personality is reflected in a country's food. Since children enjoy cooking and eating, exposing them to different foods is an effective way to enrich their overall understanding of a particular country.

The alphabets of many languages are made up of letters different from the English alphabet. We have included a few of these alphabets to highlight the differences among cultures. A simple vocabulary list has been included for each country to expose children to the existence of languages other than English.

In the primary curriculum, much of the school day is dedicated to reading and math. Social studies should not be neglected, however. Furthermore, math, reading, and language experiences can be integrated into this social studies curriculum. The cooking experiences involve science, measurement and creative verbal expression. In addition, discussing the history, geography, music, and recipes of each country will help enhance the child's vocabulary.

The political, cultural, and social conditions of the world change continuously, sometimes from day to day or even hour to hour. When using the chapters in this book, the good teacher will take advantage of current materials, including television news and magazines to get current coverage on world-wide cultural and political issues. Using outside resources with the latest information will make your students aware of the importance of getting to know all of our global neighbors.

Sample Lesson

LESSON ONE – 30-45 MINUTES

OBJECTIVES
1. The students will participate in a class discussion about Mexico.
2. Each student will locate three regions in Mexico on a tear sheet.
3. Each student will color the flag of Mexico.

LEARNING STRATEGIES
1. The teacher becomes familiar with the narrative about Mexico and lists specific information that seems relevant to the children for discussion. Also before the lesson begins, copies of the map and flag should be made for each child.
2. With the use of a large map of Mexico and a globe, the teacher and students will locate together their home state and then Mexico, so they can get an idea of where Mexico is in relation to where they are.
3. A class discussion follows. The teacher, noting the list of specific information, asks leading questions that encourage children to arrive at the appropriate answers. The following types of questions are given as examples.
    1. Let's look at the map. There is water on both sides of Mexico. What are the names of these bodies of water?
    A. The Pacific Ocean and the Gulf of Mexico.
    2. What countries touch Mexico on the map?
    A. The United States and Guatemala.
    3. Who were the original people living in Mexico before Columbus discovered the "New World?".....
  A. Indians
    4. Mexicans speak Spanish today. Why do you think this is?
    A. People from Spain conquered the Indians and brought their own language with them.

4. Print out sheets of the map and flag are passed out. The teacher will show the students a colored flag of Mexico. They discuss the flag, the Mexican terrain and the three numbered places on the map. They write in the answers and color the flag. As the children work, the teacher will observe and help individual students.
5. A Mexico Center will be set up on a table. Children are asked to contribute to the table any Mexican items that they have at home. (These will be returned when the unit is completed.)
6. Any parents who have a Mexican background are urged to participate in the activities – singing, playing an instrument, teaching a dance, cooking, etc. Item such as a serape, a sombrero, dolls, records, books, pictures by Mexican artists, etc. may be used on the table.
7. Teacher writes vocabulary words on the chalkboard for students to copy.
8. Students work will be placed on a Mexican bulletin board.

EVALUATION
Teacher notes the quality of participation in the discussion and in the other activities.

LESSON TWO – 30-45 MINUTES
Prior to this day, be sure that parents have been given a note requesting that each child be given permission to sample the foods and requesting a small donation to cover costs.

OBJECTIVES
1. The student will make tacos and taste tortillas, enchiladas, refried beans, and/or Spanish rice.

LEARNING STRATEGIES
1. The teacher will tell about Mexican family life and the foods of Mexico.
2. The children will get the chance to eat tacos and tortillas.
3. The children will participate in making tacos.

EVALUATION
Each child gets the chance to taste a tortilla and help make the tacos.

Sample Lesson

LESSON THREE – 30-45 MINUTES

OBJECTIVES

1. The children will listen to a Mexican song, "The Mexican Hat Dance".
2. All the children will play the Mexican game, dancing around the sombrero.
3. The children will make a serape with butcher paper and paints.

LEARNING STRATEGIES

1. The children listen to the song.
2. The teacher observes the students dancing.
3. The children complete their serape.

NUMEROUS ACTIVITIES CAN BE INCORPORATED INTO VARIOUS LESSON PLANS. BELOW ARE A FEW EXAMPLES.

- Have the Greek Olympics. Play foreign games such as:
  a. *Japanese tag* (played similar to our tag except the player must hold the spot where he/her was tagged)
  b. *Chinese jacks* (the jacks are 4" pieces of cloth filled with rice and tied)
  c. *Israeli klass* (game like hopscotch except the marker is pushed with a toe while the player hops)
  d. *Mexican bola* (a 1' stick with a paper cup tacked to one end a 15" string with a ball attached tied to the top. Try to make the ball land in the cup.)
- Prepare the recipes contained in each unit at home with the family or at school.
- Develop language notebooks with the numbers, vocabulary, and derivations of words presented in each chapter.
- Locate folk stories and folk songs from each country.
- Make masks with paper mache, tin foil, or construction paper when studying the culture of Mexico, Africa, Indians, and China.
- Play records or tapes of songs from each country. Try to identify what country the music is from and what instruments are used. (See Bibliography for listings of international songs.)
- Study some of the illustrations of various ethnic groups. Then draw your own ethnic costumes and cut them out for paper doll outfits.
- Discover and study the heroes of the different countries. For example: Martin Luther King, Jr., Sun Yat Sin, Pancho Villa.
- Study the art of each country. Visit museums. Make the art projects presented in each unit and have an art show. For example: Japanese origami and fans, Mexican pottery, Indian batik, American Indian basket weaving, pottery and rug weaving, African wood carving, and Polish paper cuts.
- Talk with natives of the country and have them visit the class and share their ways of life.
- Learn Native American sign language.
- Learn modern day (hearing impaired) sign language (just one or two, of course).
- Collect art/craft materials from the outdoors and make an art project (Faux artifacts, no weapons!). Include acorns, bark, sticks, leaves, rocks, pine needles, sea shells, etc.
- String or glue colored beads into wearable art.
- Name the states with Native American names.

North America

Arctic Ocean

Labrador Sea

2.

4.

5.

3.

Atlantic Ocean

1.

Pacific Ocean

IDENTIFY

1. _____
2. _____
3. _____
4. _____
5. _____

United States

THE UNITED STATES OF AMERICA

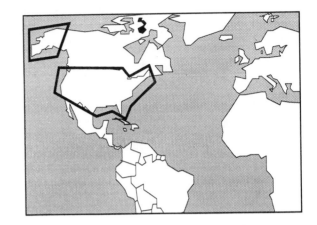

Nicknamed the Star Spangled Banner, the U.S. flag, has 13 red and white stripes for the original 13 colonies. The 50 white stars on the blue background represent each state. The Stars and Stripes is thought to have been originally designed by Betsy Ross.

United States

The United States of America is located in central North America. The bordering countries are Mexico to the south, and Canada to the north. The capital of the United States is **WASHINGTON, D.C.** The population of the U.S. is 247,100,000. The territory of the United States extends to include Hawaii and Alaska. Secondary or outlying territories held by the United States include Puerto Rico, the U.S. Virgin Islands, Guam, American Samoa, the Midway Islands and the Marshall Islands. The people of these islands are United States citizens.

LAND

The country is 3,620,000 square miles. The U.S. can be divided into eight regions.

1. *Northeastern States* are Connecticut, Maine, Massachusetts, New Hampshire, New Jersey, New York, Pennsylvania, Rhode Island, and Vermont.

2. *Southern State*s are Alabama, Arkansas, Delaware, Florida, Georgia, Kentucky, Louisiana, Maryland, Mississippi, New North Carolina, South Carolina, Tennessee, and Virginia. The Mississippi River flows through some of this area.

3. *Midwestern States* are Illinois, Indiana, Iowa, Kansas, Michigan, Minnesota, Missouri, Nebraska, North Dakota, Ohio, South Dakota, and Wisconsin. This area is basically flat, fertile ground. Also included in this area are the five Great Lakes, which contain the largest body of freshwater in the world.

4. *Rocky Mountain States* are Colorado, Idaho, Montana, Nevada, Utah, and Wyoming. The Rocky Mountains cut through this region.

5. *Southwestern States* are Arizona, New Mexico, Oklahoma, and Texas. The area is desert region. The Grand Canyon is located in this region.

6. *Pacific Coast States* are California, Oregon, and Washington. The states are located on the Pacific Ocean.

7. *Alaska* which is separated from the United States by Canada and is over 500 miles from the U.S/Canada. Mount McKinley is the highest peak in the United States.

8. *Hawaii* is located in the Pacific Ocean, over 2000 miles from the U.S. mainland. Hawaii consists over 132 islands, many volcanic.

CULTURE

The Northeast was settled by the English Puritans when the Mayflower sailed into Plymouth in 1620. With the help of the local native Americans, the Pilgrims established the Massachusetts Bay Colony, drafted their own set of laws and began their lives in the "New World". The natives taught them to hunt, fish, and farm. The first Thanksgiving was a celebration feast by the Pilgrims with their native American guests, to give thanks for the blessings they had received.

The southern region has a troubled past. The Civil War was fought between the North and the South. In Alabama, **MARTIN LUTHER KING, JR.** preached for racial equality during the early 1960s. The Southwest is where many native Americans live. **GEORGIA O'KEEFE** is a famous artist of the region, who painted bones, cacti, and the landscape. The Southwest has a recognizable regional style found in its art and food, in keeping with the land and climate.

The Pacific coast is where the gold rush of the mid-1800s was located. California, which has the greatest population, has long been known as the entertainment capital because of Hollywood.

Alaska is where native peoples called Eskimos live. Many of the Eskimos live as their ancestors did, hunting and fishing for food, and using animal skins, and furs for clothes. A parka made from whale-intestine was essential for the early Eskimo hunter. The Eskimo lifestyle revolves around the family. Babies are treated well because the Eskimos believe that the souls of their ancestors return to the world in the form of infants. Eskimo children engage in such

activities as piggyback races, and the blanket toss, which is similar to a trampoline. When Eskimos kiss, they don't use their lips – they rub their noses together.

Hawaii was the last state to join the Union in 1959. In ancient times, Hawaiians played darts, guessing games, and a bowling game using large round stones. Surfing is a popular sport.

American children attend school from age seven to age 18. The literacy rate in the United States is high, but work is being done to increase literacy to a higher percentage.

RESOURCES

The United States has an abundance of resources. In Alaska, oil, jade, and gold are produced. In Hawaii, sugarcane and pineapple are major crops. In the southern states, the major crop is cotton. The midwest produces a high amount of dairy products and grain. Along the Atlantic coast, fishing is a major industry. In the Pacific Northwest, logging is important to the economy.

RECIPES

The U.S. is called the "melting pot of the world" and our foods certainly show that idea.

*Texas Chili Con Carne*****

1 1/2 tablespoons salad oil
1 onion, chopped
1 tablespoon chili powder
2 cloves garlic, cut fine
1 pound lean ground beef, cut into 1/4" cubes
1 tablespoon flour
1/2 cup canned tomatoes, chopped
1 cup canned kidney beans, rinsed and drained
1/4 teaspoon salt
2 cups cheddar cheese, cut into 1/2" cubes

Heat the oil in a saucepan. Add the onion, chili powder, garlic, and beef. Cook over high heat, stirring constantly until meat is browned. Turn to low heat, add the flour, stir until well-blended. Add the tomatoes, cover and cook for 1 hour. Add the beans and salt to the meat mixture. Cover and cook for 20 minutes. Top with cheddar cheese. Tastes even better on the second day.

*Southern Corn Pudding*****

1 can (2 cups) cream-style corn
2 1/2 tablespoons sugar
1 egg, beaten
2 tablespoons milk
1 tablespoon flour and butter
1/4 teaspoon nutmeg
pinch of salt

Combine all ingredients in a deep bowl and. mix well. Pour into a greased baking dish. Sprinkle with flour. Bake in a 350-degree oven for 30 minutes or until the pudding is set and the top is browned.

ACTIVITIES

ACROSS

1. Came from England to settle in "New World".
2. State where Hollywood is located.
3. The Stars and _____.
4. Horseman Paul _____ who warned "The British are coming!"
5. Home of the _____.
6. Vegetable presented by the Native Americans at the feast.

DOWN

1. Fruit from Hawaii.
2. Ship the first Americans arrived in.
3. The first feast.
5. Star Spangled _____.

ACROSS 1. Pilgrims 2. California 3. Stripes 4. Revere 5. Brave 6. Corn
DOWN 1. Pineapple 2. Mayflower 3. Thanksgiving 5. Banner

Native Americans

THE NATIVE POPULATION

When Christopher Columbus landed in the Caribbean islands, he called the natives indians, believing he had landed in the East Indies. Many millions of humans in over 2,000 cultures were thus lumped together into one classification.

Pre-Columbus population estimates have ranged from a low of 8.4 million to a high of perhaps 12 million. New diseases such as smallpox, measles, diphtheria, whooping cough, and influenza introduced into America through contact with newcomers may have been responsible for over 80 million deaths.

LANGUAGE

Many hundreds of separate languages were spoken by native Americans before Columbus' discovery. Today 500 or so of America's native languages are spoken. The Navajo represent the largest group north of Mexico to speak a native-American language. Missionaries and teachers have often contributed to making European languages dominant among Native American peoples. Before long, the number of Indian languages still being spoken is expected to further diminish.

NATIVE AMERICAN CONTRIBUTIONS TO WORLD CULTURE

Many of the foods and plants common in everyday life throughout the world, were originally cultivated by the native Americans. A few of the most common are maize, beans, potatoes, sweet potatoes, tomatoes, chili peppers, cacao, squash, and maple sugar. Other items which have made an impact on the world community are rubber, a new form of cotton, tobacco, toboggans, moccasins, and snowshoes. The use of plants for medicinal value can be traced to the native Americans as well.

HOUSING AND ARCHITECTURE

Native Americans had several different means of shelter, in relation to the land region in which they lived. In the plainlands, portable teepees, tents, or wigwams made of poles and bark were used in order to move about quickly for hunting. Pit houses or igloos (houses made of blocks of ice) were traditional dwellings in the Arctic and subarctic lands. In the hot Southwest, houses made of adobe (mud) were created because the adobe kept the inside of the house cool.

NATIVE CULTURE REGIONS

Arctic and Subarctic Hunters and Fishers

The **ESKIMO** and the **ALEUT** are two native American groups found in Canada and Alaska. Vast migrating herds of caribou were hunted, along with other game. Fish provided a largely protein diet.

Northwest-Coast Fishermen

The **HAIDI**, the **SPOKAN**, the **TLINGIT**, and the **YAKIMA** are groups found on the northwestern Pacific coast of Washington and Canada. This area formed a wonderful environment for fishing because of the salmon-spawning streams.

California Foragers

Nearly 200 independent dialects existed in the area which is now present-day California. Native American groups included the **CHUMASH**, the **COSTANO**, the **MAIDU**, the **MIWOK**, the **MODOC**, the **POMO**, the **SALINAN**, the **WINTUN**, the **YOKUT**, and the **YUKOK**. Groups included in the Mission Indians were the **CAHUILLA**, the **DIEGUENO**, the **GABRILENO**, the **LUISENO**, and the **SERRANO**.

Interior Hunters

The area known as the Plateau-Basin is the area of present-day Idaho, Oregon, and Nevada. Some of the native Americans in this group include the FLATHEAD, the KUTENAI, the NEZ PERCE, and the SHUSWAP. The region was wooded, well-watered, and full of game, fruits, and good fishing. Horses were introduced to the area in 1710, and many of the groups participated in the great bison hunts. The pioneers swarmed into the Indian lands bringing disease and bloody conflict. Little remains of the traditional way of life in this area.

Desert Hunters

The area southwest of the Interior Plateau is mountainous, dry uplands and basins. Major tribes in this area included the COMANCHE, the PAIUTE, the SHOSHONI, and the UTE. Nearly all these groups spoke Shoshonean languages. Small bands spread through the inhospitable land, taking their food from the land. Nicknamed later the "diggers" by the white settlers, their summer foods included pine nuts, berries, cactus fruits, roots, and seeds, and small game. Coyotes however, were not eaten because they were believed to be endowed with supernatural power. Winters were harsh and the threat of starvation was ever-present. During the pursuit of the bison herds in the middle 17th century, many of the Basin societies took to the Great Plains. In 1805, Lewis and Clark became the first white explorers to cross the Great Basin. White pioneers then poured into the Indian lands, destroying the Basin Indian culture.

Plains-Prairie Bison Hunters

The area between the Rocky Mountains and the Mississippi River and from southern Canada to the Gulf of Mexico is known as the Great Plains. Primarily wind-swept prairie land, the tribes who made use of the land include the ARAPAHO, the BLACKFOOT, the CHEYENNE, the CROW, the Manda, the Osage, the Pawnee, and the SIOUX.

Eastern Woodlands Farmers

In the area from the Mississippi River to the Atlantic Ocean and from southern Canada to the Gulf of Mexico flourished many Indian cultures. These groups survived on farming and hunting small game in the great forests of the area. An ancient cultural tradition with these people involved the construction of over 100,000 earth mounds. On top of the mounds were temples and villages. The Northeast was inhabited by two principal groups: Iroqoian speakers, including the CAYUGA, the ERIE, the HURON, the MOHAWK, the ONEIDA, the ONONDAGA, the SENECA, and the TUSCARORA; and Alonquian speakers, including the DELAWARE, the FOX, the ILLINOIS, the KICKAPOO, the MAHICAN, the MASASSACHUSET, the MENOMINEE, the MIAMI, the MOHEGAN, the OTTAWA, the PEQUOT, the SAUK, and the SHAWNEE. In the Southeast prominent groups included the ALABAMA, the CADDO, the CHEROKEE, the CHICKASAW, the CHOCTAW, the CREEK, the NATCHEZ, the QUAPAW, and the SEMINOLE.

Southwest Cultivators and Foragers

The Southwest area of Arizona, New Mexico, portions of Utah and Colorado, and northwest Mexico is made up of hot, arid mountainous land and basins. The Southwest was the homeland of both the hunting peoples including the APACHE, and of the farming peoples including the MOJAVE, the NAVAJO, the PUEBLO, the HOPI, the ZUNI, the YAQUI, and the YUMA. As village-dwelling cultivators they constructed multi-story apartment houses focused around subterranean religious rooms called kivas.

Central American Farmers

Present-day Guatemala, Belize, Honduras, and central Mexico (southeast to the Yucatan Peninsula) was the homeland for the Indian groups including the **MAYA**, the **AZTEC**, and the **ZAPOTEC**. These civilizations developed hieroglyphic writing, bark-paper books, and maps. Today the Maya and other groups constitute the largest Indian population of the Americas.

NATIVE AMERICANS AND THE U.S.

After the Revolutionary War, the U.S. Government continued the practice of treating the native Americans as sovereign nations. Between 1778 and 1871, a total of 389 treaties were signed and ratified. These treaties were broken in the late 18th and early 19th century as white settlers moved into Indian lands.

INDIANS IN THE 20TH CENTURY

In 1990, 1,959,234 North American Indians (including Eskimos and Aleut) lived in the United States. Most native Americans live west of the Mississippi River, especially in the states of Oklahoma, New Mexico, Arizona, South Dakota, and California.

Navajo

The Navajo, numbering about 80,000, is the largest tribe in the United States. Their reservations are predominantly located in New Mexico and Arizona. They were nomadic herders of sheep, known for the blankets and rugs they made from wool. This craft is still valued highly today within their culture. The geometric designs the Navajo use in their craft are so distinctive and well-established that they have acquired names. For coloring, they use numerous dyes in their blankets made from berries, roots, flowers, and bark.

Hopi

The Hopi Tribe, numbering about 6,500, is located in Arizona. They are best known for the Kachina Dolls. These painted wooden dolls represent masked dancers, who in turn represent kachinas. Kachinas are religious figures in the Hopi religion and are similar to the Christian saints. They serve as go-betweens for mortals and the more important deities. The dolls themselves are not idols and are not worshiped or prayed to. They are used in the religious training of the young people to teach them the characteristics and names of the more than two hundred kachinas which they will see during their lifetime. The children receive the dolls as gifts during kachina ceremonies. The Hopi men carve the dolls from the root of the cottonwood tree.

The Hopi also make beautiful wicker bowls and baskets. Hopi pottery is sold for decoration as well as for cooking. Hopi also work in silver. The silverwork was encouraged by the Museum of Northern Arizona because of the unique quality and artistry of style based on their pottery designs.

Miccosukee

The Miccosukee Indians have lived in the Everglades since before Florida was admitted to the Union. In 1962, the U.S. government officially recognized the Miccosukee Tribe. The Indians now have schools, a library, a police force, and Tribal officers. Miccosukees speak both their native language and English. Some

both their native language and English. Some favorite foods are fried bread and sofkie. Tradition is strong with the Miccosukee. For instance, they still use their traditional language, medicine, clan system, and rituals. Traditional patchwork designs are found on many of their handmade clothes.

Miccosukees live in villages, an example of a real family "camp". Many live in chickees, hut-type homes. In each village, sleeping and working chickees are arranged around the central cooking chickee and its symbolic star-shaped fire. The camp traditionally belonged to the clan matriarch.

RECIPES

Baked Fish

butter
fish fillet (whatever is in season)
lemon
dash of salt, pepper, and paprika
bread crumbs

Place the fillets in a baking dish. Sprinkle with salt, pepper, paprika, and lemon juice. Sprinkle the bread crumbs over the fish. Bake in the oven at 350-degrees for 30 minutes.

Fry Bread

2 cups self-rising flour
milk or water

Add enough milk or water to make a good consistency. Knead into dough. Pat a handful of dough flat. Fry in deep fat until light brown. Eat it plain or with butter and honey. You may want to dip it into hot chili.

Indian Pudding

5 cups milk
2/3 cup molasses
1/2 cup yellow corn meal
1/4 cup sugar
dash of cinnamon, nutmeg, allspice, ginger, and salt
2 teaspoons butter

Scald 4 cups milk. Stir in other ingredients. Cook over low heat about 10 minutes until the mixture thickens. Pour into 2-quart baking dish. Pour remaining milk on top and bake in 300-degree oven for 3 hours. Serve warm or chilled with milk.

FAMOUS NATIVE AMERICANS

Geronimo (1829-1909) – Leader of the Chiricahua Apaches, he conducted a series of raids against both Mexican and American settlements in the Southwest. Geronimo finally surrendered to General Nelson Miles in 1886.

Pocohontas (1595-1617) – The daughter of the Indian chief Powhatan. She reportedly saved the life of English explorer Captain John Smith in Virginia in 1608 and subsequently married another Englishman, John Rolfe.

Sequoya (1760-1843) – Cherokee warrior who is credited with the invention of the Cherokee written language, the so-called "talking leaves".

Sitting Bull (1831-1890) – Chief of the Hunkpapa Lakota (Sioux) tribe, led his people in the struggle against white encroachment on Sioux territory. He participated in the Battle of the Little Bighorn ("Custer's Last Stand") and in the Ghost Dance uprising.

Chief Joseph (1840-1904) – Nez Perce Indian chief responsible for the tribe's skillful retreat from pursuing U.S. Army troops during the Pez Nerce War (1877). Under his leadership, the small band successfully eluded and then withstood attacks from the army during a retreat of more than 1,000 miles from Oregon to Montana, where they were forced to surrender only 38 miles from the Canadian border.

VOCABULARY

Miccosukee
breakfast – *hampole empeeke*
lunch – *empekchoobe*
dinner – *oopyah-empeeke*
basket – *shanche*
beads – *naakaashe*
doll – *yaataabe*

Navajo
Hello – *Yaeh'te*
Are you hungry? – *Dichinish nilt?*
Do you want something? – *T'a'adoo le'e'sh ninizin?*
Do you understand me? – *Da' shidinits'a'a'sh?*

Indian Words Commonly Used
teepee	wigwam
raccoon	tomahawk
caribou	chipmunk

ACTIVITIES

God's Eye

popsicle sticks
or sticks from outside
colored yarn

The God's Eye is made with two crossed sticks and yarn. The yarn is wrapped around one stick and brought over to the next stick. The process is repeated until the sticks are almost completely covered.

ACTIVITIES

Hopi Indian Pottery

playdough, modeling clay, or ceramic clay

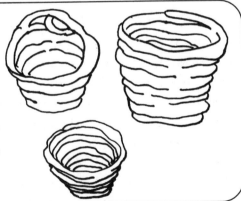

The Hopi of Arizona make beautiful wicker bowls and baskets. Hopi pottery is sold for decoration as well as for cooking. The coil pot is shown. Roll snake-like "ropes" of clay between your palms. Mount each rope or coil on top of one another to form the pots.

ACTIVITIES

The Native American Symbols Memory Game

Cut up 1 1/2" squares. On the following page is a gameboard. Cover up each square on the following page. Lift up one square at a time, trying to match the symbol pairs.

The Native American Symbols Memory Game

Mountain	Cactus Fruit	Corn	Flower
Friendship	Moon	Snake	Moon
Friendship	Turtle	Mountain	Turtle
Corn	Cactus Fruit	Snake	Flower

Mexico

Gulf of California

Sierra Madre Range

Sierra Madre Range

Gulf of Mexico

YUCATAN PENINSULA

★ MEXICO CITY

Pacific Ocean

UNITED STATES OF MEXICO

The green, white, and red stripes were introduced with the country's independence in 1821. The middle emblem of an eagle with a snake in his mouth is the Aztec founding legend.

Mexico

Mexico is the fifth largest country in land size within the Western Hemisphere. Mexico's neighbors to the north is the United States and to the south is Guatemala. Separated from the mainland of Mexico by the Gulf of California is the Baja California peninsula. The capital of Mexico is **MEXICO CITY**. The present name of Mexico was taken from the Mexica tribe, one of seven tribes inhabiting the central region of the land. Mexico gained independence from Spain in 1821.

After 1940, rapid industrial growth improved the living standards for much of the Mexican population. Through petroleum resources discovered in the 1970s and 1980s, new hope of increased economic growth has risen. With the signing of the North American Free Trade Agreement in 1993, a new era in Mexico has begun.

Mexican couple in traditional costume.

LAND

Mexico is 761,700 square miles. Mexico's land is very diverse. The country is dotted with mountains, rivers, and volcanoes. The highest point of Mexico is in the volcano **ORIZABA** at 18,855 feet. Volcanoes in the Transverse Volcanic Sierra extend east-west through the country. The **SIERRA MADRE** mountain range extends southward. The country of Mexico is located between the Gulf of Mexico and the Pacific Ocean. The land around the coastal areas, volcanoes, and rivers are fertile and productive.

CLIMATE

Due to the bodies of water that surround Mexico, Mexico's climate is hot and humid along the coastal areas. The climate turns much dryer towards the north.

CULTURE

Mexico's history is everchanging. For centuries, powerful empires flourished. The **OLMEC** developed the calendar and hieroglyphics. They lasted from 1200 – 100 B.C. Remaining monuments such as huge stone heads are still visible in parts of Mexico.

Perhaps the most brilliant civilization in South America was the **MAYA**. The origins of the Maya are shrouded in mystery. They built huge cities, and the calendar (which some say is the most accurate one devised). Religion was very important to the Maya – the Sun and Moon were sacred. The Mayan culture disappeared as mysteriously as it appeared.

Where present day Mexico City is located, lived the **TOLTEC** for nearly 400 years. The Toltec were warriors and builders.

The **AZTEC** began an empire which absorbed the Toltec and expanded the boundaries as far south as Guatemala. On the wishes of their god, the Aztec built a city on Lake Texcoco. As the Aztec grew in power, human sacrifices became more commonplace. There were two major gods for the Aztec – Huitzilopochtli, the angry god who demanded human sacrifice, and Quetzalcoatl, the loving god. Both had stone pyramids built in dedication to them. However, Quetzalcoatl was driven out by a rival god and vowed to return.

The power of the Aztec empire weakened with the arrival of the Spaniards led by Hernando Cortes. The Aztec believed Cortes to be the god Quetzalcoatl returning for his vengeance. The Spanish preceded to defeat the Aztec.

Mexicans are stereotyped in being very stoic. But when there is a fiesta (party), the true Mexican character comes out. Fiestas are held for every occasion. The *Dia de los Muertos* (Day of the Dead) is one of the most joyous fiestas. Each Mexican celebrates the spirit of a dead relative or friend. There are religious fiestas held

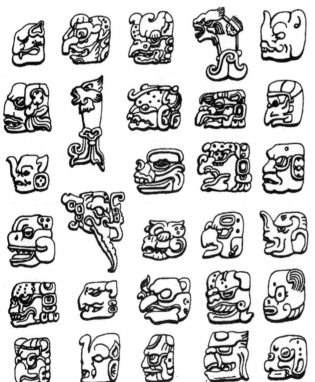

Mayan Hieroglyphics

as well, but they tend to be more solemn.

Mexico's most popular music is played by a strolling group of troubabors called mariachis. Mariachi groups typically have six-to-eight players, and they wear broad-rimmed hats and festive costumes. Most tourists are treated to a mariachi band when they go to a popular restaurant or nightclub.

The most popular sport in Mexico is soccer. Baseball, tennis and race walking are all other sports in which Mexicans excel. **FRONTON** is a game unique to Mexico. Fronton is similar to jai alai, which is also popular in Mexico. Jai alai played with wicker scoops and a ball, is probably the fastest game played in the world.

Mexican education is free for primary students. The literacy rate has improved since the 1970s. Nearly half of the population is under the age of fifteen.

RESOURCES

The Mexican economy is growing faster than any other in the world. However, due to the population increase, poverty is still a major factor for almost 40% of the country. The major crop grown in Mexico is corn. Other crops include tomatoes, chilies, onions, and limes. Mexico is rich in oil, however the oil manufacturing companies have not supplied many jobs to the Mexican people.

RECIPES

Tacos
cooked ground beef
shredded onion, cheese, lettuce, tomato
taco shells
taco seasoning and taco sauce

Prepare cooked ground beef with taco seasoning. Spoon this mixture into taco shell and top with onion and cheese. Place in oven until cheese is melted. Top with lettuce, chopped tomatoes, and taco sauce.

Nachos
round tortilla chips
taco sauce
cheddar cheese, shredded
green chilies

Put small amount of sauce, cheese, and chilies on top of chips and bake at 350-degrees for 5 minutes. Top with sour cream.

*Mexican Brown Sugar Candy
(Dulce de Piloncillo)* ***
1 cup brown sugar
1/4 cup water
1 1/2 teaspoons vinegar
1 1/2 teaspoons butter
1/2 cup broken pecans or walnuts

VOCABULARY

one – *uno*
two – *dos*
three – *tres*
four – *cuatro*
five – *cinco*
six – *seis*
seven – *siete*
eight – *ocho*
nine – *nueve*
ten – *diez*

Good afternoon – *Buenos tardes*
Good night – *Buenos noches*
Good day – *Buenos Dias*
Thank you – *Gracias*
Please – *Por favor*
What is your name? – *Como se ilamo usted?*

ACTIVITIES

Make a Brown Paper Bag Pinata
At Mexican fiestas, the children all gather around to take turns hitting the pinata. In Mexico, the pineapple is a sign of good fortune.
Large brown paper bag
tempura or acrylic paints
scissors
treats
Paint the bag as shown. Cut the top into 5" strips (long enough to be gathered together and tied).
Fill the bag with treats. At school, it might be fun to fill the bag with erasers, pencil sharpeners, etc. but nothing sharp! Tie the "leaves" together with strong yarn or ribbon. Take turns hitting the pinata with a whiffle bat.

ACTIVITIES

Make a Mexican Serape
brown kraft paper (2'x 3')
markers, paint, crayons
Lay the kraft paper on the floor and let the children create any design they choose. Choose bright and cheerful colors. They might want to cut fringe on the ends of their serapes!

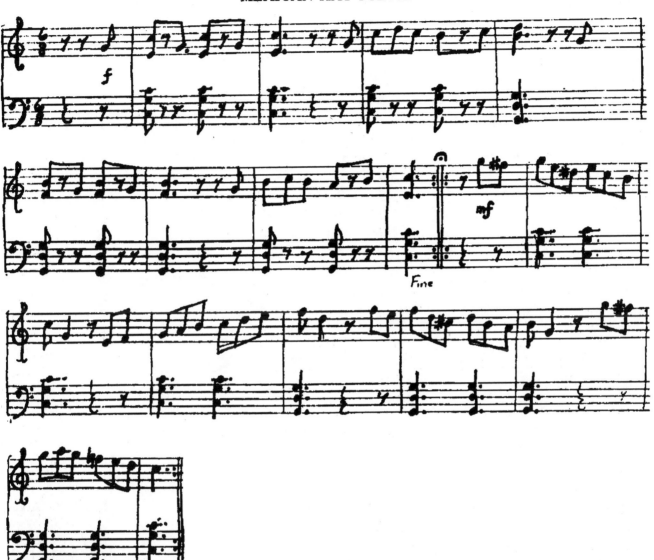

ACTIVITIES

The Mexican Hat Dance (La Raspa)

Partners face each other, left shoulder to left shoulder. Beginning right, step from heel to toe 8 times. Turn to face opposite direction (right shoulder to right shoulder) and repeat. Repeat action, facing opposite direction (left shoulder to left shoulder). Repeat the action. Hook right elbows, left hands held high. Take 8 running steps, clapping on the eighth step. Repeat action. The movements are the same for boy and girl. To begin, the girls holds her skirt and the boy holds clasped hands behind his back.

ACTIVITIES
Color in the Pyramids Jose Has Discovered

Canada

DOMINION OF CANADA

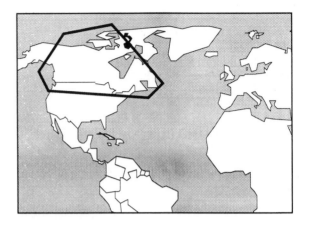

The left and right red stripes on either side of the red maple-leaf represent the Atlantic and Pacific Oceans (originally they were to be blue but altered so that the flag would keep Canada's traditional colors of red and white.) Red stands for the blood of the Canadian soldiers killed during World War I, and white for the snowy wastes of the north.

Canada

Canada is the second largest country in the world, slightly larger than the continent of Europe. The name Canada is thought to come from an Iroquois word Kanata meaning "community". The capitol is **OTTAWA**. The population is 26,000,000. About 80% of Canadians live within 100 miles of the U.S. border. Canada borders three oceans – the Pacific Ocean on the west, the Atlantic Ocean on the east, and the Arctic Ocean on the north. Canada has relations to both France and Britain. Canada was originally a French colony called New France, until the British conquest in 1763. The government of Canada is parliamentary. Canada has ten provinces: Alberta, British Columbia, Manitoba, New Brunswick, Newfoundland, Nova Scotia, Ontario, Prince Edward Island, Quebec, and Saskatchewan. The Northwest and the Yukon are territories.

LAND

The country is 3,850,350 square miles. Canada can be divided into seven separate land regions. The Appalachian region, located in eastern Canada is the continuation of the Appalachian Mountains from the U.S. It is a region of old, worn-down uplands which include the **SHICKSHOCK MOUNTAINS** of the Gaspe Peninsula.

The St. Lawrence Lower Great Lakes Lowlands make up only a small region of Canada's land but is home to over 80% of the people. It includes all of the **ST. LAWRENCE RIVER** valley, the Ontario Peninsula, and **LAKE HURON, LAKE ERIE, AND LAKE ONTARIO.**

The **CANADIAN SHIELD** covers nearly half of Canada. The region is covered by numerous lakes, due to Ice Age glaciation.

The Western Plains is the region between the Rocky Mountains and the Canadian Shield.

The Western Mountain region extends east from the Pacific coast to the Western Plains. Mountain ranges include the Rocky Mountains in the south, the Mackenzie Mountains in the north. The western range is the **ST. ELIAS MOUNTAINS**, which has the highest point in Canada –Mount Logan at 19,850 feet.

The Arctic islands are mostly covered by snow and ice.

CLIMATE

The climate is varied as to the different regions.

CULTURE

The original native inhabitants of Canada have lived there for over 10,000 years. A large native group, the **HAIDA** from British Columbia have been strong voices for maintaining indian culture within Canada.

Both French and English are the official languages. Protestant and Catholicism are the predominant religions in Canada.

Each of Canada's provinces has its own school system. In all provinces except Quebec, school is taught in English and resembles American schools.

Canadians live very much like Americans do. Some major exceptions are the French Canadians in Quebec, who speak French instead of English. The **ESKIMO** make their living by hunting, fishing, selling furs, or working in mining camps. Eskimo also ride in boats called kayaks, made from animal skins, and travel across the snow on **KOMATIKS**, sleds pulled by dogs.

Hockey is the national sport of Canada. Children play in leagues during the winter. Children learn to ski and skate at very early ages. Tobogganing and dog sled racing are also popular winter sports. Summer activities include hiking, horseback riding, and canoeing.

RESOURCES

Major mineral resources found in Canada are coal, copper, gold, iron ore, lead, nickel, silver, and zinc. The provinces of Alberta, Saskatchewan, and Manitoba are heavy agricultural lands. Major crops include apples, barley, oats, rye, wheat, sugar beets, honey, and maple products. Forests cover much of Canada which enables a thriving forestry and paper industry. Fishing is also an important industry.

RECIPES

Canadian Popovers****

2 eggs
1 cup milk
1 cup flour
1/2 teaspoon salt

Grease an 8-cup muffin tin (with butter or shortening) generously, or the batter will stick to the pan. Be sure the rims at the top are well greased. Place the muffin pan in a pre-heated 450-degree oven while batter is being made.

In a mixing bowl beat the eggs, milk, flour, and salt until well blended. Very carefully and with the use of potholders, take the hot muffin pan out of the oven. Spoon the liquid batter into the cups one-half full. Bake at 450-degrees for 15 minutes, then lower the heat to 350-degrees and bake 15-20 minutes or until well browned.

Ice Cream with Maple Topping

The maple tree is a symbol of Canada. Maple syrup is very popular in Canada. The harvesting of maple syrup is known as the sugar bush.

1 cup ice cream
maple syrup

Heat syrup and pour over the ice cream or snow. Serve in bowls.

VOCABULARY

Eskimo

boats made from seal skin – *kayaks*
house made of ice – *igloo*
sleds pulledby dogs – *komatiks*

ACTIVITIES

Make a Eskimo Soap Carving

Large cake of soft bath soap
butter knife or plastic knife
pencil
toothpick

1. Decide which animal you want to carve and draw it on your bar of soap. Draw the side view and the frontal view.
2. Using the knife, carve out the outline of the animal, cutting a little at a time.
3. Use the toothpick to carve out eyes, nose, mouth, any features that the knife would be too large to carve.
4. Round out edges by using either the knife or a damp cloth.

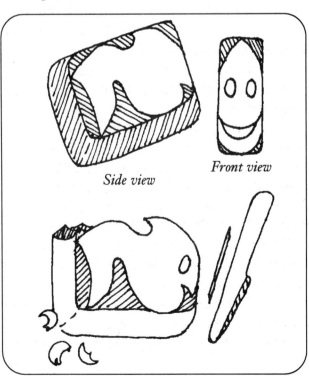

Side view   *Front view*

ACTIVITIES

Look closely at the Haida totem pole. What is missing? In the right column are the missing items. Draw the missing items and color (totem poles usually use bright oranges, yellows, and reds).

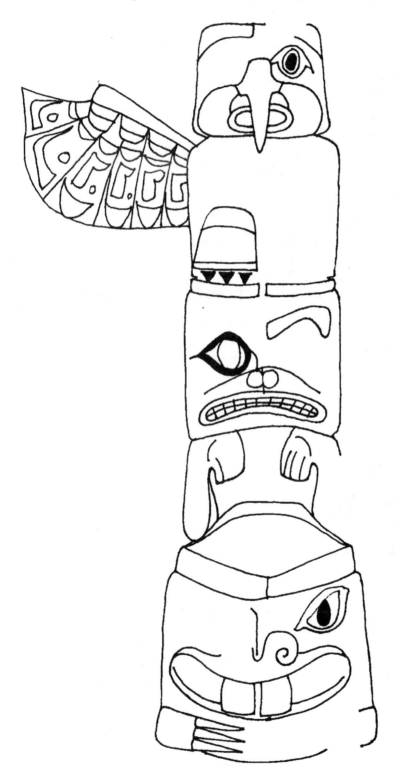

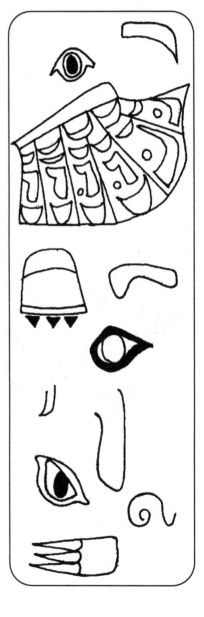

The Caribbean and Central America

IDENTIFY

1. _____
2. _____
3. _____
4. _____
5. _____

REPUBLIC OF HAITI

The flag was originally taken from the French tricolor. In 1986, the flag was changed to the present flag of a top blue stripe and the bottom red stripe.

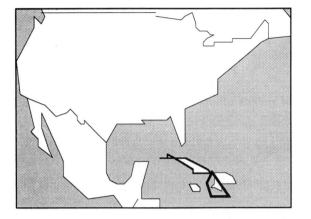

Atlantic Ocean

CAP-HAITIEN

PORT-AU-PRINCE

Caribbean Sea

Antilles Sea

Haiti shares the island of Hispaniola with the Dominican Republic. The name of Haiti is taken from the Arawak Indians. The population is 690,000. Haiti is governed by a military dictatorship who deposed President Arristide in 1986. The United Nations has imposed an embargo on Haiti in an attempt to force a return to democracy. Life in towns such as the capital of **PORT-AU-PRINCE**, and **CAP HATIEN** has become difficult without electricity and other services. Haiti is the poorest country in the Western Hemisphere.

Recently, Haiti has been going through major struggles. Many Haitians are leaving by boat, trying to find refuge within the United States.

LAND

The country is 10,710 square miles. Haiti consists of two large peninsulas which stretch west from the central area of the island. Haiti occupies 1/3 of the island.

CLIMATE

The climate of Haiti is tropical. The average annual temperatures are 80° F. During the rainy season, hurricanes devastate the land. The annual average precipitation is 60 inches.

CULTURE

Christopher Columbus discovered Haiti in 1492. The Spanish returned to this "paradise" in 1493 and were welcomed warmly by the native Arawak Indians. In return the Spanish enslaved both the Arawaks and the cannibalistic Carib Indians, also native to Haiti, and forced them to work in Spanish mines and plantations. The Indians soon died out and the Spaniards began to engage the West African slave trade to replace the Indian workers.

The French took control of Haiti in 1697, renaming the island Saint Dominique. It soon became the richest colony in the New World. The slaves on Haiti, however were badly treated. In the 18th century, led by **TOUSSAINT L. OUVERTURE** (known as the "George Washington of Haiti"), the slaves rebelled against the oppressive Haitian aristocracy. When Napoleon came to power, he sent French troops to regain control of the Haitian colony. The Haitians defeated the troops and in 1804, Haiti gained its freedom from foreign control.

In fear of the French returning, **HENRI CHRISTOPHE** built the Citadelle La Ferriere in 1808. The French never returned, and the fortress was never used. Without the French, the mines and lands of Haiti fell into disuse. The world seemed to forget Haiti. In 1917, the United States entered World War I and moved into Haiti to protect the eastern entrance to the Panama Canal. With their arrival, they brought aid to the Haitians. Twenty years later, the Americans left, and the island was again on its own.

In 1957, **PAPA DOC DUVALIER** became dictator, repressing the hope of Haiti. On his death in 1971, his son Baby Doc Duvalier continued his father's repression, until Haitians rebelled and exiled him in 1986.

The majority of the population are black, descendants of African slaves. The people of Haiti speak Creole, a French dialect unique to Haiti. French is the official language and most literature and newspapers are written in French.

The official religion is Roman Catholicism. Many of the Haitians however, practice Voodoo. **VOODOO** is a blend of traditional African and Christian beliefs. Adherents worship gods they believe control the rain, water, love, war, and all other aspects of life. The religion involves many rituals, ceremonies, and dances. Often believers try to become possessed

and the Catholic religion. Haitian artists tend to use bright colors in painting and sculpture.

RESOURCES

The economy at present is poor, due to the embargo set by the United Nations. Many Haitian families help support themselves by selling items for tourists. The major crops for Haiti are coffee and sugar.

RECIPES

The Haitian diet consists of rice, corn, beans, fruit, fish, and chicken. *Cassava* is a starchy root ground into flour.

Plat National
1 cup dried kidney beans
3 cups water
2-4 strips of bacon
1-2 medium onions
1 cup soaked rice
dash of cloves, salt, pepper
few drops of hot pepper sauce

Soak dried beans overnight in 3 cups of water, then simmer, covered, over low heat until they are tender (about one hour). Fry bacon, then saute onions in the grease. Add all the ingredients to the beans. Serve over cooked rice.

Melongene
1 eggplant, chopped
1 clove garlic, minced
1 tomato, chopped
2 tablespoons oil
1 onion, chopped
1 green pepper, chopped
salt, pepper to taste

Saute onion, pepper, and garlic in oil. Add tomato and eggplant, salt and pepper and cook for ten minutes.

by gods during these ceremonies. The UGAN is the high priest who performs the ceremonies. The DEMBALA is the snake dance, the AIDAE is the water dance (like a baptism), and the petro is a fire dance, where participants walk on coals and eat fire.

Many fine artisans come from Haiti. In the late 1980s, Haitian art became very popular in the United States. Different organizations would buy art from Haitian artists and auction the work in the U.S., giving the proceeds to much needed healthcare programs in Haiti. Haitian art is a multi-faceted form of art which has been in existence for hundreds of years. It presents a link between the world of voodoo

ACTIVITIES

The Haiti Game

2-3 players
gamepieces (or coins, checkers, etc.)
die

Roll the die to see who goes first. On the following page is a gameboard. Begin at Start. First player rolls die and moves accordingly. The winner is the player who reaches Finish first.

START

FINISH

Stop and watch a Voodoo dance.

GO BACK A SPACE

Stop and have a cup of coffee.

GO BACK 1 SPACE

Buy a piece of Haitian art.

GO AHEAD 5 SPACES

Hit on the head by a coconut.

GO BACK 2 SPACES

Catch 3 big fish.

GO 3 SPACES AHEAD

Hurricane sweeps you up.

GO BACK TO START

Caught in a tidal wave.

SKIP A TURN

Jamaica

STATE OF JAMAICA

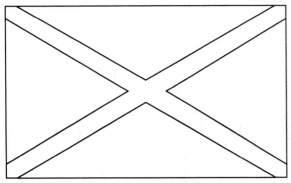

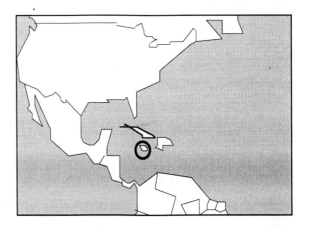

The yellow cross represents sunshine and the minerals found on Jamaica. The top and bottom green triangles represent the agricultural wealth. The right and left black triangles represent the past struggles the Jamaican people have endured.

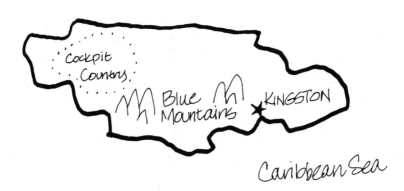

Jamaica

The island of Jamaica is an independent country located in the Caribbean Sea, approximately ninety miles south of Cuba. It is strategically important since its location controls the entrance to the Caribbean Sea. A United States naval and air base is located near Kingston. The name Jamaica comes from the Arawak Indians word for the land – Xamayca (*Land of wood and water*). **KINGSTON** is the capital. The population is 566,000. In 1962, Jamaica became an independent member of the British Commonwealth of Nations. The political system reflects the influence of the British parliamentary form of government. In Jamaica there are two major political parties: The People's Nationalist Party and The Jamaica Labor Party. In 1980, The People's National Party, a socialist party in favor of government ownership of businesses, was defeated in the national election. The Jamaica Labor Party, a socialist party which is generally pro-business and in favor of free enterprise, was elected to power.

LAND

Jamaica is 4,250 square miles. The land has very diverse land areas. The **BLUE MOUNTAINS** extend east/west in the southern part of Jamaica. Farther east are the **JOHN CROW MOUNTAINS**. Scattered among the mountains are the plains. There are over 200 rivers and streams in Jamaica. The most important river is the **GREAT RIVER**. In the western region of Jamaica is the **COCKPIT COUNTRY** – a land area full of mounds and craters, largely unexplored.

CLIMATE

The climate of Jamaica is tropical The average temperature is 75° F. The rainy season is from April to November. During this season, hurricanes and floods hit the land. The Blue Mountains average 200 inches precipitation annually, with the other parts of Jamaica averaging about 50 inches.

CULTURE

The island was first visited by Columbus in 1494, and ruled by Spain for over 150 years. Under Spanish rule, approximately 100,000 Arawak Indians died in slavery; a few hundred survived. When the British seized Jamaica in 1655, a group of Indians and Africans fled into Jamaica's mountainous areas. These former Spanish slaves became known as **MAROONS**. A mystique developed about the Maroons because of their ability to avoid capture or control by the British. They successfully evaded British rule until the early 1700s. During Spanish rule, few Africans had been imported into Jamaica as slaves. During the 18th century, under the British, however, many Africans were imported. At one point as many as 300,000 African slaves were at work on the plantations that made Jamaica the leading sugar producer in the world. Slavery was abolished in 1838.

English is the official language of Jamaica. Jamaicans predominately follow Anglican, Baptist, and Roman Catholic practices. There are however, minority religions which figure prominently in the Jamaican culture. **POCOMANIA** (practiced mainly in Kingston) is a mixture of African beliefs and Christianity. **OBEAHISM** is a form of African voodoo. **RASTAFARIANISM** which originated in Jamaica, combines east African culture with some Christian beliefs. The Rastafarians believe Ethiopia is the spiritual homeland of all black people.

The biggest contribution from Jamaica has been in the form of music. **REGGAE** is a mixture of African and European rhythms, with lyrics protesting political injustice. Since the 1970s, Reggae has been a major influence on world music. Bob Marley is among the more famous Jamaican reggae musicians.

Jamaicans excel at sports. Among the popular sports are cricket and horse-racing. Jamaicans also enjoy track and field.

The literacy rate in Jamaica is fairly high at 85%. Children attend school for free. All school children wear uniforms.

RESOURCES

Tourism is the most important industry in Jamaica. Coffee is one of their most important crops – Jamaica Blue Mountain is among the highest quality coffee produced. Other major crops include sugar cane, bananas, pineapples, allspice, and tobacco. The major mineral mined is bauxite.

RECIPES

Some popular Jamaican foods include:
Curried goat jerk pork – meat which has had peppers pounded into it, cooked over an open pit.
Red beans and rice
Pattys – pastries filled with spicy meat mixtures.
Breadfruit

Baked Bananas
6 bananas, peeled
1 orange, peeled, cut into chunks
2 tablespoons frozen orange juice
1 tablespoons lemon juice
1/2 cup sugar
dash of cinnamon and/or nutmeg

Preheat oven to 325-degrees. Combine all ingredients but bananas. Place peeled bananas in baking dish and pour mixture over them. Bake 20-30 minutes and serve.

Fish Stew
fresh fish (remove head and tail)
3 quarts water
dash of salt, pepper, and garlic
1 small onion, chopped
1/2 cup green pepper, chopped
1 16 ounce can tomatoes
1 cube chicken bouillon
leftover vegetables (potatoes, carrots, etc.)

Cook the fish in boiling water. Add salt, pepper, and garlic. Saute onion and green pepper in butter and add to soup. Add a can of tomatoes and leftover vegetables. Add 1 cube chicken bouillon and continue to cook for about 45 minutes.

Ham Banana Rolls
4 slices boiled ham
mustard
4 firm bananas
3 teaspoons melted butter
cheese sauce: cheddar cheese soup or mixture of melted cheese, milk and small quality of flour

Preheat oven to 350-degrees. Spread ham with mustard. Peel bananas and wrap in a ham slice. Brush with melted butter. Place in greased baking dish and cover with cheese sauce. Bake 30 minutes or until bananas are easily pierced with fork.

ACTIVITIES

What's Wrong With This Picture?
On the following page is a scene of a market place. In the picture are seven items which don't belong.

Cuba

REPUBLIC OF CUBA

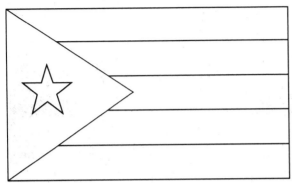

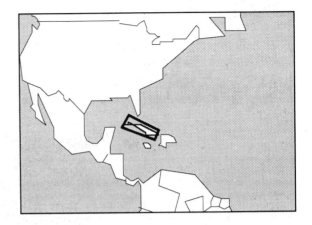

The red triangle symbolizes freedom from Spanish rule and the blood shed to obtain that freedom. Each side of the triangle represents one quality: liberty, fraternity, and equality. The blue/white/blue/white/blue stripes and the white star in the triangle were taken from the United States flag.

Gulf of Mexico

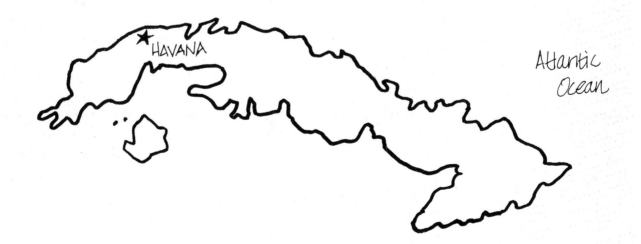

★ HAVANA

Atlantic Ocean

Cuba

Cuba is the largest of the West Indian islands. Cuba was called by the early Spanish settlers "the pearl of the Antilles". The capital is **HAVANA**, an old Spanish port. The population is 10,050,000. Columbus discovered Cuba and in the early 16th century, the Spanish settled there. Cuba remained under Spanish control for almost 400 years. In 1899, Cuba won independence from Spain with the help of the United States. Cuba has endured many leaders, some very corrupt. In 1958, Fidel Castro came to power, establishing a Communist government. Poor relations exist between the United States and Cuba because of a failed invasion attempt at the Bay of Pigs. The United States government had hopes of overthrowing the Communist government.

LAND

Cuba is 44,218 square miles. Besides the mainland, Cuba consists of 3,715 small islands. Over 1/4 of the Cuban mainland is covered by mountains. The valleys and plains offer very fertile land.

CLIMATE

Cuba has a tropical climate, similar to the other Caribbean islands. The annual average temperature is 80° F. The coolest months are January and February with an average temperature of 75° F. During the summer, the temperature is kept relatively low by the cooling, trade winds. The annual average precipitation is 65 inches. Cuba is often hit by hurricanes.

CULTURE

The official language is Spanish. Most of the population are of mixed ancestry – Spanish, African, Chinese, and Central American. Roman Catholicism is the predominant religion, although Santeria is also practiced.

SANTERIA is a mixture of Catholicism and traditional African religions.

Education is free to all Cuban children. The Cuban government has set up a countrywide literacy program. Healthcare is free to all Cubans.

RESOURCES

Sugarcane is the principal crop. Mineral resources produced are nickel, chromite, copper, iron ore, and manganese. A rare and valuable wood, the West Indian Ebony, is also produced.

RECIPES

Cuban bread is used to make cuban sandwiches which often have ham, turkey, and cheese. Cuban sandwiches are similar to the American hoagie or submarine sandwich.

Cuban Potato Omelet (Tortilla de Papas)***
1 medium potato
1 tablespoon butter
2 eggs
salt and pepper to taste

Peel the potato, cut into eighths, and then into slices. Heat a large skillet, melt a little of the butter, and add the slices. Cook over medium heat, browning the slices with a spatula.

Beat the eggs in a deep bowl. Add the salt and pepper. Mix the potato with the eggs. Allow the mixture to stand for 45 minutes.

Heat a small skillet. Grease lightly with the rest of the butter. Pour in the mixture and cook over low heat, lifting the edges to allow the uncooked egg to flow underneath. When the omelet is set, turn in with a spatula and cook the other side. Serve as a main dish or between bread as a sandwich.

The Bahamas

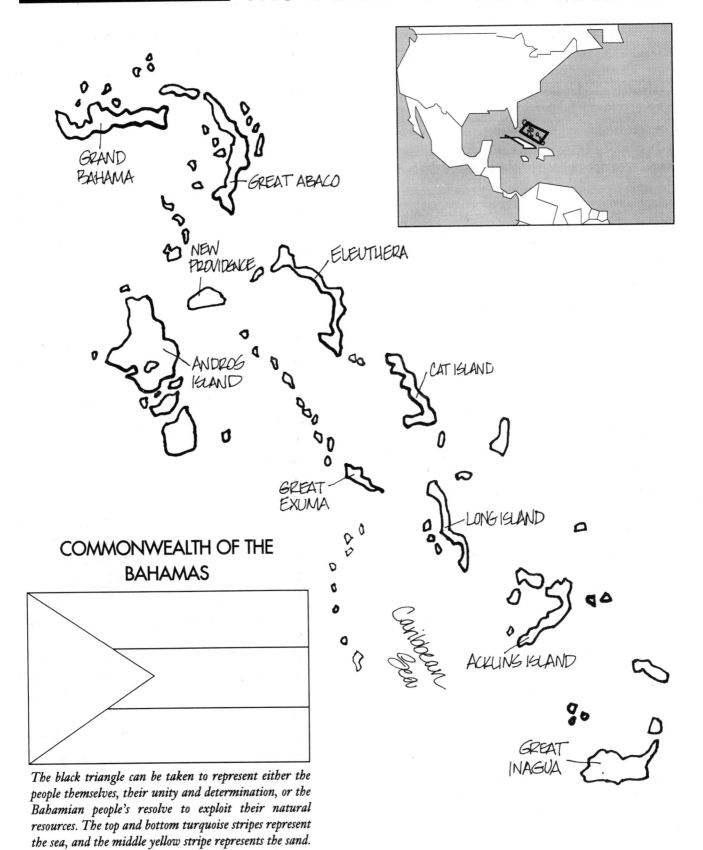

GRAND BAHAMA

GREAT ABACO

NEW PROVIDENCE

ELEUTHERA

ANDROS ISLAND

CAT ISLAND

GREAT EXUMA

LONG ISLAND

Caribbean Sea

ACKLINS ISLAND

GREAT INAGUA

COMMONWEALTH OF THE BAHAMAS

The black triangle can be taken to represent either the people themselves, their unity and determination, or the Bahamian people's resolve to exploit their natural resources. The top and bottom turquoise stripes represent the sea, and the middle yellow stripe represents the sand.

Columbus first sighted San Salvador, an island in the Bahamas, in 1492. The capital of the Bahamian islands is NASSAU, located on New Providence. The Bahamas' name come from a Spanish word bajamar (meaning "*shallow water*"). The population is 230,000. The Bahamas became independent in 1973.

LAND

The Bahamian islands are 5,400 square miles. The Bahamas consist of 700 islands, of which only 30 are inhabited. The larger islands are New Providence, Grand Bahama, Andros, and Eleuthra. The larger islands are full of low, sandy beaches.

CLIMATE

The climate is tropical. The annual average temperature is 80° F. During its rainy season, hurricanes sweep through the Bahamas.

CULTURE

The original natives of the Bahamian islands were the Arawak Indians and the fierce Carib known as LUCAYANS (island people). They were enslaved by the Spanish and taken to Hispaniola.

The Bahamas then remained uninhabited for almost a century until the English arrived. The British began to colonize the Bahamas and by the late 18th century, British control of the islands was well established. The British colonists built many houses and churches, particularly on Nassau, the most populated of the islands. The colonists established large plantations on the islands for cultivating crops, and introduced slavery to the islands. Since slave ships coming from West Africa stopped here before going on to Cuba, the Bahamian planters had first choice among the slaves for sale. In 1834, slavery was abolished in the Bahamas.

Today a large part of the Bahamian population is made up of blacks who are descendants of West African slaves.

RESOURCES

The Bahamian economy is largely dependent on real estate investment and the booming tourist trade. Fishing is also a major industry. Rum and wood also attribute to the economy.

RECIPES

The Caribbean supplies an important staple to the Bahamian diet – fish and shellfish. A favorite dish in the Bahamas is conch (pronounced "konk"). It is the meat inside the pretty pink shell that we put to our ear to hear the ocean. Although conch may be hard to find outside the Bahamas and Florida, we've included these recipes with the hope that your fish market can get you some. Conch is tough and must be pounded to tenderize the meat. Bahamian food is spicy, so use plenty of seasoning to give the conch the authentic taste of Bahamian cooking.

Conch is not an endangered species. A conch does not lose its shell, but grows up with it to an average size of 1 1/2 to 2 pounds. Conch can be eaten raw or with a dash of lime juice, or cooked in conch chowder, cracked conch, or conch fritters.

Conch Fritters
2 medium conchs finely diced
2 cups flour
2 teaspoons baking powder
1 cup water
1 stalk celery
1 onion and green pepper, chopped
1 tablespoon tomato paste
dash of salt, paprika, thyme

Combine flour, salt, and baking powder. Separately, combine celery, onions, pepper, and conch in mixing bowl. Add water and flour alternately, beating batter thoroughly after each addition. Add thyme, tomato paste, and paprika. Beat well and drop into deep fat. Fry until brown.

Cracked Conch

1 1/2 pounds conch, tenderized
3/4 cup fine bread crumbs
2 large beaten eggs
6 tablespoon lime juice
dash of allspice, garlic powder, hot pepper sauce

Mix allspice, garlic powder, and bread crumbs in shallow bowl. Dip conch into beaten eggs, then roll in bread crumb mixture. Fry until brown. Turn and fry other side. Pour lime juice and hot pepper sauce on just before serving.

Fish Caribbean

1 to 1 1/2 pounds red snapper or bluefish (head and tail removed)
1/2 lemon
1 1/2 tablespoons butter
1 medium onion, chopped
1/8 teaspoon red pepper
1 1/2 cups tomatoes, chopped
parsley or celery leaves, chopped
1/2 teaspoon oil
salt and pepper to taste

Wash the fish in cold running water. Pat it dry and slice it. Squeeze lemon juice over both sides of the fish.

Melt the butter over medium heat. Saute the onion until tender. Add the red pepper and cook one minute longer. Stir in the tomatoes, parsley or celery leaves, and salt and pepper. Simmer for five minutes. Place the pieces of the fish in the tomato sauce. Sprinkle with the salad oil. Simmer for 15 minutes.

Serve with boiled rice and spoon the fish-tomato gravy over the rice.

VOCABULARY

These Arawak words are used in the English vocabulary.

avocado	hammock
barbecue	hurricane
buccaneer	iguana
canoe	maize
cannibal	potato
cay	tobacco
guava	

ACTIVITIES

Make a Bahamian Mobile

wire hanger
yarn, string of different colors
watercolor, crayons, or markers
hole puncher
scissors
colored construction paper
glue

Decorate the shells and fish on the following page. Glue colored construction paper on the back of each shape, using a different color for each shape to make the mobile colorful. Cut out the shapes. Punch out the hole shown on the shape. Tie yarn through each shape and attach to the hanger, making each yarn different lengths and different colors.

Panama

REPUBLIC OF PANAMA

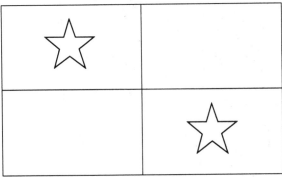

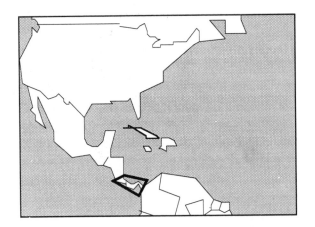

The red, white, and blue of the Panamanian flag might be adopted from the U.S. flag (the U.S. helped Panama achieve independence from Columbia). The white means purity. The top right red rectangle and the bottom right red star represent the rule of law. The bottom left blue rectangle and the top left blue star mean civic values.

Panama

Panama is the bridge between Central America and South America. The borders of Panama are to the east, the Atlantic Ocean; to the west, the Pacific Ocean; to the northwest, Costa Rica; and to the southeast, Columbia. Its most famous landmark is the **PANAMA CANAL**, sometimes called the "Crossroads of the World". The capital is Panama City. The population is almost 2.5 million.

LAND

Panama is 29,762 square miles. There are three different land regions in Panama. The lowlands which make up 87% of Panama have plains, savannas, and jungles (nearly 1/2 of Panama is rainforest). The temperate lands make up 10% of Panama. The highlands, which make up 3% of Panama, include the Tabasaru Mountains. There are over 500 rivers, although no large major river.

CLIMATE

The climate is tropical. The annual average temperature is 80° F. The rainy season lasts from April to December.

CULTURE

Panama has a varied population. Many are **MESTIZO** – people of mixed background. The three predominant native indians are the **CUNA**, the **CHOCO**, and the **GUAYMI**. Many believe these indian groups migrated south from Mexico or north from Peru, centuries before the Spanish settled. The Cuna live on the coast and are best known for mola – an art form which involves intricate hand applique work. The Choco live mainly in the rainforests and are excellent fishermen and horseback riders. The third group are the Guaymi who represent the majority native indian group.

Other groups in the Panamanian population are the Spanish, descendants from the conquistadors or conquerors. Many of the blacks are descendants from the African slave trade. There are also a minority of Chinese, who were originally brought in to work on the railroad.

The official language is Spanish but English is widely spoken. The majority of the population are Roman Catholic. However, there are many religions practiced such as Hindu, Protestant, and Islam.

Education is free for children ages seven to age fifteen. Panama has a high literacy rate at 85%, as well as good public healthcare.

Horse sports are very popular in Panama. The deep-sea fishing is among the best in the world. Water sports, like scuba diving and sailing, boxing, and baseball are also enjoyed.

Panama is most famous for the Panama Canal which allows ships to take a "short-cut" from the Atlantic to the Pacific Ocean. Work began on the canal in 1882 by the French, but was abandoned. In 1902, led by President Theodore Roosevelt, the United States began work on the canal. On May 13, 1913, the Panama Canal was completed. It was an enormously expensive project and the engineering

An example of early Panamanian Indian art.

feat of its time. Over 25,000 people died during the construction, most from malaria. The price charged for passage through the canal is high. The highest price ever paid to pass through the Canal was $89,154.62, which was paid by the ship *The Queen Elizabeth II*. The lowest price ever paid was $.36 paid in 1936 by Richard Halliburton, a swimmer.

RESOURCES

Agriculture is a large industry for Panama. Major crops are plantains and bananas. Other crops include mangoes and sugar cane. Due to the rainforest, commercial forestry is another industry important for Panama. Mahogany, kapok, and cashew trees are some of the wood obtained from the rainforest.

RECIPES

Guacamole
2 large avocados, peeled and chopped
1 tomato, peeled
1/2 onion, chopped
2 cloves garlic, chopped
2 tablespoons wine vinegar
1/2 teaspoon salt
Place all ingredients in an electric blender. Blend 60 to 90 seconds. Serve with corn chips or on a salad.

Picadillo*
2 tablespoons oil
1 large onion, chopped
1 pound ground beef
2 ripe tomatoes, chopped
1/2 cup raisins
1/3 cup pimento stuffed olives
1 green pepper
Saute onion and garlic in oil. Add meat, seasonings, and wine. Add other ingredients and cook until heated. Serve over white rice.

ACTIVITIES

Create a Mola Design
Stiff paper or cardboard
yarn, in assorted colors
glue
scissors
pencil

Pencil in a drawing or try the example on the following page. Cover the outline with yarn as the example below shows. Glue to the page, pressing the yarn down, following the outline. Cut the yarn where you began. Fill in the figure with yarn, working from the outside to the inside, keeping the yarn as close together as possible. The colors used in Mola applique are bright (orange, turquoise with black outlines).

An example of a mola design.

South America

Pacific
Ocean

Atlantic Ocean

IDENTIFY
1. _____
2. _____
3. _____
4. _____
5. _____

Brazil

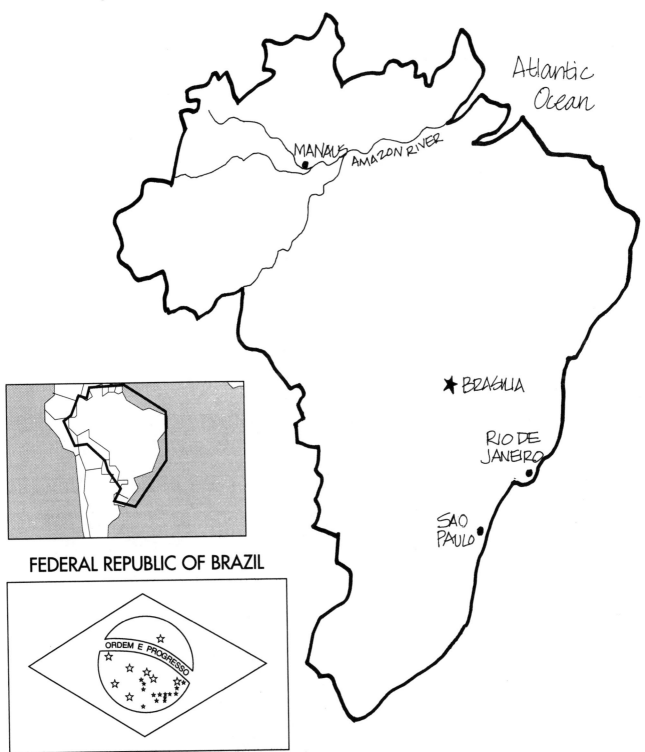

Atlantic Ocean

MANAUS AMAZON RIVER

★ BRASILIA

RIO DE JANEIRO

SAO PAULO

FEDERAL REPUBLIC OF BRAZIL

ORDEM E PROGRESSO

The flag has a lime-green background with a yellow diamond shape (called a lozenge) in the middle. In the middle of the lozenge is a blue circle representing a view of the night sky over Rio de Janeiro. The banner crossing the circle says "Order and Progress".

Brazil

Brazil is the largest country in South America and ranks fifth in size in the world. It occupies the eastern half of South America and is bordered on the east by the Atlantic Ocean. Brazil is often called a mini-South America because its shape is similar to the shape of South America. The capital is **BRASILIA**. Other large cities are **RIO DE JANEIRO**, Sao Paulo, and Manaus (which is located within the Amazon). The population is over 144 million, with half of that being under the age of 20.

A Portuguese navigator, Pedro Cabral discovered Brazil in 1500. At that time Brazil was inhabited by many Indians. During the next few hundred years, colonists from Portugal moved into the interior and built large sugar plantations. They brought with them West Africans who were made to work the plantations. Slavery was abolished in Brazil in 1888.

LAND

Brazil is 3,000,0000 square miles. Brazil has few mountains. Almost 1/2 of the land is lowlands or plains. The Amazon basin is one of the wildest, unexplored areas in the world. The **AMAZON RIVER**, which flows through Brazil, is the world's largest river. The Pantanal Basin is also largely unexplored and is a reserve for hundreds of rare or endangered animals.

CLIMATE

The majority of Brazil is below the equator, so their seasons are opposite that of the Northern Hemisphere. The climate is mostly tropical to temperate in the most southern region. Average temperatures range from 80° to 100° F in the summer and 65° F in winter. The rainy season is during the summer months (December - April).

CULTURE

A majority of the people in Brazil are Portuguese, Africans, and mulattoes. Today most of the few remaining Indians live deep in the forests along the banks of the Amazon River. In addition, there are Italians, Germans, Japanese, Jews, and Arabs living in Brazil. They all contribute to the melting pot.

RESOURCES

Brazil is rich in many resources. It has the

Brazil was the 1994 World Cup Soccer champion.

largest reserves of iron ore. Other minerals include bauxite, manganese, nickel, tin, and uranium. Brazil also produces 90% of the world's semi-precious gems, such as quartz crystal, topaz, amethyst, tourmaline, and emerald. Black diamonds which are unique to Brazil, are used mainly for manufacturing purposes. Brazil's manufacturing industry produces automobiles, ships, and textiles.

RECIPES

Brazilian Fudge Balls (Brigadeiro) ****
1 15 ounce can sweetened condensed milk
3 tablespoons cocoa
1 tablespoon butter

For rolling:
chocolate jimmies, chopped nuts, powdered sugar, or fine bread crumbs

Cook the milk, cocoa, and butter in a saucepan over low heat for 10 minutes (stirring constantly with a wooden spoon) until the mixture thickens and sticks together in a mass. Remove from heat. Empty contents onto a plate and allow to cool (about 35 minutes).

Grease hands with butter. Pick up a teaspoonful of the mixture, scoop it off with another teaspoon, drop it into your palm and roll it lightly into a ball. Dip it into any of the rolling ingredients. Enjoy!

Brazilian Rice ****
1 tablespoon salad oil
1/2 small onion, chopped
1 clove garlic, crushed
1 tablespoon chopped parsley
1/2 cup rice
1 1/3 cups boiling water
1/4 teaspoon salt

Heat the oil in a medium-sized saucepan. Add the onion, garlic, and parsley. cook and stir over medium heat until onion is golden. Add the rice, stirring constantly over low heat for 3 minutes. Carefully add the boiling water at once – the rice will "jump". Stir, add the salt, and stir again. Cover and simmer gently for 15 minutes or until the rice is cooked and the water is absorbed. Keep covered until ready to serve.

ACTIVITIES

Cat and Rat Game

All the players but two form a circle, hands clasped. The two players represent the cat and rat. The cat stands outside the circle and the rat inside. The cat knocks on the back of one of the players in the circle. That player asks, "What do you want?"

"I want to see the rat," says the cat.

"You cannot see him now," says the circle player.

"When can I see him?" asks the cat.

"At ten o'clock," says the circle player. (The player can call out any time he desires).

Immediately the circle begins moving around in rhythm as they count off the hours. All the players may call off the hours. They call, "One o'clock, ticktock! Two o'clock, ticktock!" and so on, until they reach the announced time, which in this case in ten o'clock. At this point the circle stops moving. The cat steps up again to the player whose back he tapped. He knocks again. This time the dialogue is as follows: "What do you want?"

"I want to see the rat."

"What time is it?"

"Ten o'clock!" answers the cat.

"O.K; come in!" The cat ducks in, and the rat tries to elude him by getting outside. The rat runs around the entire circle and tries to get back into the circle where he came out. The cat tries to tag him before he does.

ACTIVITIES

Create a Brazilian Carnival

In Brazil and many of the South American countries, Carnival is celebrated. Similar to the Mardi Gras festival in New Orleans, Carnival is held during the Lenten time before Easter. Elaborate costumes are worn, there is dancing in the streets, and many good things are eaten.

Make a Carnival Bonnet

Both men and women dress as wildly as they please during Carnival. Make your own Carnival hat.

paper plate
scissors
ribbon or crepe paper
glue, tape, or stapler
glitter, fake flowers, wrapping paper, bells, pipe cleaners, etc.

1. Slit a narrow hole about 1" long on opposite sides of the plate rim.
2. Push a ribbon or crepe paper about 35" long through each slit. Either tape, glue, or staple the ribbon to the top of the hat.
3. Decorate to your pleasure.

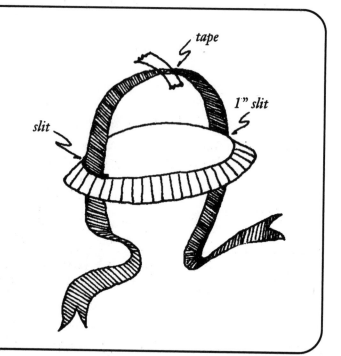

Make a Carnival Mask

Maybe instead of a hat, a mask might be fun for Carnival.

paper plate
scissors
ribbon or crepe paper
glue, tape, or stapler
glitter, fake flowers, wrapping paper, bells, pipe cleaners, etc.

1. Slit a narrow hole about 1" long on opposite sides of the plate rim.
2. Push a ribbon or crepe paper about 35" long through each slit. Either tape, glue, or staple the ribbon to the top of the hat.
3. With scissors, cut out eye and mouth holes on the opposite side of the plate (the inside).
4. Decorate to your pleasure.

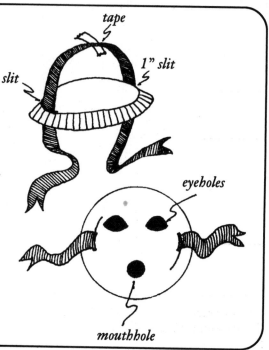

Argentina

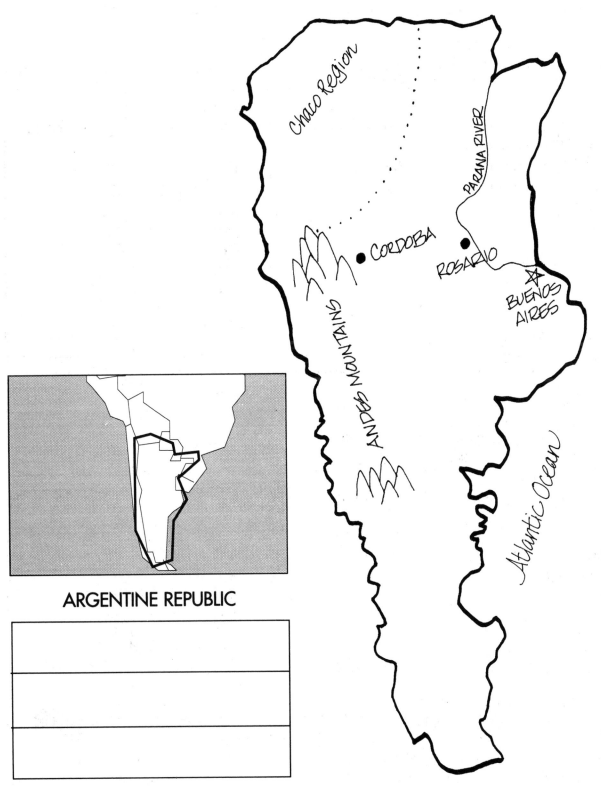

ARGENTINE REPUBLIC

The top horizontal band is baby-blue, the middle white, and the bottom band is baby-blue.

Argentina is the second largest country in Latin America. The name Argentina comes from the Latin word *argentus*, meaning silver. At present, the capital is **BUENOS AIRES** but there are plans to move the capital to ViedmaCarmen de Patagones by 1995. The population of Argentina is 32 million. About 1/3 of the population lives in Buenos Aires, about half live in the other big cities Rosario, Cordoba (in Andes), and Mendoza (in Andes). Only 1/5 of the population live in the more rural areas.

LAND

Argentina is 4,250 square miles. The **PAMPAS** are fertile plains in east central Argentina. They can be subdivided into the eastern, humid Pampas and the dry Pampas to the west. The soil of the Pampas is among the richest in the world.

The **ANDES MOUNTAINS** which border on western Argentina, are the world's second highest mountains. **MOUNT ACONCAGUA** is the Western Hemisphere's highest peak.

South and east of the Andes are plateaus called **PATAGONIA**. The Patagonia extend to the Atlantic Ocean, cut by canyons and ravines. Only 1% of the population live in the Patagonia.

The **CHACO** region lies northeast of the Andes. The Chaco is forests, plains, and jungles which lie between the **PARANA** and the **URUGUAY RIVERS**.

CLIMATE

The seasons of Argentina are opposite of the Northern Hemisphere. The climate is generally temperate. Other than the Andes, the temperatures range from 60° to 75° F. The Andes reach glacier cold temperatures. The annual precipitation is about 80 inches in the north to 30 inches in the south.

CULTURE

There were at least 20 major Indian tribes living in Argentina before the Spaniards settled. These Indians were basically nomadic and were great hunters.

The first settled Spanish smuggled goods. Eventually, the Spanish government put a halt to smuggling by allowing free trade on the entire Atlantic coast. Buenos Aires became a major port for trade.

Many different people began to appear besides the Spanish and the Indians. The **CREOLES** (children of Spanish parents) and **MESTIZOS** (mixed European and Indian blood), as well as German, Dutch, Italian, and Oriental immigrants arrived. In the beginning of the 19th century, the Creoles formed a government based in Buenos Aires.

Spanish is the official language of Argentina. There are Indian dialects spoken as well, but at a very small minority. Almost 90% of the population are Roman Catholic; the president and vice president must belong to the Roman Catholic Church before serving.

The **TANGO** originated in Argentina. It was the music of the gauchos and the lower class, but the upper class Argentinians adopted the tango as well. The **BANDONEON** is the instrument used in tango music. It is a mixture of an accordion and a concertina. Opera is the second most popular music in Argentina. There are many theaters and theater companies. The **TEATRO COLON** is among the most famous opera houses in the world.

Education is very important to Argentina. The country has the highest literacy rate in the world. Education is free from preschool to university level. School is compulsory for age 6 to age 16. Many schoolchildren wear uniforms.

Argentinians are fanatic soccer players, which they call futbol. They also enjoy tennis, and rodeos. They also play **PATO**, which originated with the gauchos. Pato is a game similar to polo, played on horses. Argentinians also enjoy the cafe society: relaxing and people-watching. A favorite game to play at the cafes is chess.

RESOURCES

The most important industry in Argentina is agriculture. Nearly 60% of the land is used for farming or livestock. Argentina is among the world's top producers of wheat, rye, and corn. Other important crops are soybeans, sunflower seeds, and grapes. Argentina has a large amount of sheep, hogs, and cattle. Besides meat, Argentina produces a high amount of hides, skins, and wool. The fishing industry is also important because of the long coastline on the Atlantic Ocean.

RECIPES

Argentina is a huge beef producer so meat is common with at least two meals a day. A favorite fruit is the tuna, the fruit of the prickly pear cactus.

Argentinian Gaucho Sweet Potato***

1 large sweet potato
1 egg yolk
2 tablespoons sugar
1/4 teaspoon salt
1 tablespoon milk

Meringue
1 egg white
pinch of salt
1 tablespoon sugar

Scrub the sweet potato. Broil in the oven (about 5 inches below the flame), turning potato on all sides until it is soft. When the potato is cool, cut it in half lengthwise and scoop out the center. Mash the potato with the egg yolk, sugar, salt, and milk until creamy. Refill the potato skins with the mixture.

To make the meringue, beat the egg white with a pinch of salt until foamy. Add the sugar, beat until peaks form. Pile the meringue high on the sweet potato filling. Bake at 350-degrees for 10 minutes or until the meringue is light brown.

Argentinian Apple Pancake****

1 egg, beaten
1 tablespoon flour
pinch of salt
2 1/2 tablespoons milk
1 1/2 tablespoons butter
1/2 apple, sliced thin
sugar for carmelizing

Mix the egg, flour, salt, and milk into a smooth batter. Melt the butter in a medium skillet, swirl it to cover bottom and sides. Saute the apple slices over medium heat until tender and browned on both sides. Pour into the batter. Cook over low heat. Lift the edges, allowing uncooked part to run under and the batter to set.

To turn the pancake over, slip it onto a plate, then slip the uncooked side back into the skillet. Almost immediately, slip pancake onto the plate again. Melt a heaping tablespoon of sugar in the skillet; it will brown quickly. Slip the well-done side of the pancake onto the syrup. Cook for 1 minute, juggling the skillet. Serve the pancake caramelized side up.

ACTIVITIES

Color in the Argentine Gaucho

What would you add to the picture of Juan, the Argentine gaucho? Would there be mountains, horses, rivers, sheep, any other gauchos?

Columbia

REPUBLIC OF COLUMBIA

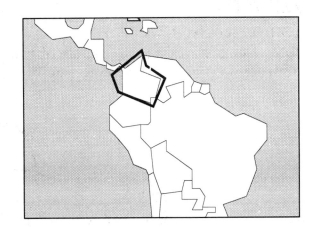

The oversized top yellow stripe represents the nation, the middle blue stripe represents the sea, and the bottom red stripe represents the liberation of the South American territories from Spain and the blood shed to attain that freedom.

Columbia is the only South American country with coastlines on both the Atlantic and Pacific oceans. The name comes from Christopher Columbus, although it is not certain whether he landed in Columbia. The capital is **BOGOTA**, one of the oldest cities on the Western Hemisphere. Other large cities include Medellin and Cartagena. The population is over 30 million. The Spanish landed in Columbia, lured by the legend of El Dorado (the golden one), a city whose streets where paved in gold. Columbia, after years of Spanish rule, is a democratic republic.

LAND

Columbia is 439,737 square miles. Columbia is extremely mountainous. The **ANDES MOUNTAINS** extend north/south along Columbia's western border. The rainforests lie in the southeast, in the Amazon Basin. The **MAGDALENA RIVER** is Columbia's chief river.

CLIMATE

Columbia's climate changes with the altitude. The lowest level has average temperatures of 80° F, with high humidity. The middle zone has temperatures of 65° F, receiving an average of 60 inches yearly. The cold zone receives snow.

CULTURE

More than 2/3 of the population live in the cities. Mestizos (people of Indian and European blood) make up nearly half the Columbian population. Nearly 20% are those of pure European blood. The **ZAMBOS** (mixed black and indian blood) make up 23%; the blacks with 6%; and the native indians make up only 1%.

The Roman Catholic Church is the national religion. The official language is Spanish.

Schooling is free and compulsory, but there are limited facilities. Healthcare is poor.

A famous Columbian writer is Gabriel Garcia Marquez, who won the Nobel Peace Prize for literature. Many handicrafts are done, mainly for tourists, which include leather work, and hand weaving.

RESOURCES

Colombia has extremely rich mineral resources. Gold, salt, coal, nickel, silver, copper, manganese, platinum, and emeralds are produced. Columbia's diverse land means different regional crops can be grown. The major crop grown is coffee (Columbia is the world's largest grower, second only to Brazil). Other crops include sugarcane, bananas, maize, rice, cotton, wheat, tobacco, cacao, and beans.

One of Columbia's major trade is the export of illegal drugs (cocaine and marijuana). This trade supports nearly 55% of the Columbian economy.

RECIPES

Maize is an important staple of the Columbian diet.
Colombian Fruit Salad***
1 ripe banana, sliced
1/4 cantaloupe, cubed
1/2 apple, peeled and diced
3/4 cup milk or cream
1 teaspoon sugar
cinnamon

Combine the banana, cantaloupe, and apple into a deep bowl. Mix the sugar and milk or cream together and pour over the fruit, keeping the banana deep in the milk so that it will not turn brown. Refrigerate. When ready to serve, spoon fruit salads into individual bowls and sprinkle cinnamon over the top.

Peru

Atlantic Ocean

Andes Mountains

AMAZON RIVER

★ LIMA

REPUBLIC OF PERU

The left and right red panels represent the blood of the independence fighters. The middle white panel is for peace/justice. The middle emblem are symbols of Peru.

Peru

Peru is one of the poorest countries in South America. The capital is **LIMA**, where nearly 1/4 of the population is located. The population is 20.2 million.

LAND

Peru is 496,225 square miles. Peru can be broken into three distinct regions. The costa which is mainly desert extends northwest towards Ecuador. The sierra where the Andean highlands are located. The selva on the east, is where the rainforests and hilly lands are located.

CULTURE

The Inca came into power, overtaking smaller Indian tribes. They located their empire within the Andes. The Inca were ruled by the Lord Inca, who was treated as a god. The Inca formed their cities by clans or *ayllus*. They were excellent sculptors, using the stone of the Andes to form their sculptures and cities. One of the major cities in Incan society was Machu Picchu. In Machu Picchu, the ruins of The Temple of the Sun show how skilled the Inca were in architectural design.

Nearly half of the Peruvian population are of Indian descent. The Roman Catholic church is the principal religion.

The official language is Spanish, but two Indian languages, Quechua and Aymara are spoken by half the Peruvian population. Quechua means "warm valley people" is also the name of the tribe, and has been spoken by the Indians since 1438, when the Lord Inca declared it to be the language spoken.

Peru has many fine arts and crafts. Chief among them are weavings. Peruvians have been weaving for over 2,000 years. Jewelry making is also a craft for which Peru is renown.

Peruvian dragon painted on pottery.

RESOURCES

Major minerals found in Peru are copper, zinc, silver, and lead, and petroleum. Coffee and cotton are among the chief crops grown. Other crops include maize, potatoes, and cassava. Peru supplies the world with its unique llama wool. Also raised are the alpaca and vicuna which are similar to the llama, but yield much more expensive wool.

Peru's biggest industry is the illegal drug trade. Peru supplies nearly 50% of the coco leaves needed for cocaine.

RECIPES

Many of the world's food have their beginnings in Peru – the potato and tomato.

Peruvian Pie of the Sierra***

(Pastel de la Sierra)

3 large potatoes, cooked, peeled and diced
2 medium tomatoes
3 tablespoons salad oil
1 large onion, chopped fine
1 clove garlic, minced
6 to 8 ounces cheddar cheese, sliced thin
2 egg whites
2 egg yolks
2 tablespoons cream
dash of salt

Cook the potatoes in a large saucepan. Bring water to a boil, then cook over high heat for 30 minutes or until tender.

Grate the tomatoes, making at least 3/4 cup. Heat the oil in a saucepan, until it is hot. Add the onion and garlic, saute until tender. Add the tomatoes, simmer over low heat for 8 minutes.

Grease the bottom and sides of an 8"x 8" baking dish. Using half of the potatoes, cover the bottom of the dish. Spoon half of the tomato sauce over the potatoes, place half of the cheese slices on the sauce.

Make another layer with the remaining potatoes. Spoon the tomato sauce over the potatoes, arrange the cheese slices on top.

Beat the egg whites (add a pinch of salt) until foamy. Mix the egg yolks, cream and salt. Fold the egg whites into the yolk mixture and spoon it over the cheese layer. Bake in a preheated oven for one hour at 350-degrees.

ACTIVITIES

Peruvian Game – Wolf

The players form a circle around the player at the center. He is the wolf. The other players call to him, "Wolf, Wolf, are you ready?"

The wolf answers, "No, I've got to put my socks on!"

Again they call, and he answers, "No, I've got to put on my shoes!" Each time he goes through the motions of putting on the piece of apparel he names. It may be his hat, his coat, his pants, his shirt, or whatever he chooses.

Suddenly, he answers, "Yes, I'm ready and here I come!" Immediately all players scatter and rush to a designated safety zone. The wolf tries to tag a player before he reaches safety. If he does, that person becomes the wolf and the game continues. The wolf may get ready on any call that suits him.

ACTIVITIES

Make Peruvian Beads

Many Peruvians supplement their income by making clay beads called *muyuchacunas* and selling them at local markets. Often, they are traded for other things such as food.

Sculpy (follow directions on package)
Acrylic paint
small paintbrushes
embroidery thread or thin yarn

1. Mold the Sculpy into balls, slice with plastic knife, and make a hole with a pencil or the end of a paintbrush.
2. Paint.

ACTIVITIES

Create a Raised-Line Design

tracing paper
thin cardboard
scissors
white glue
cotton macrame cord
gold paint (spray paint works better because it spreads evenly but can be messy)
black acrylic or tempera paint

1. Draw a design on tracing paper and copy onto the cardboard. Below are some design ideas.
2. Cut out the shape.
3. Glue the cord down over the lines so the design becomes raised with the cord.
4. When the glue has dried, paint the design with two coats of gold paint.
5. Mount the design on a black-painted cardboard background or use the design as jewelry.

East Asia

Sea of Japan

Yellow Sea

Pacific Ocean

3.

1.

South China Sea

Sulu Sea

Celebes Sea

Gulf of Thailand

Andaman Sea

4.

5.

2.

IDENTIFY

1. _____
2. _____
3. _____
4. _____
5. _____

China

PEOPLE'S REPUBLIC OF CHINA

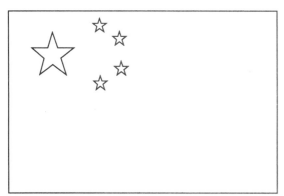

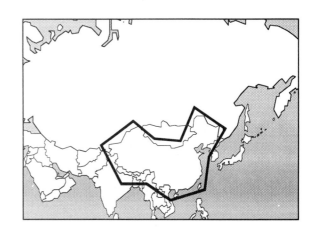

Red and yellow are the traditional colors of the country. The large yellow star represents the Communist Party and the red background also represents Communism. The four small, yellow stars are for the four sections of society.

China

The name China (the name most commonly used by foreigners) was probably taken from the **CH'IN DYNASTY** who unified the nation in 221 B.C. However, the natives of China use the name Chung Hua which means *Middle Country*. This concept originated with the idea that China was in the middle of the world.

China is the world's third largest country in land size. China is the most populated country with an estimate of nearly 1/4 of the world's population (over 1 billion).

LAND

China can be divided into three levels of elevation. The Tibetan highland is the highest with an average elevation of 13,000 feet. In the middle of the region is the Tibetan Plateau, rimmed by high mountain ranges (Kunlun Mountains, the **HIMALAYAS**; and the Karakoran and Pamir Mountains) and the Yangtze River which empties into the Pacific Ocean. **MT. EVEREST**, located on the Himalayan range is the world's highest elevation at 29,028 feet. The middle region are called the Uplands. In this region lies the **GOBI DESERT**, the Ordos Desert, and the Tsinling Mountains which divides the Yangtze river and the **HWANG HO** (*Yellow River*) basins. The third region, called the Lowlands, is where the majority of the Chinese population is located.

CLIMATE

Eastern China has heavy monsoon rains in summer and due to the Yangtze and Hwang Ho Rivers, is very prone to floods. The southeast of China has a subtropical climate with heavy summer rains. These rains are known as the Mai-yu (*Plum Rains*) because they appear when the plums are ripe. The southwest and central China have a continental climate. The uplands (the higher elevations) have subarctic conditions. The average amount of precipitation ranges from 80 inches in the areas hit by the rains to 4 inches in the desert lands.

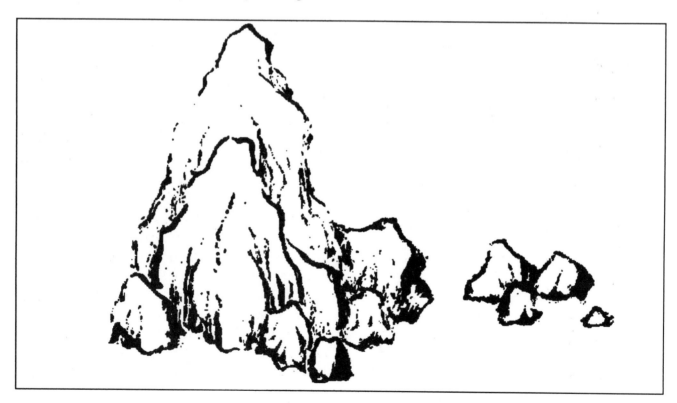

CULTURE

China's rule, until modern times, has been through a series of powerful dynasties. The first recorded history begins with the **SHANG** dynasty in the 16th century B.C. With the fall of the **CH'ING** (Manchu) dynasty, a republic was founded in 1912. The Chinese Communist party began in 1921, which led to a long civil war which ended with the Communists (led by **MAO TSE-TUNG**) taking over the country and establishing the People's Republic of China. The nationalists (who ruled pre-Communism) were led by **CHIANG KAI-SHEK**, and in 1949 retreated to the island of Taiwan. They established the Republic of China. The debate over the governments of the Republic of China and the government of Taiwan is still in dispute.

The population of China is multiracial. The mixture includes 94% **HAN** Chinese and the other percentage includes such ethnic groups as the Tibetans, Manchus, Mongols, Yis, and Koreans. The areas where these other ethnic groups are concentrated, have been established into national autonomous regions.

The Chinese language is one of the world's oldest languages. It is spoken in many different dialects. Over 800,000,000 people Chinese. Chinese is one of mankind's most difficult languages to read. Traditional written Chinese consists of many characters, each of which represents a separate word or idea, rather than letters. In traditional Chinese, a person must be able to recognize over 3,500 characters before he can read a novel, and over 10,000 characters before he can read a classical Chinese work. In 1950, due to the difficulty involved in learning to read traditional Chinese, the Communist government introduced the Chinese Alphabet to simplify the written language.

Religion in China was discouraged after the Communist party came into power. During the **CULTURAL REVOLUTION** of the 1960s, the practice of religion was discouraged even further when religious institutions were destroyed. Since 1978, the government has become much more tolerant of religious practice. Traditionally, the major religions were Buddhism and **TAOISM**. Many Chinese also believed in **ANCESTOR WORSHIP** and Confucianism, a system involving social and political values. The minority religions of Muslim and Christianity (mainly Roman Catholic) were important as well. The Chinese celebrate the Chinese New Year on October 1st. This is the anniversary of the founding of the People's Republic of China.

Each dynasty brought a new richness to the arts of China, many of which the Chinese are still renown. The Shang and **CHOU** dynasties produced great bronzes and jades – predecessors to the bronzes and jades created today. The

Chinese couple in Communist-style dress.

Chinese consider the **T'ANG** dynasty their golden age of figure painting. The T'ang also brought about the popularity of black and white landscape painting. Some of the world's best known ceramics (particularly vases) have survived from the **MING** dynasty. To this day, fine ceramics, especially porcelain, are called "china". The introduction of Buddhism from India brought the **PAGODA** (to many a symbol of China). The earliest pagodas were mere reflections of Indian pagodas but in time, established their own unique, Chinese style. **CALLIGRAPHY**, the art of brushstrokes, is attributed to the Chinese style of painting (common to all the dynasties.

China's literacy rate has improved since 1950. Children attend primary school for five to six years and middle school three years. The curriculum consists of Chinese, geography, music, and arithmetic. The secondary schools are work study schools and the students' work helps support the school. The subjects taught include science, literature, and mathematics. Chinese children start learning English at about the fourth grade level.

RESOURCES

The majority of China is rich with resources. It has many mineral resources, including the world's largest reserve of tungsten. Other resources include bauxite, iron ore, tin, lead, manganese, and mercury. Located in all but the southern part of China are the world's largest coal reserves. China is the fourth largest oil producer in the world. Due to economic reforms limiting defense-related industries, China has concentrated on textiles and has become one of the leading producers. China is a major agricultural country. The leading crops are rice, wheat, corn, and legumes (beans and peas). Cotton, because of the textile industry, is also an important crop. China has more livestock raised than any other country in the world. As of the late 1980s, China had an estimated 1 billion chickens and over 350,000,000 pigs.

RECIPES

Chinese seasonings frequently consist of the following: salt, pepper, sugar, and sesame oil. Wine, vinegar, cornstarch, and frying oil are also used. Chinese cooking instruments include the following: cleavers, chopping block, spatula, strainers, wok, and steamers.

Egg Flower Soup
3 cups clear canned chicken broth
dash of salt
chopped scallion
1 tablespoon cornstarch
2 tablespoons water
1 egg, beaten

Bring chicken broth to a boil. Separately, add water slowly to the cornstarch. Add cornstarch liquid to the broth. Stir until it begins to thicken and becomes clear. Add salt. Pour the beaten egg into the broth and continue to cook. It will cook quickly. Top with scallion.

The dragon is a symbol of fortune and happiness.

Sweet and Sour Pork

1 pound pork loin, cut up
1 tablespoon Soy Sauce
1 egg yolk
7-8 tablespoons cornstarch
1 cup pickled relish
1 green pepper
dash garlic
6 cups oil
3 tablespoons vinegar
3 tablespoons sugar
3 tablespoons ketchup
dash salt
1 1/2 teaspoon water

Soak cut up pieces of pork in soy sauce, egg yolk, and 1 tablespoon cornstarch. Mix with 6 more tablespoons of cornstarch and fry 3 minutes. Remove from pan. Reheat pan and stir-fry green pepper, garlic, and salad. Add vinegar, sugar, water, ketchup, and salt. Add 1 more teaspoon of cornstarch and water to thicken. Pour mixture over pork and serve with rice.

Stir-Fried Shrimp with Garlic

1 pound fresh shrimp
1/2 tablespoon cornstarch
oil
dash of salt
2 tablespoons chopped garlic
1/2 tablespoon chopped hot red pepper (optional)

Boil shrimp in pan of water for 3 minutes until bright pink in color. Remove, devein, and mix with cornstarch. Stir-fry shrimp, garlic, and seasonings.

VOCABULARY

The Chinese people have a special way of writing. They use characters made up of brush or pen strokes which give ideas of what is meant and pictures of words. These are called ideograms and pictographs. Special sounds are made to match each picture or idea.

people – *Jen-min*
mountain – *shan*
river – *chiang*
river – *ho*
the Chu River – *Chu Chiang*
the Yellow River – *Huang Ho*

ACTIVITIES

CHINESE CHECKERS is played on a six-pointed star, as shown. Use a commercially made board or make your own. If you make your own, paint each point of the star a different color and then shellac the entire board. If the board is flat, use discs as "men". If holes are bored in wood, use marbles. Each player uses ten men. The men are placed on the star point beginning with the point, as shown. Each player tries to get all his men across the board to fill in the opposite star point. He may move in any direction except backward, one place at a time. A man may "jump" over another man, and can even make a series of continuous jumps, in one move. The men he jumps over, however, are not removed from the board as in American checkers. The first player to fill in the opposite star point with his men wins.

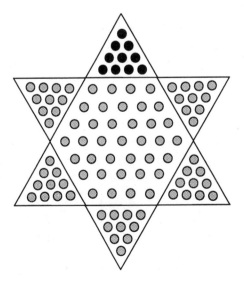

ACTIVITIES

Make a Chinese mask

crayons or paint

glitter, yarn, or any other decorations

slim stick or dowel

cardboard

tape

glue

Decorate mask. Cut out and glue mask to a piece of cardboard. Cut out eyes. Attach dowel to the back of the cardboard with mechanical tape or industrial-strength glue.

Korea

PEOPLE'S DEMOCRATIC REPUBLIC OF NORTH KOREA

The middle panel is red. The red star represents glory. The white circular background is for purity and the top/bottom stripes are for peace.

REPUBLIC OF SOUTH KOREA

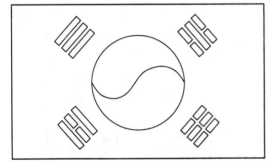

The central symbol (yin-yang) is red and blue — opposites. The white background expresses purity. The meanings of the four trigrams are clockwise from left:
1. summer/south/sky   2. autumn/west/moon
3. winter/north/earth   4. spring/east/sun

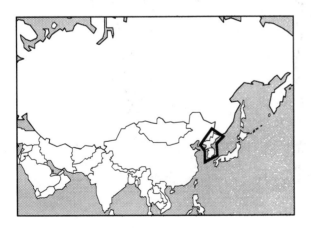

Korea

Korea is a peninsula extending southward, off the Asian mainland. Its borders are China on the north, the Russian republic on the northeast, and 120 miles east is Honshu (Japan). Because of these borders, Korea has been a cultural bridge between the Chinese and Japanese cultures. Although Korea was dominated by both China and Japan for centuries, the Koreans have maintained their own identity as a separate Asian country. The name derives from the **KORYO** dynasty (who ruled from 913 to 1392). Formerly a single nation, Korea was divided in 1945 into two separate occupation zones. The U.S.S.R. occupied the north and the U.S. the south. Since 1948, the Communist Democratic People's Republic of Korea (North Korea) and the Republic of Korea (South Korea) have been independent states. **SEOUL** is the capital of South Korea and **PYONGYANG** is the capital of the North Korea.

LAND

The country is so mountainous, only about 1/4 is arable. The narrowest point is 200 miles wide. It is bordered by the **YELLOW SEA** on the west and the Sea of Japan on the east. The irregular 5,400 mile coastline is bordered by more than 3000 islands.

The coastal lowlands offer few good harbors. The western lowlands open to the largest and richest lands for agriculture. The **KAEMA PLATEAU** rises near Wonsan to the **PAEKTUSAN** mountains, reaching 9,000 feet (highest point of Korea). The **TAEBACK** mountains rise steeply from the eastern lowlands. The **SOBACK RANGE** separates the western lowlands from the southern coast and Naktong Valley.

CLIMATE

The climate of Korea is continental but prone to extreme weather. The north of Korea has long, cold, and snowy winters and in the south the summers bring heavy rains and monsoons. The average annual precipitation in the south is 60 inches.

CULTURE

The Koreans are of the Mongoloid race. The official language of both the north and the south is Korean. The Korean alphabet, **HANGUL**, was developed during the 15th century, on the orders of King Sejong. It was the first phonetic alphabet in Asia.

The Koreans adhere to Buddhism and Confucianism. Confucianism was Korea's official religion from the the 14th century to the early 20th century. Also important to the Koreans is **SHAMANISM** – an ancient form of warding off spirits. Christianity is a minority.

Korea's rich artistic and cultural heritage reflects its Chinese influence. During the Koryo dynasty, ceramics of outstanding beauty and craftsmanship were produced. Most famous is the **CELADON** ware. This early ceramic work show the delicacy and feelings the Koreans have towards nature. Buddhism has been a major influence on the architecture

An example of the outstanding beauty of the Celadon designs.

(Buddhist shrines and temples), and metalwork. The literature of Korea is primarily poetic and draws heavily from Buddhism and Confucian traditions; **KASA**, a narrative poetry and folk poetry called **SIJA** which is chanted to **PANSORI** (drums).

Koreans are 98% literate, most of the population having completed six years of free, compulsory schooling. Nearly 75% attend secondary schools. Life expectancy has improved, due to improved healthcare. The use of herbs and acupuncture are ancient ways of healing the Koreans still use today. Koreans enjoy skiing, table tennis, and **PADUK**, a complex Oriental form of chess.

RESOURCES

Following the Korean War (1950-1953), South Korea developed a successful economy based on world-wide trade. The electronics

Painting showing the migrant worker.

industry successfully competes with that of Japan. The manufacture of textiles and footwear are also strong industries for the south. Rice is the major wet-season crop and wheat, barley, potatoes, and sweet potatoes are the principal dry-season crops. South Korea ranks third among Asian fish producers. New roads and subways were built for the 1988 Olympic games held in Seoul.

The political split of the country left North Korea with most of the mineral resources, including coal, iron ore, copper, gold, silver, and tungsten and much of the commercial forests. However, due to the migration of over 3 million northerners to the south, North Korea has a labor shortage. During the beginning of the Communist control, stress was put on machine and chemical industries in order to build an industrially self-sufficient economy and a strong military. Emphasis has switched to farm equipment industry and electric resources. At present, foreign trade is unstable.

VOCABULARY

temple – *sa*
mountain – *san*
river – *gang*
yes – *nay*
no – *anio*
please – *putokkhamnida*
good – *cho-un*

ACTIVITIES

Follow along with a traditional Korean song. The Arirang Pass is an imaginary rendezvous of lovers in the dreamland, although there is a real mountain pass called "Arirang Gogae" outside the Small East Gate of Seoul. The heroine of the story from which the Arirang Song originated comes from a folk story called "Miss Arirang".

Arirang Gogae

Arirang, Arirang, Arariyo
Arirang Pass is the long road you go.

If you leave and forsake me, my own,
Ere three miles you go, lame you'll have grown.

Wondrous time, happy time – let us delay;
Till night is over, go not away.

Arirang Mount is my Tear-Falling Hill,
So seeking my love, I cannot stay still.

The brightest of stars stud the sky so blue;
Deep in my bosom burns bitterest rue.

Man's heart is like water streaming downhill;
Woman's heart is well water – so deep and still.

Young men's love is like pinecones seeming sound,
But when the wind blows, they fall to the ground.

Birds in the morning sing simply to eat;
Birds in the evening sing for love sweet.

When man has attained to the age of a score,
The mind of a woman should be his lore.

The trees and the flowers will bloom for aye,
But the glories of youth will soon fade away.

2. Arirang (in Korean)

Arirang, Arirang, arariyo!
Arirang Gogaeto numu kanda.

Nareul burigo ganeum imeun,
Simnido mot-gas balbyung nanda.

Nolda gaso, nolda gaso,
Ibami saedorok nolda gaso.

Arirang gogaeneum noonmoore gogae;
Jungdeun-nim bogo sipusu na yugi wanne.

Chungchun hanaren byuldo manko;
Yo-nae gasamen geunsimdo manta.

Namjae maamun heureunan mool;
Yujae maamun woomoore mool:

Julmooni sarang-eun solbagwool sarang;
Baram man boolmyun-eun d'ok d'urujinda.

Naje woo-neun sae-neun bae gopa woolgo;
Bame woo-neun sae-neun im bogopa woonda.

Namjae naiga isibimyun,
Yujae maamul arujoone.

Sanchun-chomogeun julmu-gago;
Woorine chungchoon-eun neulgu ganda.

Japan

THE FLAG OF JAPAN

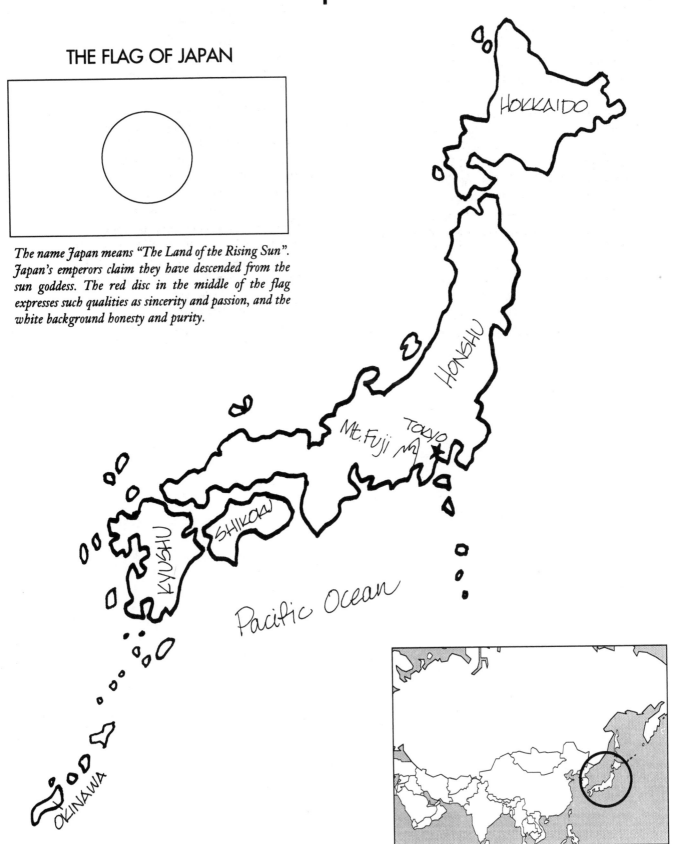

The name Japan means "The Land of the Rising Sun". Japan's emperors claim they have descended from the sun goddess. The red disc in the middle of the flag expresses such qualities as sincerity and passion, and the white background honesty and purity.

HOKKAIDO

HONSHU

Mt. Fuji

TOKYO

KYUSHU

SHIKOKU

Pacific Ocean

OKINAWA

Japan

The Japanese people call their country Nippon or Nihon, which means *origin of the sun*. The country's flag represents this concept. It contains a single red ball on a white background. The Japanese heritage is full of similar legends and symbols.

Japan's four islands cover about the same land area as California and its population density is one of the highest in the world. Japan has over 124 million inhabitants. Before World War II, Japan was the center of an empire that at times included Taiwan, Korea, Manchuria, eastern China, Indo China, and other South Pacific areas. Today Japan, greatly reduced in size, consists of four main islands – Hokkaido, Honshu, Shikoku, and Kyushu – and lesser islands that stretch for nearly 1,875 miles along the edge of Asia.

LAND

Japan's four main islands are **HOKKAIDO**, in the north; **HONSHU**, the largest and most populated, located in the center; and the southern islands of **KYUSHU** and **SHIKOKU**. Kyushu and Shikoku are separated from Honshu by the Inland Sea. Japan's islands are part of a zone of volcanic activity and mountain building, the "Ring of Fire" that rims the Pacific Ocean. The islands of Japan are actually the peaks of submerged mountain ranges. There are about 50 active volcanoes and every year about 1,500 earthquakes occur. **MOUNT FUJI**, a dormant volcano, rises to 12,388 feet. Most of the major cities lie on lowlands: **TOKYO** the largest, on the Kanto Plain, **NAGOYA** on the Nobi Plain, and **OSAKA** and **KYOTO** on the lowlands of Kansai.

CLIMATE

Japan has a climate typical of the east coast of most of North America. Hokkaido and the interior of northeastern Honshu have a humid continental climate, with short, cool summers and long, cold, and snowy winters. Towards the south, the climate is more sub-tropical with warm, long summers and short, mild winters. Typhoon season (late August to early October) brings high winds and heavy rains. The average amount of precipitation for most of Japan is 50 inches.

Japanese man in traditional costume.

CULTURE

The Japanese have developed their culture through a mixture of influences: the Chinese and the West. Chinese began settling in Japan during the 3rd century, strongly enriching the country with their language and arts. Their influence lasted until the 10th century. Western culture was introduced during the 16th century when the Dutch and British began trade.

The **MONGOLOID** people are the most dominant ethnic group in Japan. Mongoloids are characterized by an upward fold at the eyelid. A smaller minority is the **AINU**, an indigenous people who for centuries were pushed northward from their native region of the Inland Sea due to Japanese expansion. Due to Japan's historical class system, a third group, the **BURAKUMIN** or **ETA**, are often discriminated against and live in segregated communities. Another group, the **OKINAWANS** consider themselves Japanese but have unique cultural elements, including their own language.

Spoken, the Japanese language bears a strong association to Chinese. The written language of Japanese is complex, being taken from both Korean and Chinese characters. During the 9th century, two sets of characters (48 in each) were developed to bridge the gap between the Japanese and Chinese languages.

The religion of **BUDDHISM** introduced from Korea in the 6th century has a following of 75% of the Japanese population. Most Japanese Buddhists also have joining beliefs in the state religion, **SHINTO**. The oldest religion, **CONFUCIANISM** began in the 4th century.

Most Japanese arts owe their development to the arrival of the Chinese during the 6th century. Japanese literature, architecture, painting, sculpture, theater, and other art forms were greatly influenced by contact with these cultures. Japanese art is based on the beauty of

Japanese children offering their prayers to the Buddha.

nature and is very expressive. Some art forms include the woodblock print, **KABUKI** theater, **NOH** plays, and **BUNRAKI** puppetry, and unique forms of architecture and landscape design. The rich artistic heritage of Japan's past continues to be reflected in modern machine-made ceramics, textiles, and the continuation of such ancient practices as the tea ceremony, **HAIKU** poetry, and Japanese flower-arranging arts. Masters of such crafts as sword making, weaving, and lacquer designing are considered *living art treasures*.

The majority of Japan's population is literate. Education is free for all children from ages 6 up to age 15. Admission to schools of higher education is based on strict entrance examinations.

Japan's life expectancy is among the highest percent in the world. This is attributed to diet and exercise of **TAISO**. Because of the many earthquakes, the Japanese have a very enforced system of earthquake awareness.

RESOURCES

During World War II, Japan waged war against the allies but surrendered after the atomic bombing of **HIROSHIMA** and **NAGASAKI** in 1945. The country recovered quickly and became one of the world's leading industrial and trading nations. Japan produces many metallic minerals such as copper, lead, and gold. Due to it's mountainous terrain, Japanese farmland is sparse, but Japanese farmers grow tea, vegetables, and rice which is the country's chief summer crop. The Japanese produce charcoal and wood from their forests. Japan catches 1/8 of the fish caught in the world. Japan is a world leader in the electronics and the automotive industry.

RECIPES

Teriyaki Chicken

1/4 cup soy sauce
1 package boneless/skinless chicken breasts, cut into pieces
1 cup fresh mushrooms
1 cup chopped onions
1 cup bean sprouts (optional)
garlic, ginger to taste
oil

Marinate the chicken pieces in soy sauce overnight, if possible.

Saute chicken in oil until brown. Add onion, mushrooms, and soy sauce. Heat thoroughly. Add bean sprouts. Serve with cooked rice.

Fried Rice

Leftover meat or poultry scraps (ham, chicken, etc.)
2-3 eggs
1/2 teaspoon salt
1/3 cup oil
4 cups cooked rice
1 cup bean sprouts
2 tablespoons minced onion
1 teaspoon Chinese brown gravy syrup or soy sauce
garlic to taste

Brown onion in oil. Add leftover meat. Separately, scramble egg. Add egg, bean sprouts, rice, then gravy or soy sauce to the meat and onions. Heat until steaming.

You may want to try eating with chopsticks.

VOCABULARY

one – *ichi*
two – *ni*
three – *san*
four – *shi*
five – *go*
six – *roku*
seven – *nana*
eight – *hachi*
nine – *kyuh*
ten – *juh*
friend – *tomodachi*
school – *gakko*
car – *kuruma*
home – *katei*
name – *na mae*

あいうえお かきくけこ
Japanese Alphabet

ACTIVITIES

ORIGAMI is the Japanese art of paper folding. Origami has been practiced in Japan for over a thousand years by adults and children alike. The only material needed is paper. Most of the time colored paper about four to six inches square is used. Two sheets of different colored paper may be used by placing them back to back. The four basic rules of Origami are:

1. Choose a flat, hard surface as your place of work.

2. Be sure your folds straight.

3. Make your creases sharp by pressing with your thumbnail.

4. Choose paper with color, texture, and design that will add beauty to the piece. Experiment with different kinds of paper: onion skin, gift wrapping, comic strips, and others.

Origami books may be purchased at many bookstores.

Try to follow the directions below to make a hat.

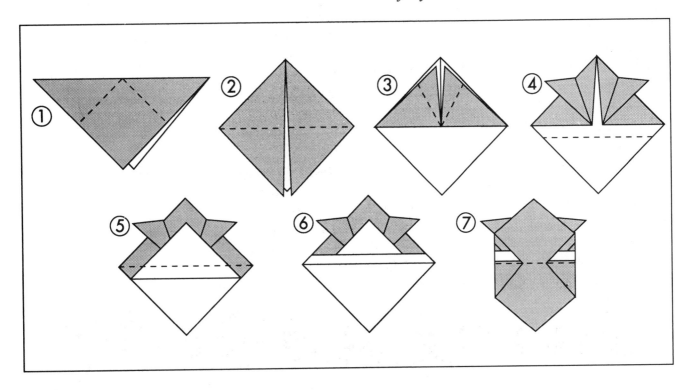

ACTIVITIES

Color Meiko in Her Kimono.

What else could you draw around her? Some ideas might be a pagoda, mountains, the sea, etc.).

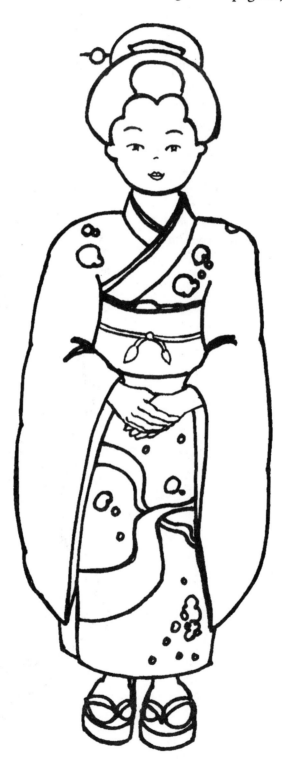

Thailand

KINGDOM OF THAILAND

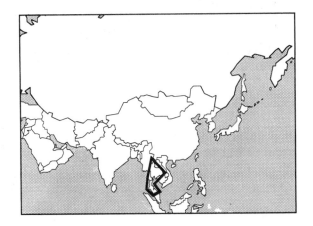

In the 19th century, the Thai flag had a white elephant – a symbol of the country (The Land of the White Elephant). The flag went through some changes and in 1917, was changed to represent solidarity with the Allies, matching the colors of the French flag –red stripes on top and bottom white stripes in between, and a blue stripe in the middle.

BANGKOK

Gulf of Thailand

Thailand

Thailand (*Land of the Free*) was formerly known as SIAM. The capital city is BANGKOK, with a population of over 3 million. During the Sokotai Empire, what is now Thailand also included parts of Burma, the Khmer Republic (Cambodia), and Malaysia. Siam was ruled by a monarchy until 1932, when a constitutional monarchy was created. In 1939, the country became a democratic country and changed the name to Thailand.

LAND

Thailand is located on the Gulf of Thailand. The country's borders are Malaysia to the east, Burma to the west, and Laos and Cambodia to the north. The country is 200,000 square miles.

CLIMATE

Thailand is a sub-tropical climate. Monsoon season lasts from May to September. The average annual temperature is 80° F. The average annual precipitation is 73 inches.

CULTURE

The Thai people originally came from southeastern China. Of the Thai there are three subgroups: the Siamese in the central plains, the LAO in the northeast, and KHON MUANG in the north. Most of the Thai speak different dialects from each other. The MALAY live in the southernmost provinces and the minority is the Chinese (mainly in Bangkok).

The official state religion in Thailand is Buddhism – 93% of the population practices Buddhism. MUSLIM is practiced by 4% – predominantly the Malay in the south.

The language of Thailand is Thai. The Thai alphabet has remain unchanged since its creation by RAMKHMHAENG, a powerful monarch (ruled 1283-1317).

Religious themes dominate Thai art. India has been a great influence. The Thai refined the art of bronze buddhas more than any other Buddhist country, using more ornamentation. Little traditional art done on paper or cloth remains due to the tropical climate. The Thai also are renown for their technique of wood carving, although now it is primarily done for tourists. The Thai history is steeped in legends – the RAMAKIEN is the Thai version of Hindu myths. RAMWONG, a dance which employs graceful hand and body movements, is a favorite event to watch.

Thai food is unique to Asia, being spiced with red hot chilies. KICKBOXING is one of the sports Thai enjoy. The literacy rate is one of the highest in East Asia. Schools are government-run and compulsory for seven years.

RESOURCES

The major crop is rice – most of the work in the rice paddies is still done manually. Other important crops are tobacco and peanuts. Major minerals mined in Thailand are iron, copper, tin, lead, zinc, and manganese. Other important industries are electrical and textiles (the Thai are famous for their silks and cottons).

RECIPES

Peanut Sauce*

1 teaspoon lemon juice
1 onion, minced
salt
1 teaspoon red pepper leaves
1 teaspoon brown sugar
1 teaspoon soy sauce
1 cup oven-heated ground peanuts

Mix and cook until heated. Serve with flank steak that has been marinated in soy sauce and cooked on bamboo skewers.

Lumpia

2 tablespoons water
1 cup flour
1 teaspoon cornstarch
dash of salt

Roll on skillet like a pancake. Brush with oil. Blot. Add a mixture of onion, celery, ground beef, pork, or other leftover meat. Fry.

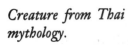

Creature from Thai mythology.

Satay (sates)

Marinate beef, pork, chicken, or shrimp in soy sauce, lime juice, and garlic. Place thin strips on bamboo skewers. Cook on a hibachi or in a broiler. Dip into a sauce of ketchup, vinegar, sugar, and water or peanut sauce.

VOCABULARY

The Thai language has 44 consonants and 32 vowels with 5 tones. A word pronounced in different tones will mean different things.

teacher – *khun kreo*
students – *mug rian*
school – *rong rian*
girl – *dek poo ying*
boy – *dek poo chia*
Greetings – *Sa wad dee*

ACTIVITIES

The customs and beliefs in Thailand are quite different from those in America. Name some of our customs and beliefs.

- The Thai believe that the head is the home of the soul. It is sacred and should not be touched.
- The feet are the least sacred part of the body. It would be an insult to point at anything with your feet or to cross your legs in front of elders.
- Women must never touch a Buddhist monk or offer to shake his hand.
- Thai always take their shoes off when entering a home or temple.

THE THAI NATIONAL ANTHEM (phonetically)

Prahte...thai, ruam leu – at neu –ah
chart chur – ah Thai...pen pracha – raj...patai khong.
Thai took su – an, yoo damrong kong wai...
dai tang mu – an duey Thau lu – an...mai...rasksa
Mak...kee, Thai nee rak saghob tae thung
rob mai klard, ekkaraj...cha mai hai krai kom...
Kee... sala...leu – at took yard pen chart
plee...ta – lerng pratate chart Thai tawee
mee chai chajo'.

ACTIVITIES

Circle the Object that Does Not Belong

In the picture below are three objects found in Thailand. Which one is not found in Thailand?

WHITE ELEPHANT

UMBRELLA

IGLOO

BOWL OF RICE

Vietnam

SOCIALIST REPUBLIC OF VIETNAM

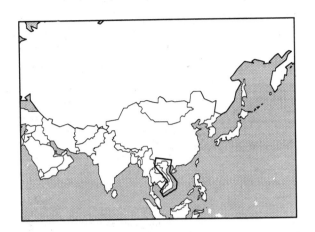

Red background and yellow star are traditional socialist colors. The flag was revised slightly in 1955 by North Vietnam with a more elongated star. In 1975, the present flag was adopted for the entire country.

Vietnam

Vietnam is a long country curved like the letter "s", south of China. The total land size of Vietnam is approximately 127,000 square miles (a little smaller that California). **HANOI** is the capital and is Vietnam's second largest city with a population of over 1.5 million people. **HO CHI MINH CITY**, known as Saigon before the Vietnam War, is the largest city with a population of over 3.5 million people. Haiphong is another important Vietnamese city. It is the manufacturing center and main seaport in that portion of the country formerly known as North Vietnam.

LAND

Vietnam is a land filled with diversity. In this country, there are mountains in the central region; plains, lush rice paddies in the northern and southern regions; and even small areas resembling deserts. About half of the country is tropical forest. The principal river of the north is the Son Hong Ha (*Red River*). In the central region is the Perfume River. The most important river in the south is the **MEKONG** (*Nine dragons*). On the deltas of these rivers are where the rice paddies are located. Vietnam is known as a *landscape filled with legend.*

CLIMATE

The climate of Vietnam varies in the north and the south. Winters in the north are dry and cool. Summers are very hot, with heavy rains and typhoons. The south has basically two seasons – wet and dry. During the wet season, the south gets many monsoons and typhoons are common along the coast. The yearly average of precipitation for Vietnam is about 59 inches.

CULTURE

According to legend, the Vietnamese are children of a dragon and a mountain fairy. Fifty of the children went with their mother, the fairy to the mountains and the other 50 went with their father, the dragon to the river. Those who went with the dragon are "Vietnamese".

For much of its history, Vietnam has been the subject of disputes and wars among other countries trying to gain or maintain control of the small country. At various times, the Japanese, French, Chinese, and **VIETMINH** Communists waged war on Vietnam soil trying to establish control. In May 1954, at the Geneva Conference, a decision was made to divide Vietnam temporarily into two zones. The northern zone, called North Vietnam, was to be controlled by the Communists and the southern zone, called South Vietnam, was to be controlled by the non-communist Vietnamese. In 1956, however, the Communists decided they wanted complete control of the country. This move by the Communists set off the **VIETNAM WAR**. Communist countries, such as China and Russia, sent aid to North Vietnam, while non-communist countries, such as the United States, sent aid to South Vietnam. The United States sent thousands of troops and millions of dollars of aid to South Vietnam. In 1973, the United States withdrew the last of its troops and the participants agreed to a ceasefire. The Communists continued fighting, however, and in April 1975, South Vietnam was defeated. Today Vietnam is one country.

The official language of Vietnam is Vietnamese. The population is made up of Vietnamese, Chinese, Cambodians, and **MONTAGNARDS**. Montagnards are dark-skinned people of mixed ethnic background and are mountain people. Most Vietnamese live on the river deltas and coastal plains, making their living as farmers or fishers. The Chinese live in the cities and the Cambodians in the rural areas. The art of Vietnam has been influenced

for centuries by the Chinese. The Chinese conquest of Vietnam lasted for nearly 1000 years, forcing the natives to adapt to Chinese customs and dress. The Chinese influence is seen in the architecture (temples and pagodas), and the painting of scrolls and panels, and the use of Calligraphy. Although, the Chinese influence on literature was great, the Vietnamese have developed their own form of folk poetry. Such crafts as jewelry making, lacquer work, and embroidery are other arts in which Vietnam has excelled.

Due to communism, religion was discouraged but Buddhism, Confucianism, and Taoism are still widely practiced. Christianity, a small minority, is also practiced in the cities.

The Vietnamese have a great respect for learning and most of the people can read and write. Most of the people use bicycles for transportation. Their diet consists mainly of fish, rice, and vegetables. In public parks, it is not uncommon to see groups of young and old practicing TAI-CHI.

RESOURCES

The major industry in Vietnam is agriculture. The most important crops are rice and rubber (which is mostly in the central region). Forestry is also strong for the Vietnamese economy, due to the amounts of tropical forests. Fisheries also attribute to the economy, due to the coastal waters and the numerous rivers throughout Vietnam. Along the coast, minerals such as iron, aluminum, lead, zinc, and manganese can be found, as well as recently discovered oil and natural gas deposits.

RECIPES

The Vietnamese people eat a lot of rice and vegetables with small pieces of shrimp, beef, or other meats. Rice, Vietnamese style, is made by adding onion, garlic, ketchup, soy sauce, carrots, and eggs to the rice.

Spring Rolls
Rice paper
Cabbage
Small pieces of meat (pork, shrimp, etc.)
Onion and/or finely chopped vegetables

Soak rice paper until it is soft. Combine other ingredients. Put mixture in rice paper, fold, and deep fry until lightly browned. Serve with soy sauce or a sauce of vinegar and carrot slivers.

Sweet Soup
1 1/2 cup sugar
5 cups water
1 can green beans
1/3 cup coconut

Combine ingredients and bring to a boil. Serve hot.

VOCABULARY

one – *mot*
two – *hai*
three – *ba*
four – *bon*
five – *nam*
six – *sau*
seven – *bay*
eight – *tam*
nine – *chin*
ten – *muoi*
Good morning/Good night – *chao ong*

ACTIVITIES

SONG OF THE VIETNAMESE CHILDREN

The children sing this song in a circle, holding hands and skipping. They change directions after each line.

Cun nhau mua chung quant la cung nhau mua vong quanh.

Cun nhau mua chung quant la ta cung nhau mua deu.

Nam tay nhau, bat tay nhau ta cung vui mua vui.

Nam tay nhau, bat tay nhau ta cung nhau mu a diw.

MID-AUTUMN FESTIVAL "TET TRUNG–THU"

The children in Vietnam celebrate the mid-autumn festival, a celebration of the full moon of the fifteenth day of the eighth month of the lunar year. The full moon brings joy to the people. During the night, the children sing and dance. They drink tea and eat cakes shaped like the round face of the moon. These cakes are called moon cakes or mid-autumn cakes. They carry lanterns, which they often make themselves. There are often contests to see who made the best lantern. After the celebration, the children gather around their parents or grandparents to watch the full moon and listen to stories of Vietnam. One such story "The Legend of Firecrackers" is told as follows:

In ancient times, there were two wicked spirits who hated mankind and played many wicked tricks on the people. Their names were Na Ong and Na Ba, husband and wife. Both of them feared light and noise, however, so they did all their nasty deeds at night.

At Tet, when the good *genii* of that neighborhood had to report to heaven, the two bad spirits were particularly bad and threw the people into a frenzy. The people learned that Na Ong and Na Ba were afraid of light and noise so they lighted their homes and exploded firecrackers to scare the bad genii away. They kept the noise and lights going strong until Tet was over and their good protectors could get back home from heaven. Then, the firecrackers and lights were no longer necessary.

In the Vietnamese calendar, the rooster is represented as the 10th cycle.

Malaysia and Singapore

FEDERATION OF MALAYSIA

The Malaysian flag was inspired by the Stars and Stripes. There are 14 red and white stripes, and the star has 14 points – a recognition of the 14 states (although Singapore's succession makes just 13 states). The star and crescent are Islamic symbols. The yellow of both the symbols represents those states that are sultanates and the blue background is a tribute to the British.

REPUBLIC OF SINGAPORE

The colors of red and white are the traditional Malaysian colors. The white stands for purity and virtue, and the red is for universal fellowship of mankind. The crescent moon signifies the youth of the state, and the five stars represent the five ideals: democracy, peace, progress, justice and equality.

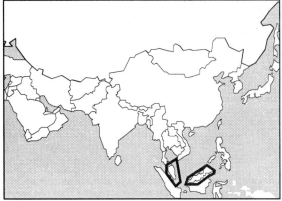

Malaysia and Singapore

Singapore (*the City of Lions*) is an island south of Malaysia. It is a forward-thinking and progressive country. This island republic maintains a unique combination of past British tradition and modern growth. Singapore is the second busiest port of the world. It was only a fishing village when Sir Raffles of the British East India Company landed in 1819 and made it a British maritime base. In 1957, full international self-government was achieved. In 1965, after years of rule by the British, Japanese, and Malaysian Republic, the country became a fully independent sovereign nation.

Malaysia, a peninsula was created in 1965 as a federation of the states of Malaysia, Sarawak, North Borneo, and Singapore (which separated later that same year). It is a constitutional monarchy. KUALA LUMPUR is the Federal capital of Malaysia.

LAND

Singapore is 240 square miles and bordered by Sumatra to the west and the eastern islands of Malaysia. Malaysia is 128,400 square miles. Almost 2/3 of Malaysia is virgin jungle and the western interior is mountainous. The highest peak in southeast Asia is MT. KINABULA.

CLIMATE

Malaysia is tropical. Monsoons occur nearly all year. The annual average precipitation is 120 inches.

CULTURE

There are four main cultures within Singapore: Chinese, Malay, Indian, and English. Religion is varied including Muslim, Hinduism, and Buddhism. English is the primary language, although Malay is also taught. Singapore children can go to schools from age six to fourteen for free.

Within Malaysia, there are Malays, Chinese, Indians and Pakistanis, and aborigines of the peninsula. The state religion is Islam but due to the freedom to worship – Buddhism, Hinduism, Sikh, Taoism, and Christianity are also practiced. The official language is Malay but again, because of all the different races, many dialects are spoken. English is taught in all schools and widely used in commerce. Education is free to all children for twelve years.

The diversity of the races of both Singapore and Malaysia produces many forms of art. Both offer BATIK art in clothing and traditional wall hangings. Painting, sculpture, ceramics, and calligraphy all are flourishing arts. All types of architecture are prominent from Chinese temples to Moorish buildings. One of the earliest Malaysian folk dances, MAK INANG, is a favorite of the Malay. At Malaysian festivals, BERSILAT – a self-defense art is demonstrated.

Malaysians enjoy soccer, ping-pong, and field hockey. Because of the surrounding waters, water sports such as scuba diving, sailing, and canoeing are also enjoyed. Both countries enjoy kite flying and often have kite competitions. Kite flying had its beginnings in the 16th century. The contests are judged by the kite's design and altitude.

RESOURCES

Singapore is known as the hub of the southeast. Because of it's close proximity to the other Asian countries, most of the economy comes from trade and tourism. Singapore in past history was known as a staging point for pirates. Malaysia on the other hand has a thriving agriculture industry. Pineapples, coconuts, rubber, palm oil, rice and timber are some primary products. Due to the amount of forests, Malaysia also has over 1/2 of the world's total animals (including the elephant, rhinoceros, the honey bear, and the tiger). Minerals found in Malaysia are oil, tin, and copper.

VOCABULARY

good-bye – *selamat tinggal*
good morning – *selamat pagi*
please – *sila*
thank you – *terima kasih*
hello, how are you? – *halo, apa khabar?*

RECIPES

There is such a variety of foods in Singapore that it is difficult to pick from a single recipe. It is a melting pot into which Asian and Western influences have been mixed.

Sample these fruits, if available. Some are not available in the U.S. Why not?

pineapple	starfruit
mangosteen	nangka
papaya	duku
chiker	jambu-air
mango	rambutan

Some favorite Chinese foods follow. Order the food at a Chinese Restaurant or find the recipe in a Chinese cookbook.

Hokkien cuisine favorite: Hokkein mee (noodles) – a mixture of thick yellow noodles and rice vermicelli (bee hoon) cooked with prawns, squid, beansprouts, and a touch of lime and red chilies.

Hakka cuisine favorite: Stewed pig's trotters and Yong Tau Foo, a fish ball recipe.

Szechuan cuisine favorite: Diced chicken with dried chilies (often very spicy food!).

Peking cuisine favorite: Peking Duck.

Malay favorites: Satay, skewers of seasoned chicken, beef, mutton grilled over charcoal, served on a bed of cool sliced cucumber and onion with a bowl of spicy peanut gravy.

Ketupat: Small rice cake.

Sotoayam: Spiced chicken broth filled with beansprouts, rice cake chunks, shreds of chicken.

Tofu dishes: Tofu is a flat, solid chunk of beancurd.

Prata dishes: Light, flaky Indian pancakes.

Pra kosong: Prata served with a bowl of thin curry gravy.

Murtabak: Prata filled with mutton and onion.

Seafood: Prawns and squid, as well as a wide variety of Japanese foods such as sushi (balls of vinegared rice topped with seafood) and sukiyaki (thinly sliced beef and vegetables cooked in a pan).

Benkang Pisang
1 cup milk
2 bananas
3 1/2 cups flour
1 tablespoon baking powder
2 tablespoons instant coffee (undissolved)
3 eggs
1/2 teaspoon salt
1/2 cup butter
1/2 cup brown sugar

Preheat oven to 350° F. Mix eggs and sugar until fluffy. In a separate bowl, mash bananas and add milk and instant coffee. Beat butter until creamy. Mix flour, baking powder, and salt. Add the banana and flour mixture alternately to the butter, a small amount at a time. Add egg mixture and beat until the batter is smooth. Pour the batter into a 8" x 8" greased baking pan. Bake for 30-45 minutes or until lightly brown on top. Serve warm or cool.

ACTIVITIES

Find the Matching Kite in the Malaysian Kite Festival

The South Pacific

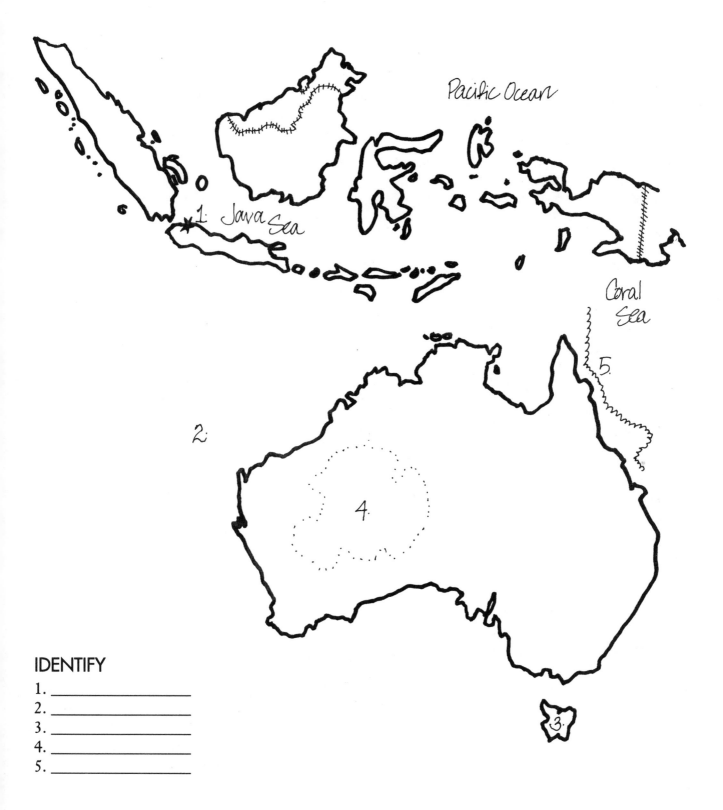

Pacific Ocean

1. Java Sea

Coral Sea

5.

2.

4

3.

IDENTIFY

1. _____
2. _____
3. _____
4. _____
5. _____

Australia

COMMONWEALTH OF AUSTRALIA

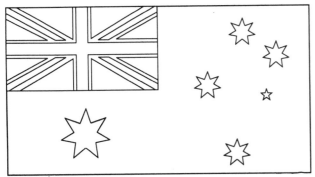

The flag is based on the United Kingdom's ensign. The constellation of stars represents the Southern Cross. Four of the smaller stars have seven points. The smallest has five points (being dimmer in the night sky). The largest star represents the Federal Commonwealth with seven points to represent each territory.

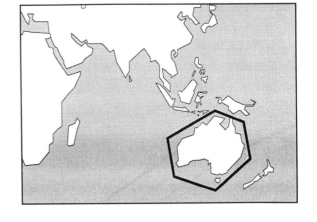

Timor Sea

Coral Sea

Great Barrier Reef

Great Dividing Range

Great Sandy Desert

Indian Ocean

SIDNEY

CANBERRA

Tasman Sea

ISLAND OF TASMANIA

Australia

Australia is an independent nation freely associated with Great Britain. The name of Australia is derived from the Latin word *australis* meaning "*south wind*". The capital is **CANBERRA** (Australia's newest city). The population of Australia is 16,500,000. Other large cities include Sidney (the largest port) and Melbourne.

The Dutch made discovery of Australia in 1607, naming it New Holland. However, they found little of value, and no land suited for settlement. The British explored the land later and claimed it their territory. The British used the territory as a prison colony for centuries. In time, Australia became settled. In 1901, the Commonwealth of Australia was founded. The Commonwealth consists of 6 states and 1 territory.

LAND

The country is 2,970,000 square miles. The main mountains are the **GREAT DIVIDING RANGE** which extend along the eastern edge of the country, and are believed to be among the oldest mountains in the world. Between the ocean and the mountains is fertile land. To the west of the mountains is tableland and deserts. The deserts cover over 1/3 of the country. Australia also includes the island of Tasmania and Norfolk Island. The **GREAT BARRIER REEF** stretches 1,200 miles along the northeastern coast.

CLIMATE

Australia is south of the equator so their summers are the northern hemisphere's winters. For the most part, the climate is warm and dry. Up in the northern peninsula, the climate is tropical. The northern region generally receives heavier rains of up to 60 inches per year. Southern and Western Australia have annual precipitation of about 9 inches.

CULTURE

The Aboriginal were the first inhabitants of Australia. They had been living in Australia for over 40,000 years. Until recently, Aboriginals were hunters and gatherers, living a nomadic life. Boomerangs (a curved tool which when thrown properly, returns to its starting point) were used by the men as a hunting weapon. They have no written language except for early Aboriginal rock paintings and carvings.

Today, many of the Aboriginal people have come into the cities, working jobs for pay. Many still live in the northern territory. Aboriginals make up little than 2% of the Australian population but seem to be increasing.

The official language of Australia is English but there are many Aborigine dialects spoken. There are all sorts of religions practiced, with the majority of the population following Christianity.

Australians enjoy water sports including surfing, swimming, sailing, and fishing. Other popular sports are cricket and tennis. Education is compulsory for ages 6 to 15.

RESOURCES

Being so set apart from all other continents has created different animal life. About 1/2 of Australia's animals are marsupials such as the kangaroo and the koala bear. Other unusual animal life includes the platypus and the spiny anteater (two of the

most primitive creatures found living) and birds like the emu (similar to the ostrich).

Australia is the largest producer and exporter of wool. Dairy products are also an important industry. Nearly 40% of export income is from agriculture. Major mineral resources found are bauxite, iron ore, tin, lead, copper, silver, gold, and zinc.

RECIPES

Australian Meat Pie

1 pound ground beef
1/2 cup ketchup
1/2 cup onion, chopped
dash of salt
1 8" pieshell
1 tablespoon Worcestershire sauce
1/2 cup evaporated milk
1/3 cup bread crumbs
1/2 teaspoon oregano
dash of pepper
1 cup shredded cheddar cheese

Combine beef, milk, ketchup, bread crumbs, onion, and dry seasonings. Put in pieshell and bake at 350-degrees about 35 minutes. Mix Worcestershire and cheese and spread on top of pie. Bake at 350-degrees until cheese melts.

Pumpkin Soup

fresh, whole pumpkin
1 cup or more of onion, chopped
2 tablespoons butter
1 cup of milk
allspice

Cube the inside of a fresh pumpkin. Cut the top off the pumpkin and keep it for a replaceable lid. Scoop the insides of the pumpkin so you can use the shell as a serving bowl. Saute 1 cup of onions (or more, if desired) in butter. Add the pumpkin, allspice, and 1 cup of milk. Put into a blender and blend until a thick soup consistency. Add more milk, if necessary. Serve in your pumpkin shell for an added touch!

VOCABULARY

dinkum Aussie – *100% Australians*
dinky dye – *everything is going well*
lift – *elevator*
fairy floss – *cotton candy*
bash – *party*
poor cow – *someone you feel sorry for*
Waltzing Matilda – *hike*

ACTIVITIES
ACROSS
1. Australia produces high amounts of this mineral.
2. Marsupial who with her baby makes big leaps.
3. Big bird, similar to the ostrich.
4. The_____-_____ Reef has lots of coral growing on it.
5. The spiny anteater eats one for breakfast
6. Without this, sheep shiver.

DOWN
1. Throw this and it will come back.
2. This creature clings to trees and always seems sad.
3. The first inhabitants of Australia.
4. An island off the mainland of Australia.
5. A game most Aussies enjoy.

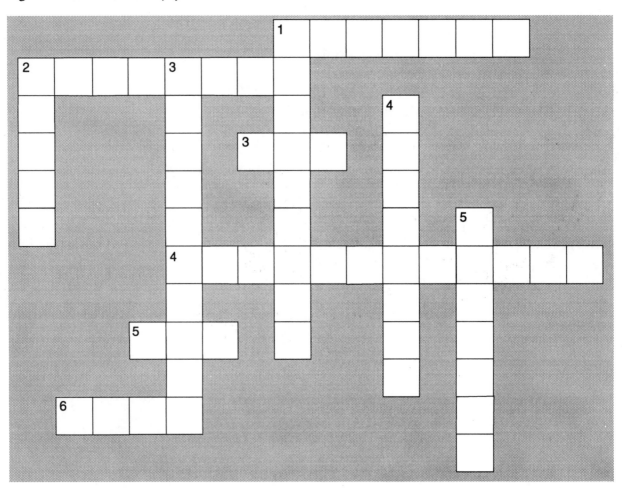

DOWN 1. Boomerang 2. Koala 3. Aboriginal 4. Tazmania 5. Cricket

ACROSS 1. Bauxite 2. Kangaroo 3. Emu 4. Great Barrier 5. Ant 6. Wool

Indonesia

REPUBLIC OF INDONESIA

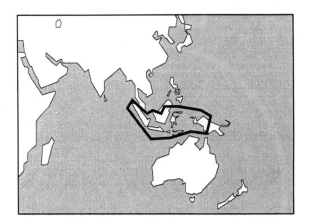

The top red stripe stands for gallantry and freedom. The bottom white stripe is for purity and justice.

Indonesia is made up of 13,677 islands stretching from the Malay Peninsula to northern Australia. To Indonesians, Indonesia is TANAH AIR KITA (meaning *"our land and water"*). Indonesia is the largest nation in southeastern Asia. With a population of 176 million, Indonesia is among the top five world's largest populated countries. The capital of Indonesia is JAKARTA. The islands of Indonesia are diverse from small one-mile wide fishing villages to BORNEO (one of the world's largest islands). Some of the islands include JAVA, where 60% of the population live; 1/2 of New Guinea; 2/3 of Borneo; Sumatra, and Sulawesi. Indonesia is a republic, led by a president who has been in office since 1968! The country became independent of the Dutch and Japanese in 1949, after centuries of rule.

LAND

Indonesia is 741,101 square miles. Most of the islands are mountainous. The islands have many volcanoes, including the volcano KRAKATOA, in western Java. Because of the volcanic ash, the land is very fertile, especially on Java and Bali. The lake KELI MUTU on the island of Flores was formed in a non-active volcanic crater. Over 80% of the islands are covered by thick, tropical rainforests.

CLIMATE

The climate of Indonesia is tropical, because the islands lie along the equator. Except for a rainy season from December to March, the weather remains hot.

CULTURE

Indonesia has over 350 ethnic groups living on its many islands. The largest majority are the JAVANESE who live in southern and central Java.

Most are rice farmers. Their culture dates back for more than one thousand years.

The second largest group are the BALINESE who live in Bali. The Balinese are the only Hindus of the islands. Art is an important aspect to their culture. Children can learn to create art by becoming apprentices to stonecarvers, wood carvers, painters, or silversmiths. Another important ethnic group are the MINANGKABOU who live in western Sumatra. They are rice farmers whose fields are built into the mountains. They use ancient farming methods, including the water buffalo to help plow. The Minangkabou are a matriarchal society; in the past they were ruled by queens and today the women are basically in charge. The Toraja people live in the southern Sulawesi mountain. They believe their ancestors arrived on Sulawesi by sea, carried their boats ashore,

A Sumatran mask

and made the boats their homes.

In the jungles of Kalimantan, over 200 groups of people live. Each tribe has different customs from each other; tattooing and body piercing are examples. In the past, many of these tribes were headhunters. Today, although headhunting is no longer practiced, some tribes still have ancient skulls decorating their homes.

Most Indonesians farm for a living. These rural Indonesians live in villages called kampong. Each Indonesian follows a traditional system called **GOTONG ROYONG** (*"mutual cooperation"*). Although most of Indonesia is poverty-stricken, this system unites the people so each share what they have with another.

Religion is very important in Indonesia. Each person must carry an identity card, listing what religion is practiced. There are five official faiths: Muslim, Hindu, Roman Catholic, Protestant, or Buddhist. Animism (worship spirits in nature) is a religion mainly practiced in the more rural areas. The majority of Indonesians tend to be Muslim. Muslim is not as strict in practice as the Middle Eastern countries, but just as much a way of life for Indonesians.

The Indonesians speak **BAHASA INDONESIA**. Each group has a different language in their village but Bahasa Indonesia is spoken in schools. The language was developed for trade to commence quickly. The language is very symbolic, poetic, and logical. Many phrases create word pictures.

Batik clothmaking is a Javanese speciality. Traditional music called **GAMELAN** (an orchestra of drums, gongs, and xylophones) accompanies shadow puppet plays called **WAYANG KULIT**. In Java and Bali, stories are told by way of dance. Each movement has a meaning.

The Indonesians enjoy many festivals, badminton, soccer, and **PENCAK SILAK**, a form of martial art.

RESOURCES

Indonesia is rich in mineral resources. Minerals produced are oil, natural gas, coal, nickel, tin, bauxite, and iron ore. Because of all the jungle land, forestry accounts for a majority industry. Some of the world's best farmland is in the Indonesian islands. Major crops include rice, palm oil, rubber, sugar, coffee, tea, pepper, and tobacco.

RECIPES

Nasi Goreng (Fried Rice)
2 cups uncooked rice
1/2 onion, chopped
3 cloves garlic, minced
4 tablespoons oil
1/2 pound shrimp, frozen
3 tablespoons soy sauce
1 thinly sliced hot red pepper (optional)
1 cucumber, sliced

While the rice is cooking, place the onions, garlic, and oil in a skillet and fry until onions are soft. Add the shrimp, and cook a few minutes longer. Add the soy sauce and hot pepper, and stir. Then add the cooked rice, and mix thoroughly. Place mixture on a serving platter, with cucumber slices around the edges.

VOCABULARY

The Bahasa Indonesia language is a combination of Arabic, Portuguese, Chinese, Dutch, Spanish, and English.
puppet master – *dalang*
child – *anak*
children – *anak-anak*
teacher – *guru*
sun (literally translated "eye of the day") – *mata hara*

ACTIVITIES

Create a Paperbag Indonesian Handpuppet

Decorate mask parts and cut out. Attach the top part to the folded part of the bag. Attach the bottom mask to the length of the bag. See bottom example.

The Indian Sub-Continent

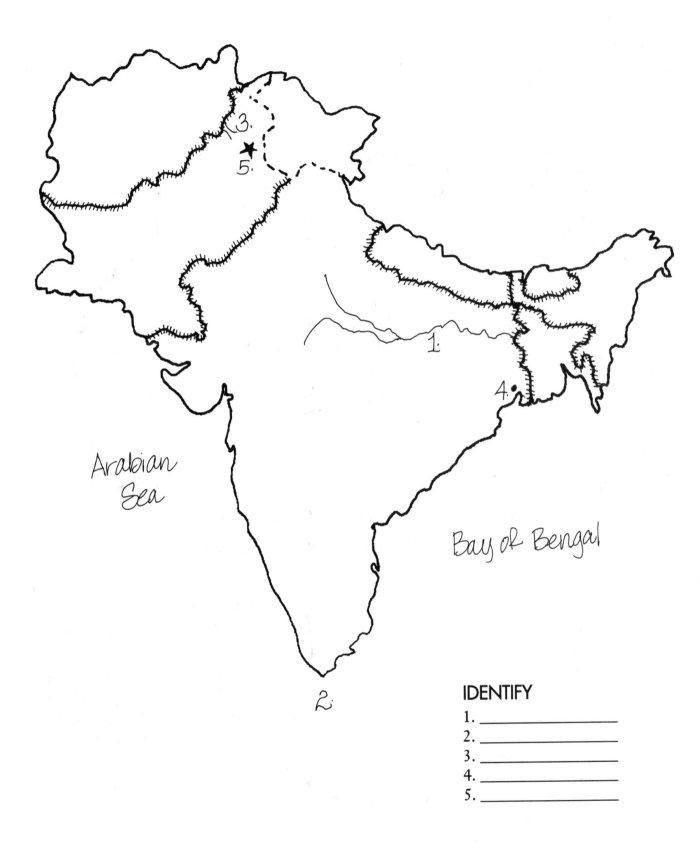

Arabian
Sea

Bay of Bengal

IDENTIFY

1. _____
2. _____
3. _____
4. _____
5. _____

India

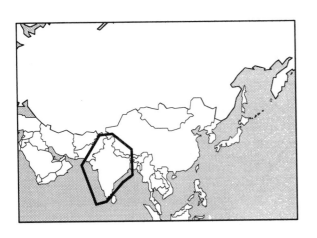

THE REPUBLIC OF INDIA

The top stripe is saffron orange meaning courage and sacrifice, the middle stripe is white representing truth and peace and the bottom stripe is green for faith, fertility, and chivalry. On the white is the image of a Buddhist dharma chakra (wheel of life).

India

India's long history of over 4500 years has left its mark in nearly all cultures of the world. The population is 845,000,000 and growing, making India the world's second most populated country next to China. The majority of the population live in rural villages. Large cities with populations of over a million include Calcutta, Bombay, Delhi, and Madras. The capital is **NEW DELHI**. India's struggle for its freedom has been long and tumultuous. In past history, India was part of the British empire. In 1947, India became a free and independent country. **MAHATMA GHANDI** led the struggle for independence with non-violence resistance.

LAND

India's land can be divided into three regions.

(1) The **HIMALAYAS**, a mountain range which rises to 18,000 feet. To the north of the Himalayas is the Karakoram Range whose 30 or more peaks rise over 24,000 feet. Between the the two mountain ranges is the valley of the Indus River. Southwest to the Himalayan range is the Vale of Kashmir.

(2) The Northern Plains, are lowlands which extend from western Pakistan to eastern Bangladesh. Through these lowlands flows the **GANGES RIVER**, considered to be a holy river.

3) The Peninsula of India in the south is where the **DECCAN PLATEAU** is located. The peninsula is surrounded by the Arabian Sea and the Indian Ocean.

CLIMATE

Most of India has a tropical monsoon climate (except the semi-arid climate of northwestern India). In summer, moisture-laden winds release heavy rains when they rise over the coast or the mountains. The summer temperatures reach an average of 85° F. Winter is dry and cool with average temperatures of 70° F. The Himalayas reach much cooler temperatures. Rainfall amounts vary from year to year which can cause problems with farming. Precipitation in the **THAR** desert is almost zero. Shillong Plateau, one of the wettest places in the world averages 428 inches annually.

CULTURE

Around 1500 B.C., Aryan tribes invaded India from the northwest and mixed with the local **DRAVIDIAN** society. From this intermingling between the Aryans and Dravidians came Hinduism and the **CASTE SYSTEM**. The caste system defines the class each person is born

Indian man wearing a turban and an Indian woman wearing a sari.

into. A person's lifestyle, language, customs and beliefs are determined by his caste. The highest caste are **BRAHMIN**. The lowest caste, the **HARIJAN** (known as the Untouchables) perform much of the manual labor in the country. Although advances have been made to limit discrimination, the caste system is very important to the Indian population. Hindus believe the only way to escape their caste is to be reborn into a new caste (called reincarnation).

India has all the principal races (Mongoloid, Europoid, Negroid, and Australoid). Nearly all major religions are practiced in India with

Ganesha, part elephant/part man is one of the principal deities within Hinduism.

Hinduism being the highest percentage at 85%. Besides Hinduism, India is attributed with the birth of Buddhism, Jainism, and Sikhism. About 11% of Indians are followers of **ISLAM**, making the country one of the four largest Muslim countries in the world.

The official language of India is Hindu. Because of past British rule, English is widely spoken. There are 15 national languages and almost 830 dialects spoken.

The majority of the architecture, sculpture, and painting was created with religious themes, dating back as early as the 4th century B.C. Hindu architecture developed from the **STUPA** (a mound in which Buddhist relics were placed) to the **GORUPAS** (huge, stone temples with thousands of halls and sculptures). The **TAJ MAHAL** is an example of Muslim architecture. Much of the stone sculpture depicts Hindu gods and goddesses. The earliest Hindu paintings on cave temple ceilings showed the life of Buddha. Within the textiles field, India has been a world leader (from the silk carpets of Kashmir to the cotton clothing and weavings).

Literacy although steadily improving, is still way below the world's average. Bicycles are very important for transportation. The games backgammon and parcheesi are believed to originated in India.

RESOURCES

India ranks among the top ten industrial nations of the world, though much of the economic growth has been absorbed by India's huge population growth. Large mineral resources found are iron ore, coal, manganese, copper, and bauxite.

Agriculture accounts for 35% of the economy. The major crops are rice, millet, wheat, and chickpeas. India produces the largest amount of tea and sugar. Due to cows being sacred in India, there is a large dairy industry.

RECIPES

The unique flavor of Indian cooking depends a lot on spices, such as cardamon, pepper, cinnamon, coriander, cumin, mustard, clove, nutmeg, mace, saffron, turmeric, garlic, and vanilla. Popular north Indian snacks are mutton kabobs and vegetable samosas. Lassi, a yogurt drink is a favorite.

Puris (Flat, round, whole wheat bread)
2 tablespoons butter
1 cup water
2 cups whole wheat flour, sifted
dash of salt
oil for frying

Mix flour and salt. Cut in butter and add water until dough is soft. Form a ball and let sit about one hour. Knead and shape dough into small balls. Roll out five inch rounds. Be sure they are thin. Fry, browning both sides.

Puris can be served with other dishes.

Chicken Curry*
4 onions, chopped
1/4 cup butter
3 pounds chicken
3 tablespoons curry powder
dash of salt
2 cups water
1 tablespoon lemon juice

Saute onion in butter. Add meat and saute 10 more minutes. Add curry and cook until chicken is browned. Add water and salt, cover and simmer about 40 minutes. Add lemon juice. Serve over rice. *Note: You may substitute cubed meat, fish, or shellfish for the chicken.*

Coconut Delight
2 cups shredded coconut
2 cups finely shredded peanuts
1/2 cup powdered sugar

Place the coconut in a preheated skillet, stirring gently. When the coconut begins to turn brown, add the chopped peanuts. Cook over a high flame, stirring constantly for two minutes.

Sprinkle with powdered sugar and remove from the heat immediately.

VOCABULARY

one – *ek*	six – *chay*
two – *do*	seven – *saat*
three – *teen*	eight – *aath*
four – *char*	nine – *nau*
five – *panch*	ten – *das*

Hello – *Namaste*
Thank You – *Dhanyavad*
Mother – *Mata*
Father – *Pita*

ACTIVITIES

Create a Shadow Puppet
cardboard or tagboard
a needle
tape
scissors
strings
crayons or paint
brads
flashlight

Draw the parts of the puppet's body and cut them out. Punch holes in the arms, legs, and head and attach them with brads to the puppet's torso. Tape a stick to the puppet's back. Tie strings to each body part and tape the string to the stick or an overhead bar. Pull the strings to move the body parts. Perform in front of a white surface (either a white wall or white sheet). Shine the flashlight onto the white background.

It is believed Shadow Play was born in India. The performance of the legendary story, Ramayana, is a favorite in India. This Hindu epic is a story of an Indian Rama who conquers evil forces. The people admire the good King Rama, a protector of the weak and poor and the purity of his Queen, Sita. Indian mythology is full of stories to use in shadow plays.

Here's a sample of a shadow puppet.

ACTIVITIES

Color the peacock, India's national bird.

Pakistan

THE ISLAMIC REPUBLIC OF PAKISTAN

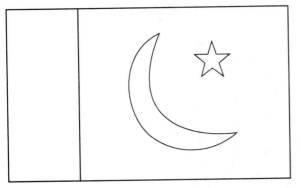

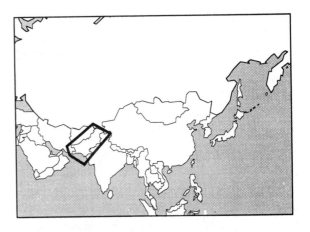

The wide green panel with the star and crescent moon represents Islam. The narrow white panel was added later to represent the tolerance of other faiths in Pakistan.

Pakistan

The name Pakistan means *"land of the pure"* in Urdu. The population is about 85 million. As a result of British rule ending in India in 1947, Pakistan became independent of India. The capital city is **ISLAMABAD**. Islamabad became the capital in 1961, after a split between East and West Pakistan. In 1971, East Pakistan split completely and became Bangladesh, leaving Pakistan as it remains today. The largest city in Pakistan is **KARACHI**, which lies on the Arabian Sea.

LAND

Pakistan is 310,404 square miles. The Arabian Sea is on the southwestern border of Pakistan. The Indus River flows north/south through the country. In northeastern Pakistan, the Karakoram Range extends through a region called Kashmir. The world's second highest mountain (28,251 feet) is part of this range – **K2** or otherwise Mount Godwin Austen. The Khyber Pass leads to the northwestern mountain border to Afghanistan.

CLIMATE

The climate is hot and dry, except in the mountains where the winters are very cold and along the coast where sea breezes cool the air. The annual precipitation ranges from 5 inches to 30 inches.

CULTURE

Pakistan is an Islamic state. Nearly 95% of the population are Muslims; majority are Sunni Muslim and about 15% are Shiite Muslims. Minority religions include Hinduism, Christianity, and Buddhism.

The official language of Pakistan is **URDU**. Punjabi is the second most widely used language. Other languages include Sindhi, Pushti, Baluchi, and Brahvi and various dialects.

English is spoken in the commerce areas and within the government.

Pakistani artisans are famous for onyx carving and elaborate copper work.

Pakistanis enjoy squash and the national sport of cricket. Other sports enjoyed are soccer, tennis, polo and field hockey.

Being a very poor country, the majority of the population do not read or write. The government has tried to make education free but not all the children have easy access to local schools.

RESOURCES

The most important industry is agriculture. About half of the population live off farming. The crops most commonly grown are rice, wheat, sugarcane, cotton, fruit, and tobacco. Textiles are the fastest growing industry. Other industries are leather and oil mills.

RECIPES

Pakistani Kima***
1 tablespoon butter
1 small onion, chopped finely
1/2 pound ground beef
1 tomato, diced
1 teaspoon salt
1 teaspoon curry powder
1/2 teaspoon paprika
1/4 teaspoon chili powder
1/4 teaspoon garlic powder
dash of pepper
1/2 cup peas, plus 2 tablespoons pea juice

Melt the butter in a heavy skillet. Add the onion and cook until tender. Add the ground beef and tomato. Stir and cook over medium heat for 15 minutes. Mix the seasonings and spices in a cup, empty it over the meat. Add the peas and liquid. Mix well. Cover and simmer over low heat for 30 minutes.

The Middle East

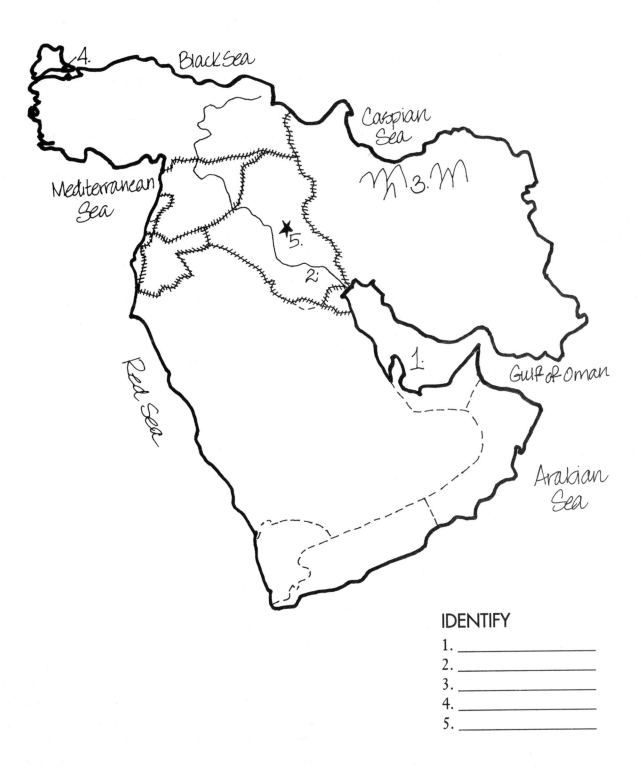

Black Sea

Caspian Sea

4.

Mediterranean Sea

3.

5.

2.

Red Sea

1.

Gulf of Oman

Arabian Sea

IDENTIFY

1. _____
2. _____
3. _____
4. _____
5. _____

Iran

ISLAMIC REPUBLIC OF IRAN

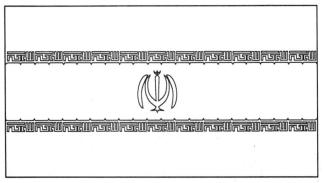

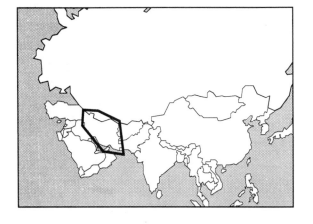

The flag's colors of green, white, and red have been used since the 18th century. The central symbol of a sword with two crescents represents a value of Allah. On the white stripe is the expression "God is Great" written 22 times in Farsi .

Caspian Sea

★TEHRAN

Elburz Mountains

●ISFAHAN

Persian Gulf

Iran

Iran is one the world's oldest countries. More than 2500 years ago, the Persian Empire was founded, ruled by such leaders as Cyrus the Great, Darius the Great, and Alexander the Great. The Aryan people founded the empire, uniting the country. The name Iran means *"Land of the Aryans"*. The capital of Iran is **TEHRAN**, the largest city.

Iran's system of government changed dramatically in 1979, when the Shah of Iran was overthrown and exiled from the country. For the next ten years, the country was led by the **AYATOLLAH KHOMEINI**, a spiritual leader of Islam. The United States began its tense relationship with Iran, when after the Shah's exile, 63 Americans were taken hostage for over 2 years.

With the death of Ayatollah Khomeini, whom many in the world considered to be a fanatic, relations with Iran and the rest of world's countries have improved.

LAND

Iran is 636,300 square miles. The country is located on a plateau. Due to geological plates within the plateau, earthquakes hit the land.

The **ELBURZ MOUNTAINS** reach east/west through Iran. Iran is strategically located in the Middle East. Bordered on the north by the Caspian Sea and Turkmenia, on the south by the Persian Gulf, on the east by Afghanistan and Pakistan, and on the west by Iraq.

CLIMATE

Iran has extreme seasons. The summers are very hot, with average temperatures of 105° F. The winters are cold, averaging 20° F. The rainy season is from October to March but is insufficient for the desert.

CULTURE

The majority of the population are **SHIITE MUSLIMS**, one of the oldest religions in the world. Other Groups, the Kurds and Turkomans are **SUNNI MUSLIMS**. A very small minority are Jews and Christians. **ZOROASTRIANISM**, the religion of the original Persians, is the religion which made impacts on Judaism, Christianity, and Islam. The official language is Persian or Farsi.

Persian rug weaving is among the finest in the world. Metal craft is abundant in Iran, with

Griffin painted on a miniature in the 10th century.

artisans working in silver and copper, using gold, turquoise, and pearls in the intricate designs. The Koran (the Muslim holy book) forbids making realistic pictures of people and animals, so Middle Eastern art is quite different than Western art. A common symbol used by metalworkers is the Hand of Fatima (or fast). The fast represents the five central figures of Islam. It is usually created as a piece of jewelry, styled in a very abstract way.

Iranians enjoy sports but have yet to compete at an international level. A sport unique to Iran is a combination of gymnastics and wrestling performed in clubs called ZURKHANEHS (meaning "house of strength). Iranians claim inventing chess and backgammon.

Iranian school children are separated by gender. Children are entitled to free school from age 6 to age 11. Heavy emphasis is placed on memorizing the Koran.

RESOURCES

The major industry in Iran is the manufacture of petroleum. The major crops are wheat, sugar beets, rice, fruits, and nuts.

RECIPES

Pork and shellfish are forbidden in the Muslim diet, so rice and bread are eaten often. The national dish is the kebab, usually made of lamb.

Persian-Style Cold Yogurt Soup

2 tablespoons golden raisins
1 cucumber
2 cups plain yogurt
3/4 teaspoon salt
1/8 teaspoon freshly ground black pepper
1 cup heavy cream
1 cup ice water
2 tablespoons very finely sliced green scallions
3 tablespoons coarsely chopped walnuts
1 tablespoon minced fresh dill

Soak the raisins in a cup of hot water for an hour, then drain. Peel and grate the cucumber. Put yogurt, salt, pepper into bowl; beat until creamy. Slowly add one cup ice water and cream, while beating. Add the other ingredients and mix well. If the soup is not to be eaten immediately, it should be refrigerated.

Dough (Persian-Style Yogurt Drink)

1/2 cup plain yogurt
1 1/2 cups ice cold water
1/4 teaspoon salt
4 ice cubes
2 sprigs fresh mint

Put the yogurt in a bowl. Slowly add ice water, while beating with a fork or whisk. Season with salt. Add ice cubes and garnish with mint.

VOCABULARY

The Farsi language is a mixture of ancient Persian and Arabic. Arabic characters and script are used to write Farsi.

leader – *imam*
religious leader – *caliph*
king – *shah*

ACTIVITIES

Persian Game – Solemn Action

Players sit in a circle to start the game. One player is designated to start the game. He makes some motion, such as pinching the nose, tickling him under the chin, etc. of the player to his right. Each player, in turn, repeats this motion with the next player to the right. Thus it goes around the circle. No player may laugh or speak. If anyone does, he drops out of the game. The last one left is the winner. *Caution: Discuss with children beforehand that no actions can hurt or be too violent.*

ACTIVITIES

Design your Own Persian Rug

    You can have your rug tell a story, or it can be made up of designs. On a piece of cardboard, glue pieces of colorful construction paper that you have cut out. Cut several pieces of yarn about an inch long and glue them on two opposite edges of the "rug" to form the fringe. Below is a Persian design that might be fun to follow.

ACTIVITIES

Write in Arabic

    Trace the Arabic characters below and then with a medium felt-tip pen, try to write the characters on your own.

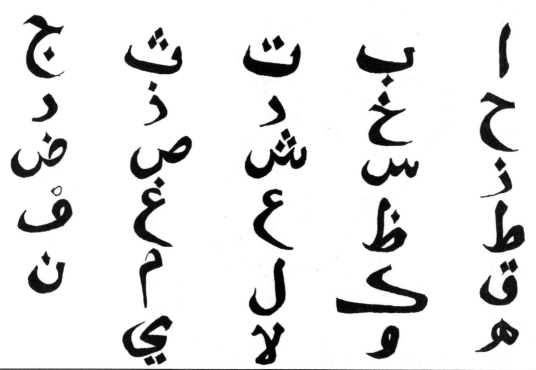

Iraq

REPUBLIC OF IRAQ

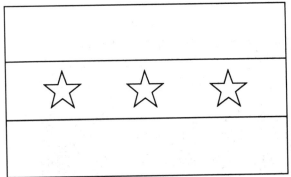

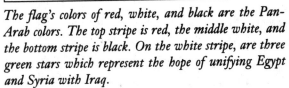

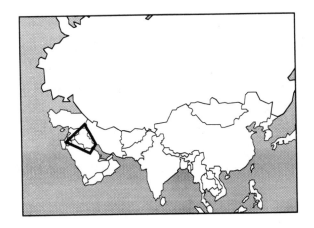

The flag's colors of red, white, and black are the Pan-Arab colors. The top stripe is red, the middle white, and the bottom stripe is black. On the white stripe, are three green stars which represent the hope of unifying Egypt and Syria with Iraq.

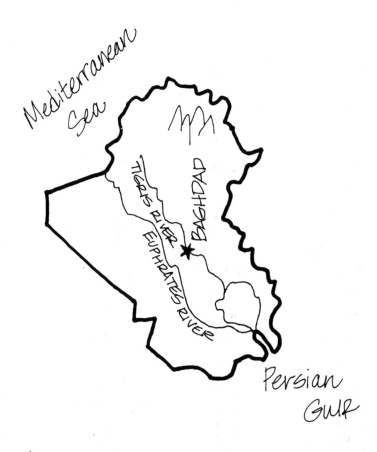

Iraq

Iraq is located in a strategic position in the Middle East. It is bordered by Iran on the east, Turkey and Syria on the north, Jordan and Saudi Arabia on the south. The land of Iraq used to be called MESOPOTAMIA – site of one the world's earlier civilizations. Mesopotamia means *"the land between the two rivers"*. The population of Iraq is 17 million, most living in urban areas. The capital of Iraq is BAGHDAD. Other large cities are Basra and Mosul. Iraq's history is filled with foreign rule. The present leader, SADDAM HUSAIN came to power in 1978. His goal is to bring Iraq back to its former glories. At present, Iraq has been greatly weakened by wars with Iran, the Gulf War, and civil wars with the northern Kurds.

LAND

Iraq is a little larger than California (169,235 square miles). It is located on the FERTILE CRESCENT. This land is roughly the area between the TIGRIS and EUPHRATES RIVERS. There is mountainous land in the north and desert in the west.

CLIMATE

Iraq has two seasons – wet and dry. The wet season occurs between November and April. The annual precipitation in most of Iraq is 5 1/2 inches (in the mountainous region it can be up to 40 inches). The dry season is from May to October. During the change of season, high winds called *sharqi* occur, causing dust-storms.

CULTURE

The majority of the people are Arabs (primarily southern Iraq). In western Iraq, the people are nomads. In the mountains are the KURDS who have their own language and culture. Through Iraq's long history, the Kurds have continually demanded their own state.

The official language is Arabic. Minority languages are Kurdish, Persian, and Turkish. Islam is the national religion, both Shiite and Sunni Muslim are practiced. The minority religions are Judaism and Christianity.

Traditional copperware can be found in Iraq, which is beaten and pressed into intricate, beautiful designs. Iraq considers itself the home of the finest Persian rugs in the world. Some of the mosques (Muslim religious temples) rival any Western architecture with their beauty and elaborate designs.

Unlike its eastern neighbor Iran, Iraqis love playing team sports, especially soccer. Although the government does not encourage women's rights, many Iraqi women have stopped wearing the traditional ABAYA (meant to protect the modesty of women).

Primary and secondary schooling are free. Both primary school and secondary last for six years each, starting at age six. There has been a push by the government to increase literacy.

RESOURCES

Iraq's major industry is oil. Iraq is one of the founding members of OPEC – Organization of Petroleum Exporting Countries. Minerals produced are gypsum, salt, and phosphates. Major crops are wheat, barley, dates, beans, and rice.

RECIPES

Hummus is served as a dip with bread or pita bread.

Hummus be Tahini
(chickpeas with sesame paste)
1 cup dried chickpeas, soaked in water overnight
1 garlic clove
3 tablespoons Tahini (sesame paste)
3/4 cup lemon juice
1 tablespoon olive oil

2 tablespoons chopped parsley
1/2 tablespoon paprika

Drain the soaked chickpeas, and cook in boiling water for 1 hour (or until well-cooked). Drain well. Save 2 tablespoons of whole chickpeas and put aside. Mash the rest of the chickpeas in a large bowl with a potato masher. Crush the garlic with a pinch of salt, and add to the chickpeas, gradually adding the Tahini, lemon juice, and 1/2 teaspoon salt. Mash well to make a creamy paste. Sprinkle with olive oil, parsley, paprika, and the whole chickpeas. Makes about 2 1/2 cups.

Z'Lata B'Khyar (Cucumber Salad)

2 cucumbers, peeled and sliced thin
1/4 teaspoon salt
1/2 cup vinegar
1/4 cup boiled water
1/2 teaspoon sugar
pepper
1/2 teaspoon crushed dried mint

Place cucumbers in a colander, sprinkle with salt and let stand for 30 minutes. In a separate bowl, mix vinegar, water, salt, sugar, and pepper to taste. Rinse cucumbers with cold water and press them between palms so they become limp. Add dressing and sprinkle with mint.

ACTIVITIES

Find the Words Relating to Iraq

- Islam
- Bedouins
- Koran
- Oil
- Nomads
- Desert
- Oase
- Soccer
- Camel
- Kurd

```
D Z A B I R A D P C S E
A R Q I O L C R E F N R
M A U C S W M U S R I Y
A T K I R O D K Z Y U S
S U O V S E C W L I O D
C I E P B L N C X H D E
U G R I J K A I E G E S
S C A M E L R M A R B E
X N G R Y O O A S E P R
S D A M O N K Y R I A T
```

ACTIVITIES

Find the Hidden Pictures in the Bazaar Stall

Kuwait

STATE OF KUWAIT

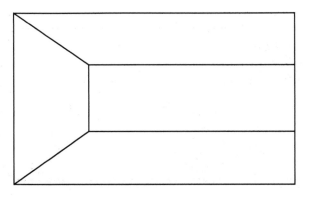

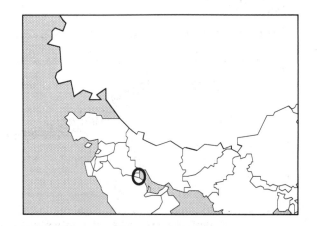

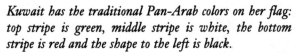

Kuwait has the traditional Pan-Arab colors on her flag: top stripe is green, middle stripe is white, the bottom stripe is red and the shape to the left is black.

KUWAIT CITY ★

Persian Gulf

Kuwait

Kuwait is a small country located in the Middle East. Kuwait means *"little fort"* in Arabic. For centuries, Kuwait has been a resting point for traders traveling between Europe and India. Kuwait was under protection of the British until 1961 when it gained its independence. Due to the oil industry and the heavy influx of international workers, little Kuwait has a population of 2 million. **KUWAIT CITY** is the capital and the largest city.

When the Ottoman Empire (Turks) fell in the early twentieth century, Kuwait was the only Middle Eastern country to remain stable. In 1914, oil was discovered in the Burgan area. In the late 1940s, full exploration of the Kuwaiti oilfields showed them to be among the most productive in the world. During the early 1990s, Iraq invaded Kuwait to gain control of the oil. However, the United Nations counterattacked and the Persian Gulf War began. Kuwait is at present rebuilding the country after the war with the help of the United Nations.

LAND

Kuwait lies west of the Persian Gulf. It borders Iraq to the northwest and Saudi Arabia to the southwest. Kuwait is only 7,000 square miles. Except for the coastline, the majority of the land is flat desert. There are ten islands which Kuwait possesses, including Failaka (dating back at least 5,000 years). There are no rivers in Kuwait, but instead **WADIS** (dried-up riverbeds which flow during rainstorms).

CLIMATE

During the summer, dust- and sand-storms are common. Temperatures can reach as high as 112° F. Winters are pleasant with gentle breezes and warm days. There is little annual precipitation.

CULTURE

The nomad tribe, the **AL-SABAH** founded Kuwait City, after a search for easier living than the desert. As they settled, the Al-Sabah established themselves as the ruling class. The Al-Sabah are still ruling Kuwait today. Originally, a small country with a population of Bedouins (nomads), Kuwait's society has changed dramatically from oil production.

Islam is the official state religion. The majority of the population are Sunni Muslims. Although many of the Bedouin have moved to more urban areas, they are an important aspect to Kuwaiti culture. Arabic and English are both the primary spoken languages. Kuwait also has a large Palestinian and Pakistani community.

The early Kuwaitis built boats called **DHOWS**. Dhows are wooden boats still made today. The dhows made it possible for trade to India and the east African coast. Pearl-diving was done off the dhows. Pearl-diving was dangerous but very important at that time for the country's economy.

Education is compulsory from age six to fourteen. Through all the schooling, boys and girls are separated from each other. Kuwait has an excellent health system which is free to Kuwaiti citizens.

Food in Kuwait are primarily the same as the other Arabic countries: falafel, pita, tea, and coffee. Kuwaitis enjoy soccer and watersports.

RESOURCES

The major industry is oil. The discovery of oil in Kuwait has caused the country to become one of the wealthiest in the world. Fishing is also important. The oil industry paved the way for **HYDROPONICS** (a technique for growing plants in difficult environments). As a result, agriculture is beginning to become an important industry as well.

Israel

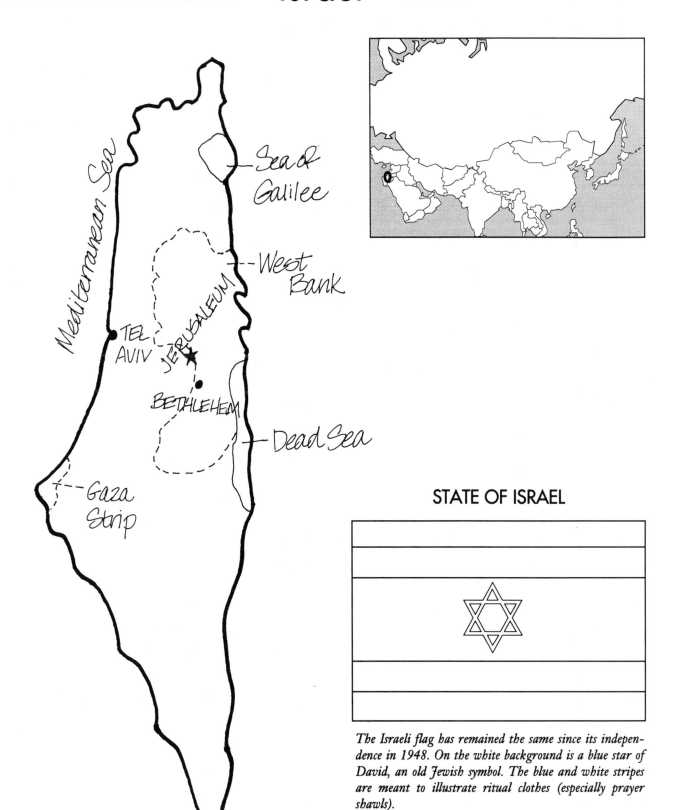

STATE OF ISRAEL

The Israeli flag has remained the same since its independence in 1948. On the white background is a blue star of David, an old Jewish symbol. The blue and white stripes are meant to illustrate ritual clothes (especially prayer shawls).

Israel

Israel is a small Middle Eastern country about the size of New Jersey. The capital of Israel is **JERUSALEM** and the population is over 4 million. The bordering countries are Lebanon, Syria, Jordan, Saudi Arabia and Egypt. Israel is a young nation but an ancient land. It became independent in 1948. Many religions consider Israel to be a holy land: Jewish, Christians, and Muslims. It was established as a homeland for the Jewish people. People from all over the world came to Israel to practice their religion in freedom. During World War II, many Jews began to emigrate to Israel. The earliest people who arrived in Israel are called **CHALUTZIM** (*pioneers*).

Continuous fighting through the years between the Israeli army and the Palestinian Liberation Organization (PLO) has made Israel a very tense area of the world. The leader of the PLO, Nassir Arafat has recently returned from a self-exile to claim Jericho as Palestinian land. Hopes of peace between the Jews of Israel and the surrounding Arab countries of Egypt, Syria, Jordan, and Iraq rest only in the people.

LAND

The land of Israel is very diverse for a country only 8,000 square miles. There are mountainous regions with fertile valleys, rich for farming. There are plains, hills, and the Negev Desert in the south. Israel is bordered by four bodies of water: the Mediterranean Sea, the Dead Sea, the Sea of Galilee, and the Gulf of Aqaba. The most important river is the Jordan River. The **DEAD SEA** is the lowest sea in the world, and the saltiest – no living things grow in the water.

CLIMATE

The climates of Israel vary as much as the land. In the north, the temperatures are more continental; along the coast, the climate is pleasant; and to the south in the desert, temperatures can reach as high as 122° F.

CULTURE

Hebrew is the official language of Israel. There are many different languages spoken, however, with a large majority speaking Arabic. Judaism makes up 90% of the population. Muslim is the minority religion. Other minority religions are Christianity and Baha'i.

Children are required to go to school for free until the age of 15. Children in Israel belong to scouts and other youth groups as they are growing up. Israeli teens (both boys and girls) must enlist in the Israel army at age 18.

RESOURCES

Many minerals come from the Dead Sea, including magnesium, sodium, calcium, potassium, and potash. In the desert, phosphates are mined.

The fastest developing industry is aircraft. The largest industry is textiles. Although no diamonds are mined, 1/2 of the world's gemstones are cut in Israel.

RECIPES

In Israel, dates are popular for desserts and holidays. Date palm trees grow mainly in desert lands. When the dates are ripe, they droop from the tree and hang in heavy bunches. The sweet dates can be eaten by themselves or added to other dessert recipes.

Honey Clusters (Taiglach)
3/4 cup flour
1 egg
1/2 teaspoon salt
1/2 cup honey
1/4 teaspoon ginger

Sift the flour and whisk the egg. Combine flour, egg, and salt in a bowl. Mix until it is doughy. Knead the dough, adding flour if it is too sticky. Divide the dough in half, roll each half into a rope 1/3 inch thick. Cut it into 1/2 inch pieces and place them on a well-greased cookie pan. Bake at 375-degrees for 15 minutes until golden brown, turning the pieces with a spatula to brown both sides.

Boil the honey with the ginger in a saucepan. Add the baked pieces and boil gently for 20 minutes, stirring gently. Pour out on a slightly greased plate. Allow to cool.

Matzo Balls
1 cup matzo meal
1/2 cup water
4 eggs, beaten
1/3 cup melted shortening
1 teaspoon salt
dash of pepper

Add water, melted shortening, salt and pepper to the beaten eggs. Mix well. Add matzo meal and stir thoroughly. Refrigerate for one hour. Form into balls and drop into soup or into 1 1/2 quarts boiling water and one tablespoon salt. Cook 20 minutes.

VOCABULARY

one – *achet*
two – *shtayim*
three – *shalosh*
four – *arba*
five – *chamash*
six – *shesh*
seven – *sheva*
eight – *shmone*
nine – *tesha*
ten – *eser*
Hello or Goodbye – *Shalom (peace)*

ACTIVITIES
The Hora
The word hora is a Croatian-Serbian word that means *tempo* or *movement*. It is a dance of Israel that portrays the flavor of the people. there are variations of steps and melodies; however, the movements follow a basic pattern. All dancers form a single circle and extend both arms to the side so that their hands rest on the shoulders of the people on either side of them. Moving clockwise, step right to the side, place left foot behind the right, and step right. Kick left foot in front of right foot while hopping on the right. Step left to the side, kick right foot across the left while hopping on the left foot. Repeat this pattern. Begin slowly and accelerate. A song sung during the Hora is Hava Nagila.

Hava Nagila
Ha-va na-gi-la, ha-va na-gi-la, ha-va na-gi-la, v'-nis'm'-ha.
Ha-va na-gi-la, ha-va na-gi-la, ha-va na-gi-la, v'-nis'm'-ha.
Ha-va n'-ra'-n'-na, ha-va n'-ra'-n'-na, ha-va n'-ra'-n'-na, v'-nis'm'-ha.
Ha-va n'-ra'-n'-na, ha-va n'-ra'-n'-na, ha-va n'-ra'-n'-na, v'-nis'm'-ha.
U-ru, u-ru a-him, u-ru a-him b'-lev sa-me-ah,
u-ru a-him, b'lv sa-me-ah,
u-ru a-him, b'lv sa-me-ah,
u-ru a-him, b'lv sa-me-ah,
u-ru a-him, u-ru a-him b'lv sa-me-ah,

ACTIVITIES
Make a Stained Glass Window
The many synagogues, churches, and mosques in Israel have beautiful stained glass windows. You can make windows for your classroom with colored cellophane and black construction paper.

Make a Stained Glass Window

In the synagogue of the Hadassah Medical Center, the Russian artist Marc Chagall created some of the finest stained glass windows in the world.

black construction paper
scissors
tissue paper or cellophane
tape
Cut out a "window" from the paper. Keep the excess paper to form a frame later. Cut out designs from the middle cutout. Tape scraps of colored tissue paper onto the back, one color for each cut. Tape the "frame" over top of the "window" and hold up to the light. Tape to the window for cheerful colors from the sun all day long.

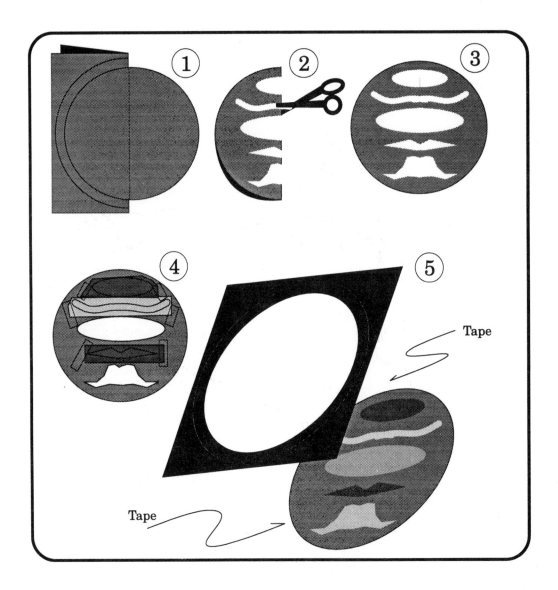

Syria

THE FLAG OF SYRIA

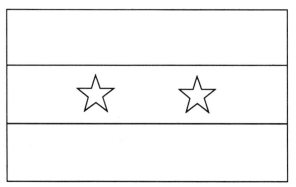

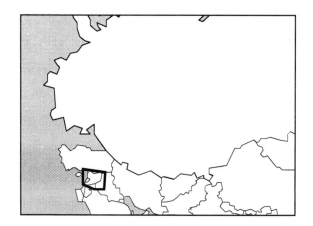

The red/white/black stripes and two green stars represents the hope of someday being joined with Egypt and Iraq.

Syria

Syria's culture has been heavily influenced by its ancient history. For thousands of years, Syria has been ruled by foreign powers: the Persian Empire, the Greeks, the Romans, the Ottoman Empires (Turks), and France and Britain. Syria became an independent state in 1946. At the same time, it's neighbor Israel became independent. Relationships with the west were deep with resentment. Fighting began between the Arab countries and Israel over land called Palestine. **DAMASCUS** is the capital and one of the world's oldest inhabited cities.

LAND

Syria is 71, 467 square miles, a relatively small country. However, Syria has some of the most fertile land in the Middle East. There are several different regions. Within the Syrian Desert, lies oases which provide the country with water. Another supply of water are the rivers which dry up during the summers. The larger rivers like the **EUPHRATES** and the Orontesi allow year-round farming. The **ANTI-LEBANON MOUNTAINS**, is a range which extends through the north and south. The Syrian Desert is rocky and full of scrub brush. Huge sand-storms sweep through the desert, re-shaping the lands. The Syrian Steppes are where especially arid lands are located.

CLIMATE

Syria is hot and dry. The high majority of the rain falls in the north coastal area. The annual average precipitation is 5 inches.

CULTURE

A small minority of the population are nomads. The nomadic shepherds travel constantly across the desert to find water and grass for their animals. They depend on camels for food and tent-making. Nearly half of the population are living in the cities located on the rivers or the sea. After Columbus discovered a new sea route in which to transport goods to the Far East, the great oasis-cities died.

Syrian has always had a closed society so the trade route did not affect the races of Syria too much. The Arabs account for 70% of the population. The **ASSYRIANS**, a northern tribe who were a very distinct group long ago, have now blended more and more into Syrian society. The **KURDS**, who are mostly nomads, do not consider themselves to be Syrian. The area in which they live is known as Kurdistan. The **BEDOUINS** are also desert nomads. They have lived their own style of life for centuries and speak the oldest form of Arabic. Modern Arabic is the official language of Syria.

Islam is the official religion of the nation. Before Islam came to Syria, most people were Christian. Jews have been living in Syria for thousands of years but due to Syria's relationship with Israel, a high amount have emigrated to Israel.

The Syrians enjoy poetry and reciting from the **KORAN** (the Muslim bible). Soccer, called football is also very popular.

The literacy rate is relatively high for the middle eastern region at 65%. Free education is compulsory for six years of elementary school.

RESOURCES

The socialist government of Syria (created by President Assad) took the troubled economy under its wing, developing industry. The mineral resources found in Syria are oil, natural gas, raw phosphate, and iron ore. The major crops produced are fruit and vegetables, cotton and silk.

Turkey

REPUBLIC OF TURKEY

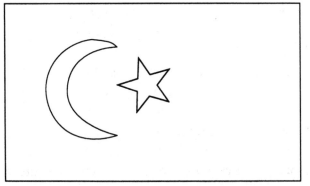

The white crescent and moon are ancient symbols of the Islam religion and the Ottoman Empire. The red background also represents Islam.

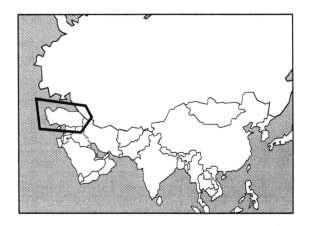

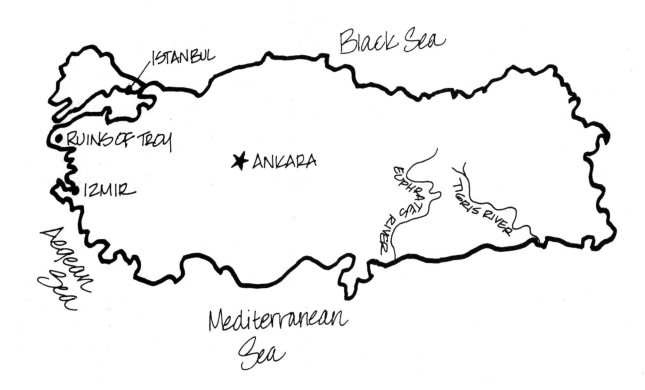

ISTANBUL

Black Sea

RUINS OF TROY

★ ANKARA

IZMIR

EUPHRATES RIVER

TIGRIS RIVER

Aegean Sea

Mediterranean Sea

Turkey

Surrounded by the Mediterranean Sea in the south, the Black Sea in the north, and the Aegean Sea in the west, Turkey has been the crossroads for important civilizations for centuries. Turkey straddles both Asia and Europe. The eastern part (97% of the country) is called Anatolia (or Asia Minor). The western part in Europe is called Thrace. ISTANBUL (formerly Constantinople) is the largest city and the most developed. The capital of Turkey (since 1923) is ANKARA. The population of the country is over 52 million.

LAND

The eastern region, or Anatolia is 80% plateau, surrounded by mountains, mostly suitable for grazing. On the Aegean coastline are fertile lowlands, perfect for agriculture. The Smal Andalou Mountains extend along the Black Sea through Anatolia. The TAURUS MOUNTAINS extend along the Mediterranean Sea. The highest mountains in the east are extinct volcanoes. Two of the most important rivers, the Euphrates and the Tigris, flow through central Turkey.

The western region or Thrace, are plains bordered on the north by the Istranca Mountains. The STRAITS (channels) join the Aegean Sea to the Black Sea.

CLIMATE

Turkey's climate is influenced by the land. The northern coastal region of Anatolia is hot in the summer and cold in the winter. The southern coastal region is known as the "Turkish Riveria" – a land of palm trees and beaches. The eastern region is dry, but receives heavy snows and bitter colds in the mountains.

CULTURE

The first people of Turkey were the Hittites. The Hittite Empire flourished, bringing different cultures into the land. The Assyrians eventually absorbed the Hittites into their empire. In the 8th century, the Greeks began settling on the western shores, founding such cities as Troy. Power struggles erupted between the Greeks and the Persian Empire. Alexander the Great finally overthrew all other other powers and gained Turkey, creating the Macedonian Empire. After Alexander's death, the empire crumbled and came under power of the Romans. The Roman Emperor, Constantine christianized the people of Turkey. He also built Constantinople, making it the center of the Christian Roman (or Byzantine) Empire. The Byzantine Empire survived for over one thousand years.

The Turks began arriving in the 10th century, forced out of Turkistan by the Mongols. The Turks formed the Ottoman Empire, overthrowing the Byzantines. In 1453, Constantinople was renamed Istanbul and Islam replaced Christianity.

Today there are many different ethnic groups in Turkey. The Kurds who live in the southeastern region, represent the largest non-Turkish minority. The majority of the population are Muslims but due to Westernization by the government, many have abandoned the strict practice of Islam. Turkey allows freedom of religion (very rare among the Islamic Middle Eastern countries). Turkish is the commonly spoken language. Turkish is a form of Arabic.

The Turkish government has improved the education system from past years. Literacy is steadily improving, mainly in men. Soccer is the most important sport in Turkey. Backgammon is also enjoyed by many of the men as they sit in local cafes.

Turkish art before the 20th century was mainly paintings called miniatures. Today, hammered brass and copper, jewelry, and rug design are among the arts sold in street markets.

On April 23rd of each year, a special holiday called Children's Day is celebrated. The Turkish believe the future of their country rests on the children. On this day, there is no school and everything is free for children all day long. Movies, ice cream, candy – the children do not have to pay for anything and can enjoy their special day!

RESOURCES

Agriculture is the most important industry for Turkey. The chief crops are tobacco and cotton. Other crops are figs, apricots, grapes, oranges, olives, and nuts. Angora goats produce mohair, an expensive wool.

Turkey has many mineral resources but due to lack of funds are unable to produce many of them. Coal is abundant. Chromite, iron ore, and manganese are minerals produced.

Tourism has become a major industry in Turkey, mainly due to Turkey's non-involvement with other Middle Eastern countries.

RECIPES

Turks enjoy shish kebobs, Baklava, and strong Turkish coffee.

Turkish Pilav***
1 quart water
1 teaspoon salt
1/2 cup rice
10 almonds or 1 tablespoon pine nuts
2 tablespoons butter
1/4 cup raisins or dried currants

Boil the water with salt. Add rice and boil for 15 minutes (until rice is tender, not mushy). Drain rice. Soak almonds in boiling water to remove skins, then rinse in cold water. Cut the almonds into slivers. Heat the slivers in the butter in a large saucepan over low heat. Add rice and raisins. Salt to taste. Mix well and serve hot.

Turkish Bean Flatterer (Fasulya Piazi)****
1 1/2 cups lima beans or small white beans
1/2 small onion, sliced paper thin
sprig of parsley, chopped
2 tablespoons olive oil
1 tablespoon lemon juice or vinegar
salt and pepper to taste
1 hard-cooked egg
1 medium tomato

Rinse the beans in cold water and drain. Lightly mix the beans with onion and parsley. Add the olive oil and lemon juice and mix well.

Transfer the mixture to a serving dish. Cut egg in half, then cut each half into thirds. Cut tomato into eighths, and arrange the egg and tomato slices on the bean mixture. Chill until ready to serve.

Turkish Cookies
1/2 pound sweet butter
1 cup sugar, granulated
2 cups flour, sifted
1/4 cup blanched almonds

Preheat oven to 350-degrees. Cream the butter thoroughly. Add the sugar and flour and mix. Roll or pat the dough on a floured board. The dough should be at about 1/2 inch thickness. Use small 1 inch cookie cutters to cut into different shapes.

Put the cookie dough onto a greased cookie sheet. Place one almond on each cookie. Leave space between each cookie as they spread while they bake. Bake 10 to 15 minutes at 350-degrees. Remove carefully when they are done.

ACTIVITIES

Make a Turkish Brass Hammering

sheet of brass or copper foil, 6 inches square (found in craft stores)
scissors
fine felt-tip marker
ball-point pen
1/2 inch stiff cardboard or plywood (slightly larger than the sheet of foil)
black spraypaint, acrylic, or tempera
fine sandpaper
rubber cement or small brads

1. Make sketches on scrap paper. Below are some examples of Turkish designs.
2. Cut a piece of metal foil not larger than 6" X 8" Smooth down the edges and any bumps with the round part of a large spoon. Place the metal foil on a flat surface and rub the spoon around the rough edges.
3. Draw your design on the metal with the felt-tip marker. A felt-tip is used so that it will not make any indentations into the sheet of metal. The side with the drawing will be the reverse of your brass hammering. If a different shape than a square or rectangle is needed, cut the required shape and smooth the rough edges down with the spoon.
4. Place the foil on a thick pad of newspapers and press hard over the lines and areas you want to press out with a ball-point pen (the end of a small paintbrush works well, too!). Turn the foil over and you will see your design has been raised from the background.
5. Paint the cardboard black with a few coats of paint. Mount the foil onto the cardboard, spreading rubber cement on both the cardboard and the back of the foil so it will adhere better. If using plywood, sand the surface first and then paint it black. Nail the foil to the background with small brads. Space the brads evenly to make them part of the design.

Africa

Mediterranean Sea

Red Sea

Indian Ocean

Atlantic Ocean

IDENTIFY

1. _____
2. _____
3. _____
4. _____
5. _____

Egypt

ARAB REPUBLIC OF EGYPT

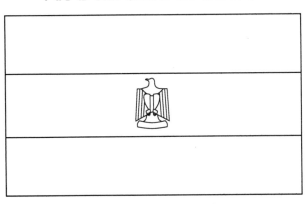

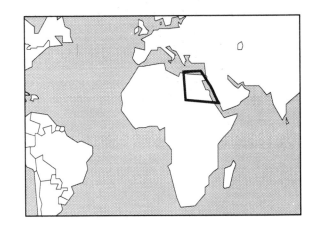

The flag has been changed many times as different unities with countries have broken off. The present flag has wide red/white/black stripes with a golden eagle in the middle (Egyptian arms).

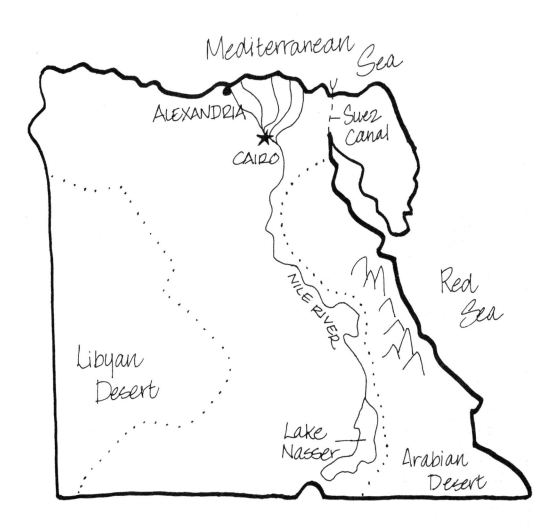

Egypt

Egypt is known as the *land of the sun*. Egypt produced one of the earliest and most glorious civilizations. Its history extends to 5000 years before the birth of Christ. The population of Egypt is over 45 million. Most Egyptians live along the **NILE RIVER**, in small towns and rural villages. **CAIRO** is the capital of Egypt and the largest city in Africa.

LAND

The country is 385,000 square miles. Egypt is bordered by the Mediterranean Sea to the north, and the Red Sea to the west. The Eastern Desert (which is part of the Libyan desert) and the Western Desert (or the Arabian Desert) make up 95% of the country. The Nile River flows through the country north/south and is one of the world's largest rivers. To the south of the Nile, is the **ASWAN DAM** and **LAKE NASSER** (the world's largest man-made lake).

CLIMATE

During the summers, the temperatures in the north average 80° F and in the winters 50° F. The further south, the annual temperatures rise by almost 30 degrees. Even with all the surrounding bodies of water, Egypt suffers from droughts due to almost non-existent annual precipitation.

CULTURE

Egypt's ancient history attracts a high tourist industry. Many of the structures were built as lasting monuments for the **PHARAOHS** (kings) who were believed to have supreme power. The **GREAT PYRAMIDS OF GIZA** (southwest of Cairo) were built as tombs for the pharaohs on their death. The pharaohs were mummified, placed inside, and then the pyramids sealed up. The Pyramid of Cheops was built over 20 years, using 100,000 men. **THE VALLEY OF THE KINGS**, on the west bank of the Nile are carved underground tombs. The most famous of the tombs is that of **KING TUTANKHAMEN** (King Tut). The **SPHINX**, another popular monument is gradually eroding away by the Giza winds. The Alexandria Library is one of of the world's largest libraries, housing magnificent Egyptian art.

HIEROGLYPHICS was a system of writing the ancient Egyptians used. The Egyptians also were one of the first civilizations to use paper, made from papyrus.

Egypt is one of the more modernized Arab states, yet still steeped in tradition. In larger cities, women dress in western style clothing alongside women who still wear the long, black garments (*melayas*) with veils covering their faces. Islam is the official religion. Nearly 90% of the population is Islamic. Arabic is the official language. It is written and read left to right. English is widely spoken in the more metropolitan cities of **ALEXANDRIA** and Cairo.

Children between the ages of six and fifteen must attend schools. They take the usual courses American children take but also classes in their religion, Islam. Literacy is relatively low at this time (nearly 70% of the people do not know how to read or write).

The Egyptian people enjoy a form of cards (*kutshina*), backgammon (*tawla*), and dominoes. Soccer is Egypt's favorite team sport. Children enjoy playing hopscotch and a version of jacks (using marbles instead). Street markets, besides being popular with tourists, are good opportunities for the population to socialize with each other.

RESOURCES

Egypt has many mineral resources: gypsum, iron ore, manganese, salt, and malachite (used to make copper). The major crop is cotton. Others include beans, corn, millet, onions, potatoes, rice, sugarcane, and wheat. Egypt's agriculture industry is due in part to ancient irrigation systems using the Nile River. The country also produces a high quality of petroleum. The **SUEZ CANAL** was built to export large quantities of oil out of Egypt.

RECIPES

Egyptians enjoy traditional middle eastern dishes such as kebabs, fresh dates, figs, and turkish coffee or spiced hot tea.

Falafel

1 packet falafel mix (available at any Greek food store)
Pita Bread
Sesame Tahini
Tomatoes, onions, cucumbers, finely chopped

Mix the falafel (a fine powder of ground chickpeas) according to the package directions. Warm pita bread, cut in half, and make a pocket. Coat pocket with Tahini. Insert falafel balls. Top with tomatoes, onions, and cucumbers.

Hieroglyphics are pictures which represent sounds. How would you write your name if you were an Egyptian? Make up your own hieroglyphics.

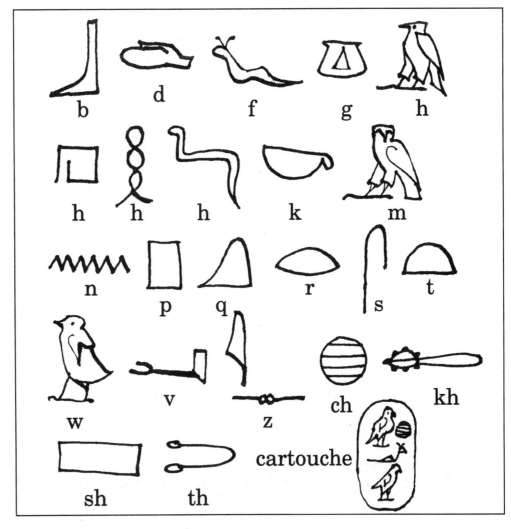

VOCABULARY

School – *med-ressa*

How are you? – *Keef-Halek*

Fine – *Bahee*

Goodbye (literal translation: Peace be with you) – *Ma-ah Saalam*

Thank you – *Shook-ran*

You are welcome! – *Ahlan wa sahlan!*

ACTIVITIES

Color in Pasha the nomad boy on his pet camel. What is behind them? What is his camel's name?

Libya

POPULAR SOCIALIST LIBYAN ARAB JAMAHIRIYAH

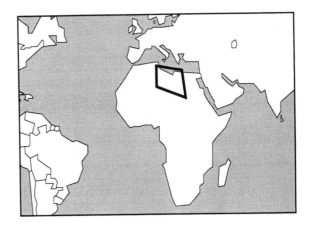

The flag is a solid green to represent the nation's complete devotion to Islam, and for the "green" revolution dictated by Moammar Gaddafi.

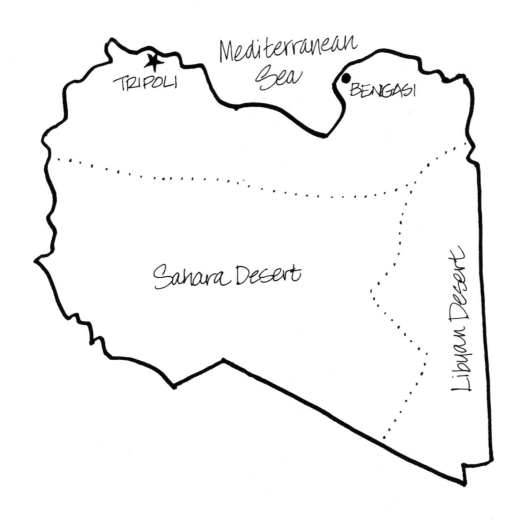

TRIPOLI

Mediterranean Sea

BENGASI

Sahara Desert

Libyan Desert

Libya

Libya is a large country located in the center of the North African coast on the Mediterranean Sea. Libya's name comes from a Berber tribe called the Lebu. The capital is **TRIPOLI**, where the majority of the people are located. Libya's past history of foreign rule, has caused the government to have tighter control on the country. Today Libya has tense relations with a few countries, due in part to the fanaticism of its leader, **MOAMMAR AL-GADDIFI**.

LAND

Libya is 679,362 square miles. Most of the land is desert and unliveable. Part of the **SAHARAN DESERT** reaches into Libya. The northeastern desert is called the Libyan Desert.

Libyan couple in traditional dress. Both are wearing a barracan *which wraps the body from head to toe.*

The cactus is the national plant of Libya. There are many plateaus in the land.

CLIMATE

The climate of Libya is hot and dry. Average summer temperatures are 110° F and winter temperatures can range from 45° to 90° F. In northern Libya along the coast, temperatures are more mild. Strong, dry winds sweep through and cause the temperature to rise.

CULTURE

Arabs at 90%, are the largest group of people living in Libya. The **BERBERS**, living in rural villages are the largest non-Arab minority. Libya is a patriarchal society – until recently, women were never seen in public without veils covering all their body but one eye. Arabic is the national language.

Libya's official religion is Islam which is strictly enforced. The sect of Islam practiced is Sunni. Sunni Muslims pray five times a day. Religion and government are closely tied together.

Libya is renown for its gold embroidery. The oil industry has decreased the number of artisans working on Libyan handicrafts.

Education is free and required up to the completion of 12th grade. Literacy is at a high rate. Healthcare is free for all the population. Soccer is a favorite game to play and watch.

RESOURCES

Oil is the major industry in Libya, accounting for 55% of the economy. A large deposit of iron ore can be found, along with gypsum, limestone, and salt. Even with Libya's reliance on the oil industry, 1/5 of the population are farmers. Water supply is a problem. Major crops are barley, wheat, millet, olives, and dates. Much citrus is grown. Livestock (including sheep, cows, and chickens) is a growing industry – more wool and hides are being exported.

RECIPES

Cous Cous (serves 4)

All ingredients can be found at a gourmet shop.

1 box cous cous
1 chicken (cut up)
1/2 cup olive or corn oil
4 large onions, chopped
salt to taste
red pepper to taste
1 teaspoon cumin powder
1/2 can tomato paste
1 can hommos (chickpeas)
2 potatoes, chopped
4 carrots, chopped
3 zucchinis, chopped
1 teaspoon cinnamon

Put the oil in a deep pot and heat. When hot, add the onions and saute. Then add the tomato paste, pepper, cumin, and salt. Stir until mixed with oil and onions, then add the chicken. Add 5 cups of waters and let simmer for a few minutes. Then taste to see if more salt or other spices need to be added. Add vegetables. Let cook until chicken is done.

In the meantime, start to prepare the cous cous. Follow directions of the box. When cous cous has been cooked, place on a large platter and add cinnamon to it. Stir it in. Then top with the sauce, the meat, and the vegetables. Do not put all the sauce on at once unless you like it soupy. Serve with radishes on the side.

Libyan Soup

1 pound lamb, cut into cubes
1 large onion, chopped
2 tablespoons tomato paste
2 tablespoons oil
1 bunch parsley, chopped
1 tomato, chopped
1 lemon
1 1/2 teaspoon each of salt, pepper, red pepper, and turmeric
1/2 can chickpeas
3 tablespoons shorba pasta (orzo)
1 tablespoon dry mint (optional)

Place pot on low flame; add lamb and onions. When onions are soft, add the oil; stir and cover. Add the tomato paste, half the parsley, and the chopped tomato; stir. Add the juice of the lemon, salt, the pepper, and turmeric. Add 1 cup water. Cover and cook about 15 minutes.

Add the rest of the parsley, cover and cook for a few minutes. Then add 3 more cups of water and cook another 15 minutes. Add 1/2 can of chickpeas and the shorba pasta. Cook 10 minutes or until lamb and pasta are done.

To serve, put soup in individual bowls and sprinkle dried mint on top. Shorba is the Libyan word for soup. Shorba pasta is a tiny pasta similar in shape and size to a grain of rice. Orzo is the Greek name, and can be bought under this name in the United States.

VOCABULARY

school – *med-ressa*
How are you? – *Keef-Halek*
Fine – *Bahee*
Thank you – *Shukran*
Goodbye (or Peace be with you) – *Mah Saalama*
prayer – *salat*

ACTIVITIES

Choose the Item that Does Not Belong

In the picture below are three objects native to Libya. Which objects are not found in Libya?

Kenya

REPUBLIC OF KENYA

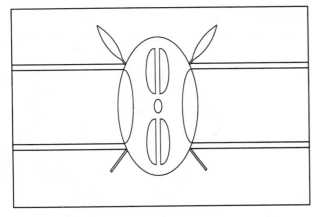

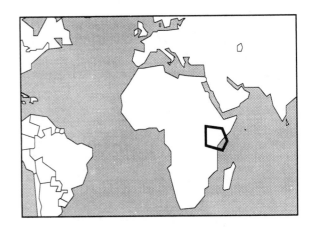

The black, red, and green stripes represent the Black liberation struggle. The thin white stripes represent purity and peace. The weapons represent Kenya's will to defend its freedom.

Kenya

Kenya is the safari center of the world. Located on the equator, Kenya is bordered by Tanzania to the south, Uganda to the west, Sudan to the northwest, Ethiopia to the north, and Somalia to the northeast. The capital is NAIROBI. Nairobi is an international city and one of the most important in Africa. The population is over 23 million. The motto for Kenya is *harambee* (Swahili for pull together). This motto represents the people's united effort to stabilize the nation. Kenya became independent from Britain in 1963, after much civil conflict. Kenya, through the effort of its people has the opportunity to become quite powerful in Africa as it builds its economy and government.

LAND

Kenya is 225,000 square miles. The northeastern region of Kenya is desert. The southwestern region where the majority of the population are located, is mountainous, semi-fertile land. Kenya is part of the GREAT RIFT VALLEY – a deep fissure extending for more than 3000 miles. MT. KENYA is an extinct volcano and the second highest mountain in Kenya. Kenya has many water sources, including the Indian Ocean on its eastern coast, and the Tana River. Kenya is also home to Lake Victoria, the world's second largest freshwater body.

CLIMATE

The climate of Kenya is based on two seasons – rainy and dry. The rainy season runs from April to December. In the long rains of April-June, precipitation averages 40 inches.

CULTURE

Kenya has over 30 ethnic groups. The Bantu-speaking people make up over 50% of the population. The BANTU can be broken up into sub-groups – the Kikuyu and Luhya. The Nilotic peoples originally came from Sudan near the Nile. The main sub-group of the Nilotic are the LUO who make up 13% of the population. Another Nilotic people but much smaller in number than the Luo, are the MASAI. The Masai are among the most famous of the different native peoples because of their reputation as fierce warriors. The Cushtic peoples of the desert of Kenya are primarily nomads and account for a very small minority.

English and KISWAHILI are the official languages in Kenya. Kenyans can practice any religion they choose. Due to missionaries in the 1800s, Christianity is practiced by over half of the population. Traditional beliefs are still practiced by a good percentage of the population, primarily in the more rural areas. The minority is Islam, practiced by 5% of the populations, mainly along the coast.

Much of Kenya's literature is told orally. Storytelling is considered an art in Kenya. Swahili poetry is sung or recited.

The government has begun to stress education although the literacy rate is still low. Many children are taught within their own ethnic group.

Kenyans enjoy soccer, track and field, and water sports. Kenyan athletes are becoming noticed for their distance running.

RESOURCES

Kenya's economy depends a great deal on tourism. Wildlife at national game parks include elephants, giraffes, buffalo, rhinoceroses, zebras, antelope, lions, cheetahs, and monkeys. Many reptiles live in Kenya, including the python, and large crocodiles.

The major crops raised in Kenya are coffee, tea, maize, sweet potatoes, pineapples, coconuts, bananas, and cotton.

RECIPES

A common staple of the Kenyan diet is a mash made of maize and water.

Samosas

Make a pastry with flour, salt, oil, and water. Roll pastry out and cut into triangles. Be sure the pastry is thin.

Filling:

mincemeat or ground meat
dash of ginger
cinnamon
powdered cloves
2 tablespoons chopped parsley
1 clove garlic, crushed
2 tablespoons water
1 cup green chili pepper, chopped & seeded
chopped onion

Saute mincemeat until browned. Add spices and simmer. Stir in onions and parsley. Put a spoonful of the filling on each pastry triangle and fold the triangle over on itself, sealing the edges. Fry the samosas in hot oil until brown.

Samosas are a popular snack in Kenya.

Irio

3-4 ears of white corn
3-4 potatoes
1/2 cup dried chickpeas, cooked
water
salt to taste

Boil the corn until the kernels are soft. Cut them from the cob. Put chickpeas and corn in cold water and bring to a boil. Reduce heat and simmer for 2 hours. Add potatoes to separate cooking water and cook until soft. Mash potatoes, corn, and peas together and add salt to taste. The dish may be served with stew or another meat. Irio is a dish of the Kikuyu tribe.

VOCABULARY

People in Kenya speak Bantu and Nilotic languages. Bantu means person. Bantu is made up of many similar languages. Look how the word "bantu" is sounded out in several of them:

Chewa – *ba-nt-ul*
Ganda – *aba-ntu*
Kwena – *ba-tU*
Swahili – *wa-tu*

Other words from Kenya:

to teach – *xU-rut-a*
teacher – *m U-rut-i*
student – *m U-rut-iw-a*
Hello – *Jambo*

ACTIVITIES

The Kenyan Safari Memory Game

Cut up 1 1/2" squares. On the following page is a gameboard. Cover up each square on the following page. Lift up one square at a time, trying to match the animal pairs.

Baboon   Elephant   Flamingo

Hippopotam   Hyena   Ostrich

Wildebeest   Zebra

The Kenyan Safari Memory Game

Nigeria

FEDERATION OF NIGERIA

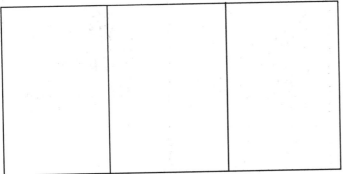

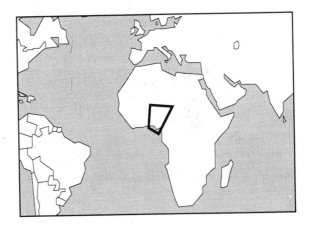

The right and left green panels represent the importance of agriculture and the forests to the country. The middle white panel represents Nigeria's desire for peace and unity.

Nigeria

Nigeria is located in western Africa, named after the Niger River. Nigeria is the most populated and the most prosperous nation in Africa. Within its borders, live a population of about 110,000,000 people. The capital of Nigeria is LAGOS. Other large populated cities are Kano and Ibadan (built in 1450 by the Yoruba people). Nigeria became an independent nation from Britain in 1960. Since then, the country has had many coups and civil wars. It now has a democratic constitution.

LAND

Much of Nigeria is located on the SUDAN, a sub-desert steppe. The Niger River which flows for 2500 miles through Nigeria, empties into the Atlantic Ocean from a hundred different mouths. Located inland are low mountains. At the northeastern tip of Nigeria is Lake Chad. Nigeria's coastal area is on the Gulf of Guinea. The country is 356,667 square miles.

CLIMATE

The climate is hot and humid along the western coast and dry in the north of the country.

CULTURE

The main ethnic groups in Nigeria are the Hausa, Ibo, and the Yoruba. Hostilities existed between these three groups which extended into civil wars but now all groups are united. The earliest civilization in Nigeria is believed to have been the NOK, who were known for their amazing pottery and metalcraft.

English is the official language. There is a great variety of languages which are tonal in quality. Because of this the "talking drum" was used to communicate over long distances.

Nigeria's education system is improving at a slow rate, but is one of the top African countries in literacy. The changes in the education system are being made as the economy faces greater growth.

RESOURCES

Resources found in Nigeria are iron and a high quality of oil. Major crops are yams, plantains, bananas, palm oil, peanuts, and rubber.

RECIPES

Groundnut (Peanut) Soup*
1 tomato
1 potato
1 onion
2 cups water
1 beef bouillon cube
dash of salt
1 cup shelled unsalted roasted peanuts
2 tablespoons rice

Peel and dice the potato and onion. Dice the tomato. Place in a saucepan with water, bouillon cube and salt. Boil for about 30 minutes. Chop the peanuts and combine with the milk. Add the peanut mixture and rice to the saucepan and simmer for 30 minutes. Serve in soup bowls.

Fufu
yams
salt
pepper

Boil peeled yams in a saucepan with salt and pepper until they are soft (about 25 minutes). Let the yams cool, then mash them until soft and free from lumps. Roll the yams into small balls. Serve warm.

Yams are very popular in many African countries. West African yams are different from ours, but you may adapt the recipe with yams or sweet potatoes.

VOCABULARY

one – *otu*
two – *abuo*
three – *ato*
four – *ano*
five – *ise*
six – *isi*
seven – *asaa*
eight – *asato*
nine – *tolu*
ten – *iri*
Come– *Bia*
Go – *Ga*

ACTIVITIES

Create an African Batik

wax
brush
dye
newspaper
fabric
iron

1. Lightly pencil sketch design on cotton fabric.
2. Apply melted wax to design area. Every area not covered by wax will be dyed.
3. Let wax semi-dry. Run waxed design under cold water.
4. Put the fabric into a dye-bath. Allow fabric to remain until 2 shades darker than desired.
5. Take fabric out of dye and rinse in cold running water until excess dye is removed.
6. Allow fabric to dye.
7. Sandwich the dried fabric between newspaper (or newsprint) and press with medium iron to remove wax.

If more than one color is desired, repeat steps 1-6, using the darker dye bath each time. The African batiks use a variety of colors, including yellow, orange, red, and black. The batiks can also be any variety of designs. Batiks

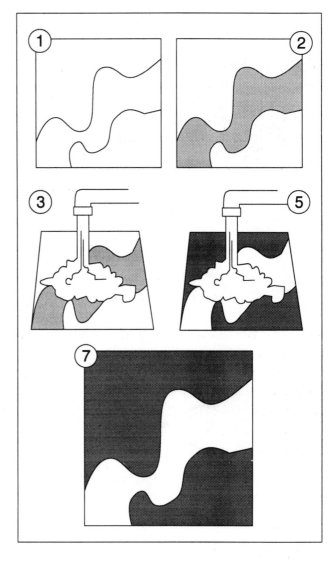

are then made into wall hangings, clothing, anything! You might want to use the designs on the next page for your batiks.

Create an African Mask

markers, crayons, or paint
glitter, feathers, and other decorations
medium brown paper bag
glue or tape

After decorating the mask, glue onto a paper bag. Cut out the eyes. Make as festive as you want!

Create an African Mask

South Africa

REPUBLIC OF SOUTH AFRICA

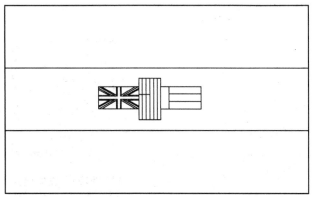

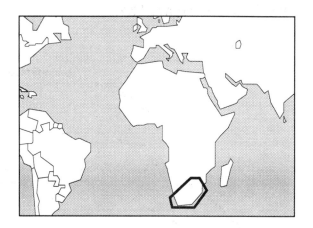

The top stripe is orange, the middle stripe is white, and the bottom stripe is blue. In the middle of the white stripe is an emblem of other country flags: United Kingdom and The Netherlands.

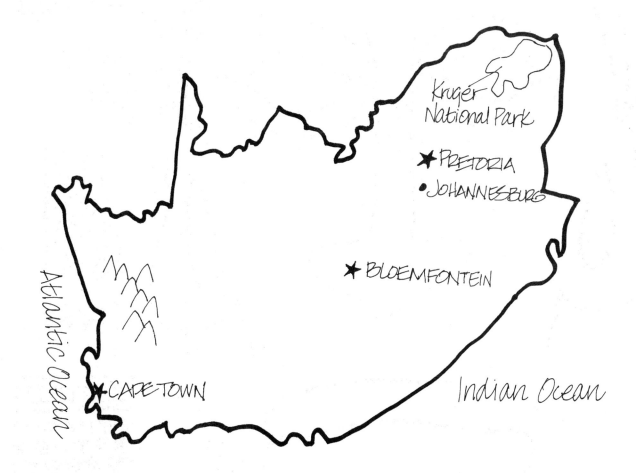

South Africa

The natural resources of gold and diamonds has made South Africa a wealthy country. South Africa is located at the tip of Africa. It has three official capitals: **PRETORIA**, the administrative capital; Cape Town, the legislative capital; and Bloemfontein, the judicial capital. The largest city of **JOHANNESBURG** began as a mining camp for gold.

Until very recently, South Africa has had a system of laws called **APARTHEID** (*apartness* in Dutch). This system was begun by the white people to protect their power and maintain their privileges. Apartheid segregates whites from non-whites, putting all the power into the white hands. Civil wars have been going on in South Africa for years because of apartheid. Because of the South African policy on apartheid, the country has not been able to participate in the United Nations nor the Olympic Games until recently (late 1994).

NELSON MANDELA, the leader of the African National Congress (ANC) has been a symbol of the Black's struggle for many years. Imprisoned for life by the Afrikaan government, Mandela was released with the help of the United Nations. With his release, many Blacks rallied around him. Although fighting still exists in many divisions, apartheid has broken down. In 1994, Mandela became president of South Africa, joining forces with Vice Prime Minister de Klerk. For the first time since the South African government was established, Blacks have gained the rights lost to them by the Afrikaners.

LAND

The country is 471,445 square miles (almost the size of Alaska). In the center of South Africa is a huge plateau. Deserts cover much of the western region. The eastern half of South Africa is more diverse. Along the Indian Ocean coast are tropical rainforests. Inland grow pine forests. Further inland are stark, brown mountains. Kruger National Park is a huge reserve for the abundance of wildlife.

CLIMATE

The majority of the country has mild climates. In the mountainous areas, snow is on the ground all year. Along the coasts, the climate is tropical.

CULTURE

South Africa has many ethnic groups. The government divided the groups into four racial categories. The Blacks (or Africans) are the largest group with over 70% of the population. Within this category are subgroups: the **ZULU** and the **XHOSA** who are the largest groups, the Sotho, the Tswana, the Shangan, and the Swazi. There have been civil wars between the different groups (called tribalism) even though they are united against apartheid.

The second category, the whites make up 15% of the population. More than half of that percentage are Afrikaners. The Afrikaners began settling in South Africa over 300 years ago. The Afrikaners were the creators of apartheid. The minority group of the whites

are the English-speaking whites. They arrived during the gold and diamond rushes and are relatively new to the country.

The third category are the colored people. The colored are a mixture of all the groups. Although still heavily segregated against, the colored maintain higher rights than the Africans. In the 1980s, the colored began to side with the Blacks against apartheid.

The fourth category and the smallest are the Asians – mainly Indians and Pakistanis.

The practice of any religion is allowed. Originally, most Africans followed traditional African beliefs. Most Black South Africans practice Christianity. The Afrikaners follow the Dutch Reformed Church. The English-speaking whites and many non-whites follow the Anglican church which doesn't segregate like the Dutch Reformed. **Reverend Desmond Tutu**, who won the Nobel Peace Prize for his non-violence efforts against apartheid, became the first black Anglican bishop. Minority religions mainly practiced by the Asians, are Buddhism and Hinduism. **Afrikaan** (a form of Dutch) and English are the official languages. There are many different languages within the different sub-groups.

Black South African art combines religious themes with traditional African beliefs, in the form of masks, wood sculpture, and pottery. South African literature has shown the world many of the struggles the country has gone through.

Sports are very important to all the different groups in South Africa. The Afrikaners enjoy rugby football, the English-speaking whites enjoy cricket, and many of the Blacks excel at soccer.

RESOURCES

More than 1/2 of the world's gold is mined in South Africa. The country is the world's largest producer of diamonds. Other mineral resources are large deposits of platinum, uranium, copper, manganese, chromium, and coal. Major crops raised are corn, wheat, sugarcane, fruit, and wool. Many Africans raise sheep.

Girl in traditional N'Bele dress.

South Africa **151**

ACTIVITIES
Mine for South African Diamonds
The mining of Diamonds has shaped the destiny of South Africa. Can you find the diamond in the mine that matches the one to the right?

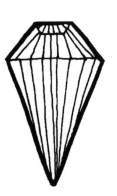

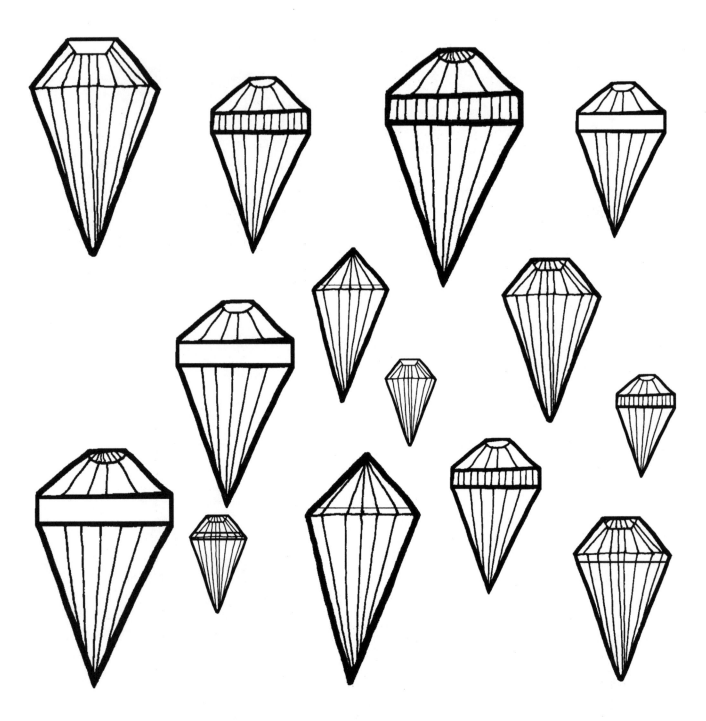

Angola

PEOPLE'S REPUBLIC OF ANGOLA

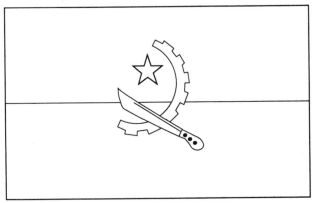

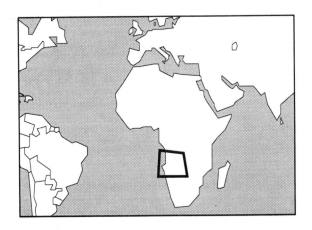

The red stripe on top represents the spilled blood of the freedom fighters and the black stripe on the bottom represents Africa. The yellow symbol in the middle represents the country's natural wealth.

LUANDA

CUANZA RIVER

Atlantic Ocean

Namib Desert

The name Angola derives from the Ndongo people's name for their king – *ngola*. Angola's capital is LUANDA. The population at 9 million is small in comparison to the size of the country. Much of Angola's history has been ruled by the Portuguese. On November 11, 1975, Angola finally gained its independence of Portugal. However, civil wars followed and backed by Cuba and China, a Marxist government followed.

LAND

Angola is 482,500 square miles. The Atlantic Ocean is the western border. To the east is Zambia, to the north is Zaire, and to the south is Namibia. The majority of Angola is made up of tablelands. A small province of Angola, Cabinda, actually lies within Zaire. The country has many rivers, the most important being the CUANZA RIVER. South Angola is desert region known as the NAMIB DESERT. Much of the north region is jungle.

CLIMATE

Angola has two seasons – wet and dry. The rainy season's annual precipitation can vary from 5 inches along the coast to 60 inches in the central region. The dry season brings on cold, foggy air and is called *cacimbo*.

CULTURE

The earliest people in Angola were the SAN (bushmen). The Bantu came next, arriving from central Africa. They had skill with ironworking which enabled them to form large kingdoms. During the fifteenth century, the Portuguese arrived. Portugal profited from their slave trade of Angolan natives for almost 300 years until slavery was abolished. However, their exploitation of the Angolan people continued for five centuries.

There are two major ethnic groups. The largest is the OVIMBUNDU, who make up 38% of the population. Other African peoples are still resentful of the traitor role the Ovimbundu played in the slave trade. The second largest are the MBUNDU people. The BAKONGO, the LUNDA, and the CHOKWE make up about 25% of Angola's population. The smallest group are the San.

When the Portuguese were in Angola, the official religion became Catholicism. However, nearly half of the Angolan people have continued to follow their traditional African religion. The remainder follow some form of Christianity. Angola's official language is Portuguese. Many African languages and dialects are also used.

All the Chokwe art have ritual meaning or practical uses, rather than just aesthetic purposes. Their basketry and pottery are equally as practical. The Muhuila people are known for their beautiful beadwork.

Angolans enjoy playing soccer and basketball. Since their independence, the Angolans have begun making themselves noticed in world games. Their track and field teams are up and coming.

Education is a problem within Angola. There are a serious lack of teachers. Many children only attend school for four years. Healthcare in Angola is poor, due to the many civil wars. In the past, witch doctors were called in to work with the sick person.

RESOURCES

Angolan economy is based almost entirely on its oil industry. Angola major mineral deposits are diamonds, iron ore, phosphates, gold, and uranium. The major crops raised are coffee, cotton, beans, sugarcane, palm oil and tobacco. Fishing is an important industry because of Angola's long coastline. Angola is a poor country due to all the warfare, however the large deposits of oil and diamonds could eventually bring some stability to the country in coming years.

ACTIVITIES

The following story called a singing tale and is one told throughout Africa. The song is included on the next page.

Once upon a time there was a village with a lot of fruit trees. People came from other villages to buy the fruit from this market.

The father of a family in this fruit-tree village had four children, all of them girls. But one of the girls, Ijomah, was a stepchild. Her mother had died when Ijomah was young and her father had married again. It was then that Ijomah's troubles began. Her stepmother, Nnekeh, never liked her. She only loved her own children and completely neglected Ijomah. Worse than that, she made the girl do all the hard work and did not even give her enough food.

Ijomah's father was too busy as a trader to know what was going on. The few times he was at home Ijomah complained to him in secret, but her father never wanted to offend his second wife. Instead, he asked Ijomah to be patient and occasionally gave her money for food.

Ijomah's mother had loved to plant flowers. After she died, Ijomah continued to tend the garden. Nnekeh often sent her own children to pick all the brightest and most beautiful flowers, but always once a month Ijomah took roses to her mother's grave. She would have taken the roses more often, but Nnekeh never gave her the chance. At times Ijomah cried over the loss of her mother and over her own sad state. But things never changed.

One day Nnekeh went to the market and bought some juicy red fruit called odala. Of course, Nnekeh only gave the fruit to her own children, and Ijomah had none. But after her half sisters had eaten their odala, Ijomah saw that they had thrown away the seeds. She collected the seeds and planted them in her garden.

When she woke up one day, she found little plants sprouting from the seeds. She was very happy and took great care to make the plants grow up strong and healthy. Early every morning, Ijomah would go to her garden to water the plants. As she watered them, she sang this song: *(sing first verse in song)*

Each morning Ijomah sang her song and watered the odala plants she loved so much.

Soon the plants grew into trees, and one day Ijomah saw the first fruit beginning to grow. She was so happy. She never stopped singing her song. But when the fruit began to ripen, Nnekeh said the trees belonged to her children, not just to Ijomah. Ijomah was very unhappy. She told Nnekeh that the trees and fruit were hers, but Nnekeh said: "I bought the odala in the market, and without them you would have no trees!"

As soon as the fruit were fully ripe, people came to Ijomah's garden to buy them. Very many people came because the odala were were so big and sweet. Ijomah wanted to sell the fruit and have money to buy some the beautiful things that her stepmother would never allow her to have.

Nnekeh was furiously angry. She raged at Ijomah and refused to let her sell the odala. She herself would be the one to sell them. Ijomah was so unhappy she could not sleep that night. Very early the next morning, she crept to the garden, stood sadly by her odala trees and started singing: *(sing the second verse)*

As she finished the song, the odala trees began to shrivel until they were all withered up.

When daylight came, the people came to buy to the fruit. But all the people found were shriveled trees and withered fruit. Everyone was annoyed. Nnekeh was so ashamed, she started shouting like an angry general in the army. She knew very well, she said, that her crafty stepdaughter had played a trick on her.

"But if Nnekeh wants to," said Ijomah, "she can bring the trees to life again. If the trees are hers, they will obey her! If they belong to me, they will obey me!"

Nnekeh looked at the shriveled trees, but there was nothing she could do. She tried to pounce on Ijomah, but the people grabbed her and pulled her away. Then they asked Ijomah whether she could do anything to the trees. Ijomah smiled and started singing: *(sing the first verse)*

While she sang, the trees began to grow! New green leaves sprouted from the withered branches, and soon the trees were loaded with even bigger fruit than before. When the villagers saw that, they knew the stepmother was wrong. The fruit belonged to Ijomah, and Nnekeh had been trying to take them away from her.

So the villagers bought fruit from Ijomah. They bought and bought. They carried away basketloads of fruit and still there was more to buy. No one had ever seen so many odala or tasted fruit so fine and sweet. Soon Ijomah was the richest person in the village. She had money to buy all the things she wanted, and her stepmother never troubled her again.

FIRST VERSE

Odala me so	My odala! grow
Nda	Please
Odala me so	My odala! grow
Nda	Please
So, so, so	Grow, grow, grow
Nda	Please
Nwunye nna mo-o	My father's wife
Nda	Please
Nwunye nna mo-o	My father's wife
Nda	Please
Zora odala na afia	Bought odala from the market
Nda	Please
Lacha, lacha, lacha	Ate, ate, ate
Nda	Please
Lacha bo nwa di a	Ate and did not give her stepdaughter
Nda.	Please.

SECOND VERSE

Odala mo	My odala! die
Nda	Please
Odala mo	My odala! die
Nda	Please
Mo, mo, mo	Die, die, die
Nda	Please
Nwunye nna mo-o	My father's wife
Nda	Please
Nwunye nna mo-o	My father's wife
Nda	Please
Zora odala na afia	Bought odala from the market
Nda	Please
Lacha, lacha, lacha	Ate, ate, ate
Nda	Please
Lacha bo nwa di a	Ate and did not give her stepdaughter
Nda	Please
Odala mo.	My odala! die.

Europe

North
Sea

Baltic
Sea

Atlantic
Ocean

English Channel

1.

3.

4.

5.

2.

Adriatic Sea

Aegean
Sea

IDENTIFY

1. _____
2. _____
3. _____
4. _____
5. _____

Spain

KINGDOM OF SPAIN

The original colors were red and white instead of red and yellow. The original colors dated back to the 9th century. In 1981, the flag as it is today was adopted.

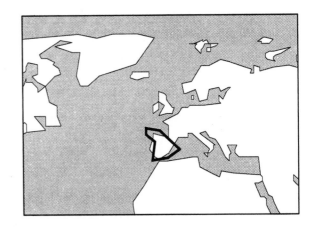

Bay of Biscay

Atlantic Ocean

Pyrenees

BARCELONA

✈ MADRID

Mediterranean Sea

· TOLEDO

Iberian Peninsula

Strait of Gibraltar

Spain

Spain is the second largest western European country. The capital of Spain is **MADRID**. The population is 38,865,000. Other large cities are Toledo and Barcelona. During the Golden Age of Spain, Columbus discovered America. Spain began to extend its borders outside of the mainland, making it the most powerful nation in the Old World. However, due to the American Revolution (Spain fought with the Americans against England), the Spanish-American War, and many civil wars, much of the land Spain had claimed were lost.

LAND

Spain is 190,000 square miles (with an additional 4,000 miles of islands). Spain's mainland is often called the Iberian Peninsula. It consists of a central plateau ringed by mountains. Extending east/west through Spain are the **PYRENEES**, which form a natural border with France. Besides the mainland, Spain contains the Balearic Islands and the Canary Islands.

CLIMATE

The climate is varied. In the central region, the weather is dry, with hot summers and cold winters. The central region has an annual precipitation of 15 inches. Towards the north, the temperatures are more moderate, with an annual precipitation of 38 inches.

CULTURE

The groups of Spaniards are classified more by cultural differences than ethnic groups. These groups include the Castillians of central Spain; the Basques of the north; the Catalans of the northeast; the Galicians of the northwest; and the Andanisians of the south.

The official language of Spain is Spanish. Other languages spoken are Catalan, Basque, and Galician. Most Spanish are Roman Catholics. There is no official religion in Spain.

Different cultures like the Celts, the Romans, and the Moors all contributed to make Spain what it is today. Today much Roman art and architecture is intact, after 20 centuries. The Moors contributed to the architecture, creating Islamic mosques and ceramics.

Important artists that have come from Spain are Francisco Goya, Juan Gris, Velazquez, and Salvador Dali. **PABLO PICASSO** is probably the most famous Spanish painter, leaving his mark in modern times.

Spanish music is often performed with guitar and castanets. Flamenco is sung by Spanish Gypsies (*gitanos*). To dance flamenco, it is said the dancer has to be possessed by *duende* (the demon of inspiration). An important fiesta (or religious feast) is the bullfight (*corrida*) in October. Before the actual fight, a herd of bulls are let loose in the town and the townspeople run ahead, leading the bulls to the arena. Spaniards have a passion for soccer with children learning to play at a very young age.

RESOURCES

Most important crops are wheat, barley, corn, nuts, and fruit (grapes mainly for wine production). The Spanish have industrially developed (instead of relying solely of agriculture). They are among the top five shipbuilding nations in the world. Fishing has always been important and at present, Spain is among the world's top five fishing nations.

There are small amounts of mercury, sulfur, manganese, tin, and zinc produced. Forestry, although slightly suffering, has remained one of their more important resources.

Tourism is a growing industry for Spain. The Mediterranean beaches are ranked among the best. Many tourists enjoy visiting Barcelona and Toledo.

RECIPES

Fish and seafood are important staples to the Spanish diet. Wine is drunk with every meal except for breakfast.

Paella

yellow paella rice
canned fish: shrimp, oysters, clams, sardines, etc.
garlic salt
mushrooms
stuffed green olives

Cook rice as directed. Place in baking dish with other ingredients. Cook until completely heated. The Spanish serve paella with lemon wedges and shellfish on top. Garlic bread adds to the meal.

Leche Frita (Dried Custard Squares)

1/2 cup cornstarch
3 cups milk
1/2 cup plus 2 tablespoons sugar
2 eggs, slightly beaten
1 cup fine bread crumbs, trimmed of crusts
4 tablespoons butter
2 tablespoons oil

In a 2-quart saucepan, combine cornstarch and 1 cup milk. Stir until the cornstarch dissolves. Stir in the remaining milk and 1/2 cup sugar. Bring to a boil over high heat, stirring constantly until the mixture thickens. Pour into a shallow 9 inch baking dish. Spread evenly and refrigerate for four hours. Cut into squares. Dip the squares into the beaten eggs and then into the crumbs. Place on sheet of waxed paper. Melt butter in the oil and brown the squares on each side. Sprinkle with cinnamon and sugar. Eat!

Seville Bread Puffs (Torrejas) ****

3 slices white bread, cut in half
1 egg, well beaten with a dash of salt
3/4 cup milk

orange juice
cinnamon

Generously grease a 8"x 8" baking dish with margarine, greasing the sides and the bottom. Dip the bread in the milk, place the bread to the side of the bowl to drain, then dip it into the beaten egg, coating both sides.

Arrange bread in the baking dish. Bake in a preheated 375-degree oven for 40 minutes until crispy brown.

To serve, sprinkle with orange juice, dust lightly with cinnamon. Or, dust with a mixture of cinnamon and sugar.

VOCABULARY

one – *uno*	two – *dos*
three – *tres*	four – *cuatro*
five – *cinco*	six – *seis*
seven – *sente*	eight – *ocho*
nine – *nueve*	ten – *diez*

English words borrowed from Spanish

fiesta	chili con carne
rodeo	bronco
mustang	patio
adobe	armada
mosquito	lariat
mesa	arroyo
canyon	coyote
plaza	guerrilla
embargo	

ACTIVITIES

Color in the Flamenco Dancer

Maria is a gypsy flamenco dancer. Can you add anything to the picture – a rose in her mouth, other flamenco dancers, an audience?

Italy

REPUBLIC OF ITALY

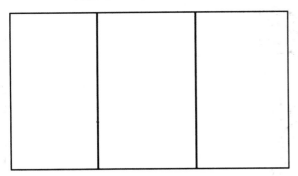

The flag has vertical stripes of green, white, and red. Taken from the French color but green used in place of blue.

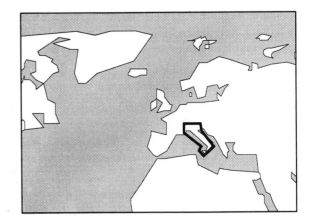

Italy

Italy is a long, narrow peninsula which lies in the Mediterranean Sea. Italy is shaped like a boot. At the toe of the boot is the island of Sicily and at the knee of the boot is the other Italian island of Sardinia. The capital of Italy is **ROME**. The population is over 58 million with 60% living in the cities. Italy's past history is full of civil wars within the land, the two World Wars, emperors, kings, and invading tribes. The influence of the Roman Empire and the Renaissance is still heavily felt in every culture within the world.

LAND

Italy is 116,000 square miles. The peninsula is surrounded by water; the Adriatic Sea to the east, the Ionian Sea to the south, the Tyrrhenian Sea to the west, and the Ligurian Sea to the northwest. The two islands of Sicily and Sardinia are surrounded by the Mediterranean Sea.

Italy can be divided up into three land regions. The Continental region of Italy includes Italy's only sizable lowlands, the North Italian Plain and the Alps, which curve around the Po River Valley.

The Peninsular region of Italy is all of the Italian peninsula south the North Italian Plain. It includes the **APENNINES** mountain range, broad lowlands, and the southern coast. The southern coastline is rocky and steep. **VESUVIUS**, located near Naples is Europe's only active mainland volcano.

The insular region of Italy includes the islands of Sicily and Sardinia, and many smaller islands. Two active volcanoes – Stromboli and Vulcano are located on islands north of Sicily. Frequent earthquakes hit throughout Italy.

CLIMATE

Northern Italy has a mountain climate. During the winter, the Alps reach temperatures of 33° F. The northern Peninsular region has a continental climate, and the southern Peninsular region has a Mediterranean climate. Winter temperatures in the south reach 45° F in Rome and 53° F in Sicily. Summer temperatures for much of Italy average 75° F. Annual precipitation averages 43 inches in the north and 14 inches in the south.

CULTURE

The peoples of Italy are mixtures from all the different cultures the Roman Empire came into contact with. The northern people of Italy are very different from the southern people. The northerners tend to be blond-haired and blue-eyed, descendants of the northern Germans who settled in the north after the Fall of Rome. They are also far more influenced by their European neighbors. Because of the fertile Po Valley, the northern peoples of Italy tend to have a higher standard of living.

The southern half of Italy was settled by the Arabs, French, and Spanish, which accounts for their darker skin and hair coloring.

The official language is Italian, although many dialects are spoken. When the Roman Empire was in power, Latin was the official language. Italian is an offspring of Latin. Because so many different dialects are spoken, there is a standardized Italian which helps unify the people of Italy.

Over 95% of the population is Roman Catholic. The Pope (or leader) of the Roman Catholic Church lives in the Vatican City. The Vatican City, although its location is in Rome, is the smallest independent country in the world (only 108 acres).

Italy's rich heritage of art, literature, and architecture is still in evidence. Glassblowing is an art practiced even today. The leather products of Italy are among the finest in the world. The craft of lace making is practiced in small mountain villages. Opera began in Italy, and among the finest operas performed are by Italian composers.

All children between the ages of six and fourteen must attend school. Italians are soccer fanatics. Bicycle racing and skiing are also enjoyed.

RESOURCES

The only minerals produced in Italy are mercury and sulfur. The major industry is metal. Many Italians work in manufacturing plants which produce typewriters, sewing machines, and aircraft equipment. Leather is also a major product produced. The majority of agriculture is centered around the Po Valley. Major crops include grain, fruit, and vegetables. Also grown in the Po Valley are the artichoke and the finnocchi, a licorice-tasting plant.

Tourism accounts for a great deal of industry. The cities of Italy are filled with monuments to its past history. These include Venice with its **GONDOLAS** (long, flat-bottomed boats); Milan, Italy's second largest city; Florence, considered among the prettiest cities in Europe; and Rome. In Rome, tourists flock to the Colosseum, the Sistine Chapel, and St. Peter's Church. In Bologna, the Children's Book Fair has been held annually for 29 years.

RECIPES

Spaghetti
1 medium onion, chopped
1 green pepper, chopped
clove of garlic
1 pound ground beef or turkey
1/2 teaspoon chili pepper
1/3 can tomato paste
parmesan cheese

1 cup mushrooms
1 tablespoon ketchup
ripe, stuffed olives, chopped
olive oil
2 tablespoons butter
1 box spaghetti noodles, cooked

Saute onions and garlic, add meat. Add other ingredients and simmer for awhile. Pour over spaghetti and serve. Add garlic bread to complete the meal.

Lasagna
Cook lasagna noodles (8 ounce box) in 4 cups of water. Prepare the following meat mixture:

2 tablespoons olive oil
1-2 pounds ground beef
1 tablespoon garlic
3/4 cup onion
16 oz. can tomato paste
1 can tomato sauce
tomatoes (optional)
dash of salt, oregano, basil, and pepper

Cheese filling
mozzarella cheese (approximately 1 pound)
ricotta or cottage cheese (1 carton)

Cook and drain noodles. In a shallow baking pan, alternate layers of noodles, meat mixture, and cheese. Sprinkle with parmesan cheese. Bake at 350 degrees for 1 hour.

VOCABULARY

one – *uno*	hello/goodbye – *ciao*
two – *due*	How are you? – *Come stai?*
three – *tre*	Fine – *Bene*
four – *quattro*	Thankyou – *Grazie*
five – *cinque*	
six – *sei*	
seven – *sette*	
eight – *otto*	
nine – *nove*	
ten – *dieci*	

FAMOUS ITALIANS

Julius Caesar – general in Roman army

Christopher Columbus – explorer who discovered America

Frederico Fellini – 20th century movie director

Galileo – astronomer and scientist

Niccolo Machiavelli – political philosopher

Marcus Antonius (Mark Antony) – Roman general who committed suicide with Egyptian Queen Cleopatra

Benito Mussolini – Fascist dictator during World War II

Giacomo Puccini – opera composer (*Madame Butterfly*)

Spartacus – Roman slave revolt leader and gladiator

Leonardo da Vinci – painter, sculptor, architect, and engineer (Renaissance man)

Antonio Vivaldi – classical music composer (*The Four Seasons*)

ACTIVITIES

Unscramble the Italian Names

Using the list above, try unscrambling the below words. Some might be two words.

PLBSCROOSUIHREHUMTR   _____   _____

LEGAILO   _____

FLINRDOFIRECEEI   _____   _____

ECGLAAERMLNH   _____

ICPCAGCIONOMUI   _____   _____

ACTIVITIES

Italian Game – Follow Through Tag*

Up to twenty players form a circle, clasping hands and holding up arms to make arches. One player, the runner, stands inside the circle; and another, the chaser, stands outside.

The chaser tries to catch the runner, but he must follow the exact route of the runner, going under the same arms. When he catches him or gives up, two more players are selected to be runner and chaser.

Switzerland

CONFEDERATION OF SWITZERLAND

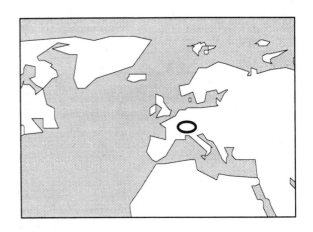

During the 13th century, the current emblem of the cross was put on the flag to represent the struggle for liberty from the Holy Roman Empire. Today the white flag on the red background represents neutrality. It is the only national flag to be square.

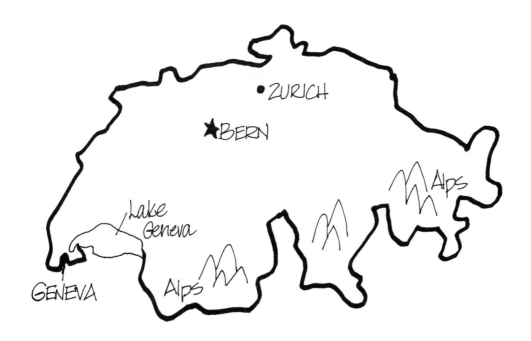

Switzerland

Switzerland is a peaceful country made up of lakes, mountains, modern cities, and old-world villages. **BERN** is the capital of Switzerland. The government is democratic and is built upon the Swiss Constitution of 1848, in which they achieved the neutral position within the world community. Although not a member of the United Nations, Switzerland is host to many world-wide conferences.

LAND

Switzerland is 15,942 square miles. Over 60% is covered by the **ALPS**, the largest mountain range in Europe. The Alps make up the southern border with Italy. Many glaciers move through the Alps changing the shape of the range. The older Jura Mountains extend along the western border with France. **JURA** is where the word *Jurassic* comes from. Central Switzerland is a fertile plateau. Important bodies of water are **LAKE GENEVA** and the **RHONE RIVER**.

CLIMATE

The climate varies greatly due to the mountain ranges.

CULTURE

Switzerland has three official languages: German (which the majority of the population speak), French, and Italian. There is complete freedom of religion. Children are required to attend school from age six to fourteen years. Switzerland has many boarding schools.

Different children's festivals are held to celebrate the beginning of summer and the end of spring. The St. Gallen Children's Festival, which began in 1824, is held every two years simply to honor children.

Swiss literature has produced two of the most famous children's books: *Swiss Family Robinson* by the Wyss family and *Heidi* by Johanna Spyri.

Skiing, hiking, camping, and bicycling are popular sports. **HORNUSSEN** is a national game, similar to baseball. A popular swiss card game is called **JASS**.

RESOURCES

Tourism is important to the economy of Switzerland. Dairy products make up an important agricultural industry. Swiss chocolate and cheese are renown. Swiss manufacturing produces leather, textiles, and watches. Switzerland is also an important banking center to many of the world's countries.

RECIPES

Chocolate Fondue
Chocolate sauce
powdered sugar
coconut
fruit (apples, oranges, strawberries, etc.)

Heat the chocolate sauce in a fondue pot. Dip the fruits into the sauce, then into the coconut or sugar. *Note: Dip the fruits into lemon juice before serving to prevent them from darkening.*

ACTIVITY

Draw a Watercolor Mountain

You will need tissues or napkins and watercolors. Wet the paper and then apply the tissue to form mountain shapes. Use watercolors to define the outline. The texture of the mountains will result when the paint bleeds through the tissue. Fill in the rest of the picture with watercolor wash while the paper is wet. A person, house, or trees may be added, if desired.

France

REPUBLIC OF FRANCE

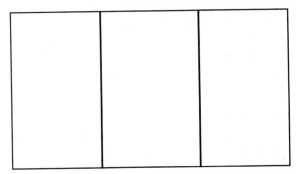

The right blue panel and the left red panel represent Paris, the white panel represents the Bourbons. This flag has inspired many other flags of the world.

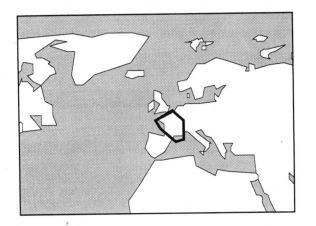

France is the largest country in western Europe. The name France is taken from the Frank tribe. **PARIS** "the city of lights" is the capital and home to 1/6 of the French population. The population of France is almost 56 million. Other large cities are Marseille, Lyon, and Toulouse. France is a democratic republic. The French have had many problems with their government starting with the French Revolution, where Louis XVI and his wife Marie Antoinette lost their heads to the guillotine; to **NAPOLEON BONAPARTE**, and his ever-spreading empire.

LAND

France is 212,900 square miles. The **RHINE RIVER** forms the German border, as well as the Jura Mountains. Other major rivers include the Loire, and the Seine. The **PYRENEES** mountains range extend from Spain into France. However, the French Alps are the highest mountains in France. Most of central France is made up of a plateau called **MASSIF CENTRAL**.

CLIMATE

The climate varies with the altitude. The west coast has a very rainy climate, the inland areas has a mixture of mild summers and cold winters in the north, and hot summers and mild winters in the south. The mountains receive the most precipitation. The Alps often have glaciers forming. The Mediterranean areas has hot summers and mild winters.

CULTURE

Since its beginnings, Paris has played a role in high fashion, painting, sculpture, architecture, and literature. The contributions the French have made to the arts is invaluable. Much of the great artwork in the world is housed at the Louvre in Paris, one of the largest art museums in the world.

Architecture is one of the areas where past French excelled. The Chartres cathedral is an example of French Gothic style, with high vaulted ceilings and stained glass. Another style of architecture is Baroque. Louis XIV's palace at Versailles is an example of how ornamental Baroque can be.

Painting and sculpture is where the French truly excelled. The French Revolution allowed artistic freedom. From the Revolution came Eugene Delacroix and Jean Francois Millet who were realism painters, painting what they saw rather than what they were told to paint.

In the 19th century, a style of painting called impressionism was created in Paris by Eduard Manet, Claude Monet, Pierre-Auguste Renoir, and Edgar Degas.

While impressionists were making their mark on the canvas, writers in Paris were forming a new movement called romanticism. Victor Hugo wrote *The Hunchback of Notre Dame* and Alexandre Dumas wrote *The Three Musketeers* during this period.

Another famous Frenchman, although not in the field of art, is Louis Pasteur, a chemist who made possible the single most important discovery in modern times. He perfected his germ theory of disease. Because of his work, we now use antiseptics for protection against infections.

French is the official language, although there are other dialects spoken. Provencal is spoken in Provence, Briton is spoken in Brittany, as well as Flemish, German, Basque, and Catalan.

The majority of the French are Roman Catholics, and a small percentage are Muslims, Protestants, and Jews.

The French are fanatic bicycle riders. Many French train for the Tour de France – a world famous bike race which takes place every year. Soccer is also important to the French. The game of **PETANQUE**, which is similar to bowling is played in Normandy.

French schoolchildren attend school on Saturdays but have Wednesdays free. Children between the ages of 6 to 16 must attend school.

RESOURCES

Agriculture is important to the French economy. The leading crop is wheat. Other major crops include chicory, fruits, hops, rye, and tobacco. Grapes are produced in most of France for wine production.

Mineral resources found include iron ore, bauxite, coal, gypsum, lead, zinc, and copper.

Tourism is one of the more important industries for the French. Tourists come not only to visit the Eiffel Tower and Notre Dame in Paris, but also the French countryside where wineries are located; Brittany; and the Mediterranean beaches at Cannes.

RECIPES

The French are well-known for their cuisine. Breakfasts are light, with lunch being the main meal of the day. Cheese and fruit are often included as courses. Wine is often drunk at both lunch and dinner. French baked goods include croissants, long loaves of bread, and pastries.

Crepes

2 eggs
2/3 cup milk
1 tablespoon melted shortening
1/2 cup sifted all-purpose flour
dash of sugar

Beat eggs. Add milk and shortening. Sift milk, salt, and sugar together and add to eggs. Beat until smooth. Drop batter on greased crepe griddle. Cook until brown. Turn once. You may fill your crepe with almost anything: meats such as roast beef or hamburger; vegetables such as squash or broccoli; or desserts such as chocolate chips or fresh fruits.

Quiche

1 9" pieshell
12 bacon slices
4 eggs
2 cups heavy cream
dash of salt, nutmeg, sugar, and pepper
1 cup swiss cheese

Heat oven to 425-degrees. Fry and crumble bacon. Beat together other ingredients, except cheese. Sprinkle pie shell with cheese and bacon. Pour mixture on top. Bake at 425-degrees for 15 minutes. Reduce heat to 300-degrees and bake for 40 minutes. To test for doneness, insert a knife or toothpick in the middle of the quiche. If it comes out clean, the quiche is done!

French Dressing

1/4 cup salad oil
1/2 cup sugar
3/4 cup vinegar
1 can tomato soup
1 teaspoon salt
1 clove garlic

Combine all ingredients and blend well. Pour dressing on salad or over sandwiches.

VOCABULARY

one – *un*
two – *deux*
three – *trois*
four – *quartre*
five – *cinq*
six – *six*
seven – *sept*
eight – *huit*
nine – *nuif*
ten – *dix*
Hello – *Bonjour*
Goodbye – *Adieu*
Goodnight – *Bonsoir*
Thankyou – *Merci*

ACTIVITIES
French Songs
FRÈRE JACQUES

Lightly   *Traditional*

Frè - re Jac - ques, Frè - re Jac - ques,
Are you sleep - ing, are you sleep - ing,

Dor - mez - vous? Dor - mez - vous?
Bro - ther John, Bro - ther John?

Son - nez les ma - ti - nes, son - nez les ma - ti - nes,
Morn - ing bells are ring - ing, morn - ing bells are ring - ing,

Din, din, don; din, din, don.
Ding, ding, dong; ding, ding, dong.

WHERE IS THUMBKIN? *(Sung to the tune of Frere Jacques)*
1. Where is Thumbkin? Where is Thumbkin?
   Here I am, Here I am.
   How are you to-day, Sir?
   Very well, I thank you.
   Run a-way, run a-way.
2. Where is Pointer? Where is Pointer?
3. Where is Tall Man? Where is Tall Man?
4. Where is Ring Man? Where is Ring Man?

KINGDOM OF THE NETHERLANDS

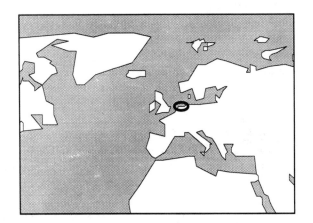

The top stripe is red, the middle white, and the bottom stripe is blue — taken from the French tricolor. Originally the red stripe was orange.

The Netherlands, also known as Holland, is a country located in western Europe. The country is also referred to as the *"land of water"*. The capital is **AMSTERDAM** and the population is over 14 million.

LAND

The Netherlands are 15,892 square miles. It can be divided into four regions. The Dunes region, which includes the West Frisian Islands, consists of mainly infertile land. The Polders region has rich, fertile land and the greatest density of population. The Sands regions has dry soil which has to be irrigated. The Southern Uplands has the highest elevation and the most fertile land. The two major rivers are the **RHINE** and the **MAAS RIVER**. There is no major mountain or range.

CLIMATE

The climate is damp. Summers are milk, usually averaging 60° F. Winters are cold, averaging 30° F. The annual precipitation is 30 inches.

CULTURE

Dutch is the national language of the Netherlands. In addition to Dutch, the government recognizes Frisian as another official language. The Netherlands offers religious freedom. There are no official religions, however 1/3 are Protestant, 1/3 are Catholic, and the rest are minority religions.

Famous painters from the Netherlands include Hieronymous Bosch and **VINCENT VAN GOGH**. Another famous figure is **ANNE FRANK**, a Jewish girl during World War II, who wrote her famous diary while hiding from the Nazis in Amsterdam.

A symbol of Holland is the Dutch wooden shoes, called **KLOMPEN**. Klompen are used to protect feet from damp ground. Today, people all over the world wear similar shoes called clogs, which are derived from the Dutch klompen.

Dutch children must attend school from age 6 to 16. The Netherlands have excellent healthcare. Life expectancy is among the highest in the world.

Soccer is the most popular sport. Dutch also enjoy bicycle riding, swimming, and sailing. Ice skating is a popular winter sport. When the canals freeze over for the first time each winter, the schools declare a holiday and everyone goes skating! The children of Holland play many games that are similar to American games, such as leap frog (*Haasje Over*), jump rope (*Touwtje*), and hide-n-seek (*Verstoppertje*), Hop Scotch (*Hinkelen*), Tag (*Krifgergfe*), and Yoyo (*Jojo*).

RESOURCES

The major crops are barley, oats, wheat, potatoes, and sugar beets. Dairy products are also important. Fishing is a big industry. The manufacturing industry produces electronic equipment, and textiles. Holland is known for its beautiful flowers, particularly tulips! Dutch tulips are flown all over the world.

There are no major mineral resources except for salt, natural gas, and petroleum.

Since the altitude of the land in Holland is very low and being almost surrounded by the North Sea, the Dutch people constructed dikes along the shoreline and canal banks. They extend inland from the sea into Holland to prevent flooding and destruction of the land. To construct a dike, the people first built a core of packed sand. Then they covered the sand with with heavy clay, and then planted grass with long roots on top. Finally, they strengthened the side of the dike facing the water by reinforcing it with logs of wood and large blocks of stone.

The Dutch use wind as a source of energy by means of windmills. Windmills are tall structures which harness the power of the wind to do work. For instance, they are used for grinding and (storing) grain. They are also used as pumps.

RECIPES

Tomato soup with Meatballs (Tomatensoep met Balletjes)****

Soup

1 onion
1 stalk celery, sliced
1 carrot, diced
2 cups canned tomatoes
beef bone or beef bouillon
6 cups water
1/2 teaspoon salt

Combine onion, celery, carrot, tomatoes, beef stock, water, and salt and bring to a boil in a large saucepan. Simmer on low heat for 1 1/2 hours or until vegetables are cooked. Strain the soup, and mash the vegetables. Combine the soup and vegetables back into the saucepan, adding 2 cups water. Salt to taste.

Meatballs

1/2 pound ground beef
1 egg, beaten
2 teaspoons bread crumbs, crust cut off

Mix the beef, egg, and bread crumbs. Form into small meatballs. Bring the soup to a boil, and then turn the heat to medium. Drop the meatballs in and cook for 10 minutes.

VOCABULARY

Mother – *Moeder*
Father – *Vader*
boy – *jongen*
girl – *meisje*
Yes – *Ja*
No – *Nee*
right – *rechts*
left – *links*

ACTIVITIES

Pretty Little Dutch Girl Song

I am a pretty little Dutch girl.
As pretty as pretty can be, be, be.
And all the boys in my hometown
Are crazy over me, me, me.

My mother wanted peaches,
My mother wanted pears,
My mother wanted fifty cents
To mend the broken stairs.

My boyfriend gave me peaches.
My boyfriend gave me pears
My boyfriend gave me fifty cents
And kissed me on the stairs.

My mother ate the peaches,
My brother ate the pears,
My father ate the fifty cents
And fell right down the stairs.

My mother called the doctor,
My brother called the nurse,
But all my father really did
Was stay in bed at Gravenhurst.

ACTIVITIES

Find the Difference in Each Dutch Item

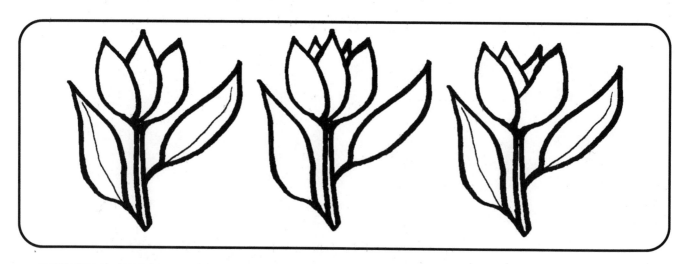

Germany

FEDERAL REPUBLIC OF GERMANY

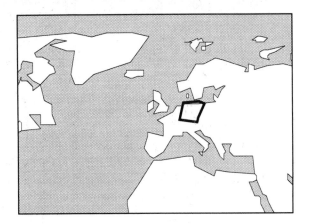

The top black stripe is for gunpowder, the middle red stripe is for blood, and the yellow bottom stripe means the flame. In 1990, this flag was adopted by Unified Germany.

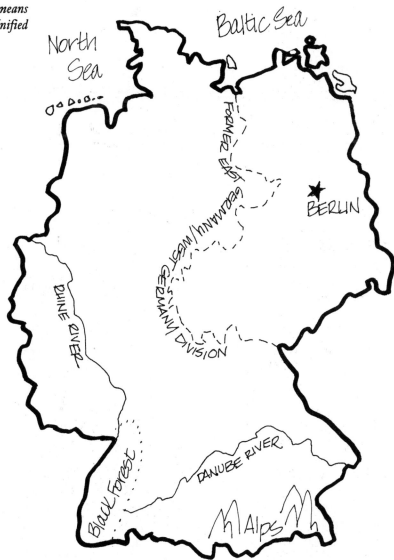

Germany

After World War II, Germany was divided into two states: the Federal Republic of Germany (West Germany) and the German Democratic Republic (East Germany). In 1990, the East German Communist regime collapsed, and East Germany became unified with the Federal Republic. This collapse was signified most by the **BERLIN WALL** (an actual wall which separated the two Germanys) being torn down. **BERLIN** is the capital of the Federal Republic. The population is nearly 80 million. Before World War II, Adolf Hitler rose to power. Because of his views on particular races, many people were sent to concentration camps (in particular Jews). In order to gain more power, and rid his empire of what *he* didn't like, he invaded Poland. World War II was started which when over, seriously crippled the German economy. Since then, Germany has been faced with economic problems, trying to overcome their debt from World War II.

LAND

Germany is 137,854 square miles. The German Lowlands is part of the Great Plain of Europe. This region extends south to the Baltic Sea. The Baltic and North Sea coasts have infertile soils which require intensive fertilization. South of the lowlands is a belt of highly fertile land. This region is called the Southern Transitional Borderlands. It has many bays and waterways such as **COLOGNE BAY** and Mittelland Canal. The Central Uplands are filled with forests, hills, inactive volcanoes, and plateaus. The Black Forest and **BOHEMIAN FOREST** are located in the southeast. The Harz Mountains, the Thuringian Forest, and Saxon Uplands are also located in the southeast. The Rhine River valley flows from Bingen to Bonn. The Alpine Foreland are northeast of the Alps. The **DANUBE RIVER** is a major navigable river.

CLIMATE

Germany has a mild climate. The coldest month is January with an average temperature of 30° F. July, the hottest month, reaches an average of 65° F. Much of the rain occurs during the summer with an average precipitation of 30 inches.

CULTURE

German is the official language, however, many dialects are spoken. Nearly 1/2 of the population are Protestants, belonging to the Lutheran Church. A large percentage are Roman Catholics, and a small percentage are Jews.

The tradition of the great German classical music began in the 1700s with Johann Bach and Frederick Handel. Later German composers include Wolfgang Mozart, Ludwig von Beethoven, Franz Schubert, and Richard Wagner.

The Brothers Grimm at the end of the 19th century created some of the most widely read stories ever such as *Hansel and Grethel, Little Red Cap (Little Red Riding Hood), Cinderella,* and *Rumpelstiltskin.*

Fussball (soccer) is by far the most popular sport. Germans have excelled in the Olympic Games in gymnastics, swimming, and skiing.

The Autobahnen, a superhighway is an achievement in transportation which the Germans are particularly proud. On the autobahnen, there is no speed limit, so it's not uncommon to see cars going 125 miles per hour!

In Bavaria in October, Germans from all around gather for Oktoberfest, a sixteen day festival. People wear native costumes, drink beer in beer halls, and listen to oompah bands. This tradition of Oktoberfest has spread to much of the world.

Education is free for children from the ages of 6 to 14. The word kindergarten comes from Germany – children attend kindergarten from ages 3 to 6. The literacy rate is over 99% – one of the highest in the world.

RESOURCES

Manufacturing is the country's strongest industry. Manufacturing was an important factor for the regrowth of Germany after World War II. Main products within the manufacturing industry are scientific instruments, textiles, and chemicals.

Much of Germany's soil is infertile. However, the Rhineland Moselle River valley produce grapes for fine wines.

RECIPES

Pretzels are popular and can be served with mustard. Some of the sausages served in Germany with German potato salad and sauerkraut are:

Bratwurst (made of pork and veal with a tangy flavor)

Bauernwurst (farmer's sausage containing mustard seeds)

Knockwurst (smoked/cooked beef sausage)

Currywurst (char-grilled veal sausage with curry sauce)

Munich Weisswurst (pork and veal sausage made with mild spices and parsley)

Weiner Schnitzel

veal cutlets

salt

flour

eggs

bread crumbs (quantity depends on how many cutlets you are fixing)

Dip the cutlets into beaten eggs, then into the flour and bread crumbs. Fry in hot oil until golden brown.

Bauernfruhstuck
(German Farmer's Breakfast)

6 bacon slices

1 green pepper, sliced

2 tablespoons onion, chopped

3 boiled potatoes, peeled and cubed

1/2 cup grated cheese

6 eggs

Fry bacon and drain off all but 3 tablespoons oil. Add vegetables and seasonings. Cook about 5 minutes until potatoes are brown. Sprinkle cheese over contents and stir. Break eggs into pan over vegetables and cook until eggs are done.

VOCABULARY

one – *eins*

two – *zwei*

three – *drei*

four – *vier*

five – *funf*

six – *sechs*

seven – *sieben*

eight – *acht*

nine – *neun*

ten – *zehn*

English words borrowed from German

hamburger

pretzel

delicatessen

sauerkraut

kindergarten

ACTIVITIES

Read a Brothers Grimm Story

In the library, find an original adaptation of Cinderella or any other story. Read it to the children and discuss the differences between the Disney movies and the original. Be aware that some Grimm stories can be scary for kids.

ACTIVITIES

Make a Special Day Cone

On the first day of school in Germany, cones filled with candy or cookies are given to the children to make the day a little less scary. A good idea might be to adapt this idea for the first day back from Christmas or Easter vacation.

posterboard or stiff construction paper (at least 12"x 12")
crepe or tissue paper
scissors
scotch tape
stapler
white glue
decorations (glitter, markers, ribbon, crayons, gift wrap, colored paper, yarn)

1. Draw an arc on the paper and cut out on the line.
2. Roll the paper into a cone, so that the edges overlap a few inches.
3. Tape or staple together.
4. Cut a piece of the crepe or tissue paper about 7"x 7". Glue inside the cone about 2-3 inches from the top.
5. Decorate the cone as festive as possible.
6. Fill the cone with cookies, candies, or small goodies and tie the top with yarn or ribbon.

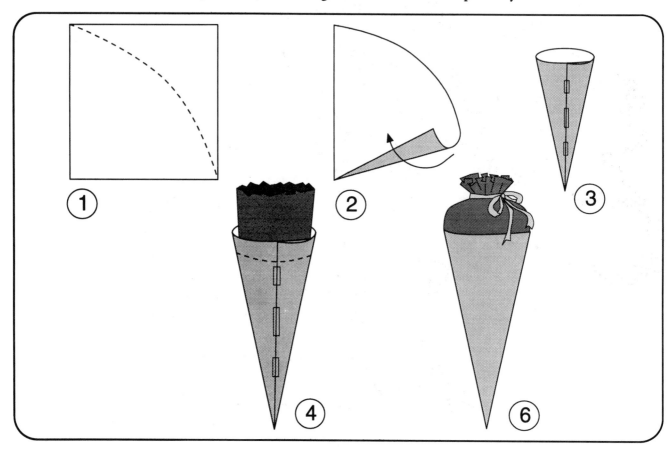

United Kingdom

Atlantic Ocean

North Sea

GLASGOW

EDINBURGH

Irish Sea

SHANNON RIVER

DUBLIN

Pennine Chain

St. George's Channel

CARDIFF

LONDON

THAMES RIVER

English Channel

England

England is a land rich in legends of fairies and witches, and tales of kings and queens. England is located on the southeastern part of the island of Great Britain. The capital is **LONDON**. The population is almost 50 million, with nearly 70% concentrated in the cities. England is a constitutional monarchy, but much of the power is through Parliament. England has endured centuries of war and battle with its neighbors, and has been a major power in the world community.

LAND

England is 50,362 square miles. The land of England is very hilly, with only a small mountain chain, the Pennine. The major rivers running through England are the Severn, the Trent, and the **THAMES RIVER** which runs flow through London.

CLIMATE

The weather is never hot nor cold. In the summer, the average temperature is 80° F. In the winter, the average temperature is 40° F. It rarely ever snows in England, but does receive a lot of rain, with an average of 34 inches a year.

CULTURE

Some of the first peoples of England were the Beaker Folk – named because of their advanced knowledge of tool making. The next group to arrive were the Celts who brought with them their culture, which shaped what is now England. Britannia, as England was called, was invaded by the Romans, led by Julius Caesar. The Romans brought with them Christianity.

England offers religious freedom, but the Church of England is the official state church. Nearly half of the population belong to the Church of England. Other religious groups are Roman Catholics, Jews, Muslims, and Hindus. The official language is English.

England has produced some of the best-loved writers in the world. Charles Dickens who wrote *Oliver Twist* and *A Christmas Carol*. William Shakespeare delighted the English world with his plays – *King Lear*, *Macbeth* are a few of the best known. Lewis Carroll, a famous children's book writer wrote *Alice in Wonderland*. Other children's book writers include C.S. Lewis, author of *The Chronicles of Narnia*; J.R.R. Tolkien, author of *The Lord of the Rings*; and Beatrix Potter, author of *The Tale of Peter Rabbit*.

Many famous musicians in the United States are from England – The Beatles, The Who, and the Rolling Stones are a few of the most popular.

The English have a passion for football (soccer). Many English also enjoy cricket, which originated in England. Other popular sports include rugby, polo, horse racing, rowing, and fox hunting.

Children must attend school from ages 5 to age 16. There are many boarding schools. Oxford University, one of the most famous and oldest universities in the world is located in London.

UNITED KINGDOM OF GREAT BRITAIN

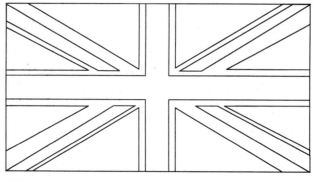

The flag is called the Union Jack. The background is blue. There are two white crosses with red crosses inside them.

RESOURCES

England although lacking in many mineral resources, produces coal and iron ore. Agriculture, although not as important as in the past, produces livestock (cattle and sheep), dairy products, fruit, barley, potatoes, and wheat. Manufacturing produces chemicals, automobiles, woolen and cotton textiles, and silverware.

England has a high tourism industry. People from all over the world, go to London to see the Tower of London, the British Museum, Madame Tussaud's Wax Museum, and Big Ben. Other places in England to see are Stratford-on-Avon, where William Shakespeare was born; Stonehenge; and the White Cliffs of Dover.

RECIPES

English meals typically consist of a meat (roast beef or a joint of lamb), vegetables, or a meat pie. A common meal served throughout England is Fish and Chips (French Fries) served in newspaper. The English also enjoy tea and set out special times during the day in which to enjoy their tea with cakes or cookies.

Sugar Crisps
1/2 stick butter
1/4 cup sugar
1/2 cup flour
drop of vanilla
2 teaspoons milk

Mix the butter and sugar together. Slowly add the flour. Add the vanilla and part of the milk. (Add more milk, if it seems too dry). Place the mixture in balls on an ungreased cookie sheet and bake in a 350-degree oven for 10 minutes. Serve crisps with hot tea. The British are known for teatime. You can do as they do and have your tea time, too.

Yorkshire Pudding
2 eggs
1 cup flour
1 cup milk
3 tablespoons oil
dash of salt

Beat eggs and gradually flour and milk, alternating. Add salt. Refrigerate for two or more hours. Heat oil in 425-degree oven in a 10 inch pie pan. Remove from oven and stir batter into the hot dish. Cook in oven for about 30 minutes, until the pudding has risen and browned. Serve with beef.

VOCABULARY

Geoffrey Chaucer wrote *The Canterbury Tales* in the 14th century. Here is a sampling of the olde English the tales were originally written in.

Whan that Aprile with his shores sote
the droote of March hath pierced to the roote
and bathed everie vein in swiche liqueor
of which vertu engendered is the fleur

Translation
When in April the sweet showers fall
And pierce the drought of March to the root, and all
The veins are bathed in liquor of such power
As brings about the engendering of the flower.

ACTIVITIES

Sing a Traditional English Song
THE MUFFIN MAN

Bouncy   F   Gmi.   G⁷   C   Traditional

1. Oh, do you know the muf-fin man, the muf-fin man, the muf-fin man,
2. Oh, yes, I know the muf-fin man, the muf-fin man, the muf-fin man,

Bouncy   F   Gmi.   G⁷   C

1. Oh, do you know the muf-fin man, the muf-fin man, the muf-fin man,
2. Oh, yes, I know the muf-fin man, the muf-fin man, the muf-fin man,

Who lives on Drury Lane.

ACTIVITIES

King (or Queen) for a Day!

This activity enables each child to have a special day. After everybody makes their crowns, have a vote on who should be king or queen for the day. The king/queen could be responsible for passing out papers, being first in line, etc. Make sure each child knows they will get their chance, too. This could also work on birthdays.

yellow construction paper
scissors
glitter, yarn, markers, crayons, or tempura paint, anything in which to decorate a crown
stapler or tape
1. Draw out and cut crown. Decorate.
2. Roll into a tube and staple or tape together (staples might hold better).

Scotland

Scotland located north of England, is about the size of South Carolina. The population of Scotland is over 5 million. The capital of Scotland is **EDINBURGH**. Besides the capital the major cities are Glasgow, Aberdeen, and Dundee. Scotland is bordered on the east by the North Sea, and to the north and west by the Atlantic Ocean. Scotland is part of the United Kingdom, so its government is a constitutional monarchy. However, the government is run by a prime minister.

LAND

Scotland is 30,416 square miles. Besides the mainland, there are about 780 islands, many small and uninhabited. The larger islands are Harris, the Shetlands, and Fair Isle.

There are three different regions in Scotland. In the north are the **HIGHLANDS AND ISLANDS** which are 3/4 mountains. The famous lake Loch Ness is located in the Highlands. **LOCH NESS** is where the infamous Lochness Monster is believed to inhabit. The central region of Scotland is called the **LOWLANDS**. The majority of the Scottish population live in the Lowlands. The third region is the **BORDER COUNTRY**. The Tweed River separates Scotland from England.

CLIMATE

During June, daylight lasts up to 20 hours a day, because of the northerly position of Scotland. On the Shetlands, the most northerly islands, it is never really dark during midsummer. There is a great deal of rain.

CULTURE

Scottish families can be broken down into clans. The word **CLAN** comes from a Gaelic word *clann* meaning "children". Each clan can be recognized by their tartans. Tartans are the plaid which is used in their dress and crests. There are over 250 tartans in Scotland. The men of Scotland wear kilts, which originally was a length of tartan wrapped around the body and belted. Now kilts are skirts, predominantly worn by the men. Women wear kilts only in the Highlands for dancing.

Because of the Scot's past history of being warlike, there are many castles in Scotland. Many are ruined but in Edinburgh, the city is built around a castle in excellent shape.

The official language is English. Gaelic is spoken in the Isles and the Highlands. Scots, a dialect still used, has many words which cannot be interpreted into English.

The principal religion is the Church of Scotland (the kirk), or the Presbyterian church. However, there is religious freedom in Scotland. Other religious groups include Roman Catholics, Jews, and many minority religions.

Scotland has a long history of poetry. Robert Burns is the national poet of Scotland. He wrote during the 18th century. Sir Walter Scott, who also wrote during the 18th century, is the second best-known literary figure of Scotland.

Robert Louis Stevenson, who was born in Scotland, wrote *Treasure Island* and *The Strange*

SCOTLAND

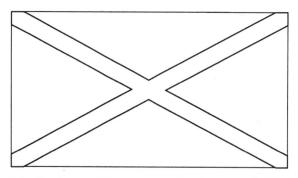

The flag has a white cross on a blue background. The origins of this flag are unknown.

Case of Dr. Jekyll and Mr. Hyde.

Although Scotland has contributed to the literary world, music is what the Scots are best known for, particularly bagpipe music. "Big music" bagpiping is called **PIBROCHS** (warlike tunes). "Little music" usually accompanies Scottish dances, like the reel and the Highland fling.

Scots enjoy both modern and traditional dancing, danced to the bagpipe. An old custom, the sword dance, is danced over two crossed swords. Scottish people also enjoy soccer and golf which was invented in Scotland during the 12th century. **SHINTY** (similar to field hockey) is a popular sport played in the north.

Children attend school from age 5 to age 16. After primary school, children have a choice of attending vocational schools, which prepare them for a career.

RESOURCES

In the coastal areas, fishing is the biggest industry. Crops grown in the fertile areas are oats, barley, wheat, and potatoes. Sheep are also raised. Scotland is famous for its wool products. Whiskey is also produced in Scotland – it is known as Scotch.

VOCABULARY

lake – *loch*
mountain – *ben*
narrow valley – *glen*
wide valley – *strath*
twilight – *the gloaming*

RECIPES

Some of the favorite foods of the Scots are herring, mutton stew, roast beef, and lamb.
*Scottish Shortbread**
1 cup butter
2 cups flour

Man wearing his clan's tartan. Can you design his kilt?

1/2 cup sifted confectioners' sugar
dash of salt

Cream butter. Sift together dry ingredients. Blend into butter and pat into an ungreased 9"X 9" inch pan. Pierce with a fork ever 1/2 inch. Bake at 325-degrees for 30 minutes. Cut into squares and serve.

Wales

The capital of Wales is **CARDIFF**. The population is 2,790,462. Wales is part of the United Kingdom, a constitutional monarchy.

LAND

Wales is 8,018 square miles. The **CAMBRIAN MOUNTAINS** cover 2/3 of the country. Wales is bordered to the east by England and the west by the Irish Sea. The major rivers are the Severn and the Wye which both flow easterly into England.

CLIMATE

The climate of Wales is unpredictable. It is dependent on the Atlantic air masses. The average annual precipitation is 53 inches.

CULTURE

The history of Wales is built upon many legends. The most famous legends are that of King Arthur. Much of the history is written in the form of poetry. Poets and singers have always been celebrated in Wales. Dylan Thomas is one of the more famous poets in modern times to have lived and worked in Wales. He is famous for *A Child's Christmas in Wales*.

The official language is English and Welsh. Welsh is a form of the Celtic language. Welsh is making a comeback within Wales, as a form of solidarity.

Children must attend school from the ages 5 to 16. Rugby is a popular sport in Wales. Soccer is also popular, but not as much as rugby.

RESOURCES

Major crops include barley, hay, and potatoes. Livestock (sheep and cattle) are also raised. Wales has very few mineral resources. Coal, limestone, and slate are the only major producing minerals.

RECIPES

Roast lamb and beef are favorite main dishes. The leek is the most important vegetable in Wales.

Welsh Cakes***

1 1/2 cups flour
4 tablespoons margarine
4 tablespoons sugar
1/3 cup raisins
1 egg
1/4 teaspoon salt
1 tablespoon milk

Sift the flour and mix with the margarine, making a crumbly mixture. Add the sugar and raisins. Mix well. Beat the egg with the salt, stir in the milk. Add to the flour mixture, knead, making a stiff dough. Roll 1/4" thick on a floured board, cut with the floured edge of a cookie cutter. Grease a skillet, heat, then turn the heat low. Cook the cakes until golden-brown on both sides.

THE PRINCIPALITY OF WALES

The flag has two stripes, the top stripe white, and the bottom stripe green. On the center of the stripes is a red dragon. The dragon has been the national symbol of Wales for nearly 2,000 years.

Ireland

Ireland is a land full of myths and magic and tales of "little people". The Emerald Isle received its nickname because of its brilliant emerald and olive green fields. They are particularly brilliant when seen from the air. **DUBLIN** is the capital. The Republic of Ireland gained independence from Britain in 1921.

LAND

Ireland is 27,136 square miles. It is bordered on the south, west, northwest, and north by the Atlantic Ocean. To the east is the Irish Sea. Ireland has three types of land areas: the seacoasts which total 1,738 miles; the mountains in the west and southwest, which include the **MOUNTAINS OF DONEGAL** and **KERRY**; and the central plain inland, where much of the fertile land is located. Many rivers and lakes are in Ireland, including the **RIVER SHANNON**, and the Lakes of Killarney in Kerry.

CLIMATE

Ireland has a mild climate. Summer temperatures average 60° F. Winter temperatures averages 40° F. Average precipitation ranges from 60 inches in the mountains to 36 inches in the central plains.

CULTURE

Gaelic was the spoken language for over 2,000 years. When the English came into power, Gaelic was outlawed. Nowadays, only 25% of the population can speak Gaelic.

Over 95% of the population are Catholic. Some of the minority religions are Church of Ireland, Methodist, and Presbyterian. Christianity came to Ireland in 432 A.D. when St. Patrick, a Briton, brought the religion to the isle. During his lifetime, he converted many of the Irish to the Catholic faith. He also preserved the Celt's customs, however-

er, unless they were in direct conflict with the Catholic religion.

Ireland has a history of great writers. Some of Ireland's best-known writers are Jonathon Swift who wrote *Gulliver's Travels*; George Bernard Shaw, who won a Nobel Prize for literature and wrote the play *Pygmalion*; and James Joyce, considered one of modern day's greatest writers.

The Irish have a long history of music. Folk dances include the Irish jig. Folk songs are usually accompanied by the harp, fiddle, or flute.

The sport of **HURLING** (similar to field hockey) is a favorite sport. Gaelic football (a mixture of rugby and soccer), horseback riding, and horse racing are also popular.

RESOURCES

Major mineral resources found are zinc, lead, copper, and silver. Peat is also produced and is an important source of fuel. There are also recently-found deposits of petroleum and natural gas. With over 2/3 of the land suitable for farming, agriculture plays a big role in their economy. Major crops grown are wheat, oats, barley, potatoes, and hay.

An example of elaborate Celtic knotwork.

RECIPES

The Irish enjoy potatoes, cabbage, and Irish stew. An Irish beverage is heavy, dark beer (called stout).

Irish Stew*

2 pounds lamb, cut into chunks
2 tablespoons flour
dash of salt, pepper, garlic, sugar
2 onions, chopped
6-8 carrots, chopped
4-6 potatoes, chopped

Roll lamb in flour, salt and pepper. Fry in hot oil. Add garlic and onion. Add water and sugar and simmer about one hour. Add carrots, potatoes, and more onions (if desired). Cook until vegetables are tender.

Irish Candy*

2 egg whites
1 teaspoon vanilla
3/4 cup granulated sugar
1 package (6 oz.) chocolate bits
1/4 cup nuts (optional)
1/8 teaspoon cream of tartar
1/8 teaspoon salt

Beat egg white, salt, cream of tartar, and vanilla until peaks form. Gradually add sugar and beat until stiff. Fold in chocolate and nuts. Drop onto cookie sheets. Bake at 300-degrees for 25 minutes.

Irish Buttermilk Oaten Bread****

1 1/2 cups fine oatmeal
1 1/2 cups buttermilk
1 3/4 cups flour
1 1/2 teaspoons baking soda
1 teaspoon salt
1 1/2 tablespoons sugar

A day before making bread, mix the oatmeal with the buttermilk in a bowl. Cover and let stand overnight.

The next day, sift the flour, baking soda, salt, and sugar into a deep mixing bowl. Stir in the oatmeal mixture, knead it with your hand, making a soft ball of dough. Dust with flour if the dough is sticky.

On a lightly floured surface, roll out the dough into a round loaf (cup the dough into your hands to make a nice round shape). Cut the loaf into quarters, using a floured butter knife. Cut all the way through, but do not separate the sections. Place on a lightly floured baking tray. Bake in a pre-heated oven at 350-degrees for 50 minutes or until well-browned. For a special treat, mix 1/2 cup raisins into the dough just before shaping the loaf.

VOCABULARY

Gaelic

one – *aon*	six – *se*
two – *do*	seven – *seacht*
three – *tri*	eight – *ocht*
four – *ceathar*	nine – *naci*
five – *cuig*	ten – *deich*
father – *athar*	mother – *mathar*
boy – *buachall*	girl – *cailin*
no – *nih-ea*	yes – *sea*

REPUBLIC OF IRELAND

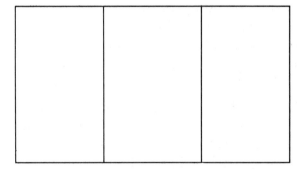

The green stripe on the left represents the ancient Celts and the Catholics. The middle white stripe represents the hope of peace. The right orange stripe represents the Protestants.

ACTIVITIES

Games in the United Kingdom

CHARLIE OVER THE WATER*

The game goes back to the exile of Charles II of England in France. He was urged by the Scots to come back over the water.

Twenty or more players form a circle. "Charlie" stands in the center facing two players who hold a stick 12 inches above and parallel to the ground to represent a bridge. The circle players join hands and skip around the circle singing:

> Charlie over the water
> Charlie over the sea
> Charlie catch a blackbird
> Can't catch me.

As the last line is said, Charlie jumps over the stick and runs to tag the circle players before they stoop. If he is successful, the tagged player becomes Charlie, if not, he must be Charlie again.

WEE BOLOGNA MAN**

This game is played by Scottish children. Similar to Simon Sez.

A leader stands in front of 20 or more players. The players might form a circle around the leader so everyone can be seen. The leaders says:

> I'm the Wee Bologna Man;
> Always do the best you can
> To follow the Wee Bologna Man

He then goes through the motions of playing some instrument – a drum, a flute, a guitar, etc. Or he imitates an orchestra leader, majorette, drum major, etc. The rest of the players follow his motions.

A good leader switches his motions quickly to confuse the other players. Each time he changes to another movement, he must repeat the rhyme. Leaders may be changed often by the simple process of pointing or calling the name of another player. The action should be fast.

STEALING STICKS*

This game is played by both English and Scottish children.

This game calls for 20 or more players. The playing area, a large field, is marked into two equal parts. Six sticks are placed in a small goal at the end of each part. The players are divided into two equal groups and take their places, one team in each part of the field. The players are to touch their opponent's goal without being tagged and bring one stick at a time back to their own goal. No player may be tagged if he has secured a stick and is returning to his own goal. If he is tagged while in the opponent's territory before reaching the goal, he becomes a prisoner until one of his team comes and tags him. If a team has lost any of its members to the other side as prisoners, that team cannot retrieve any more sticks until all the prisoners are "freed". Whichever team retrieves all its sticks first, wins.

Scandinavia

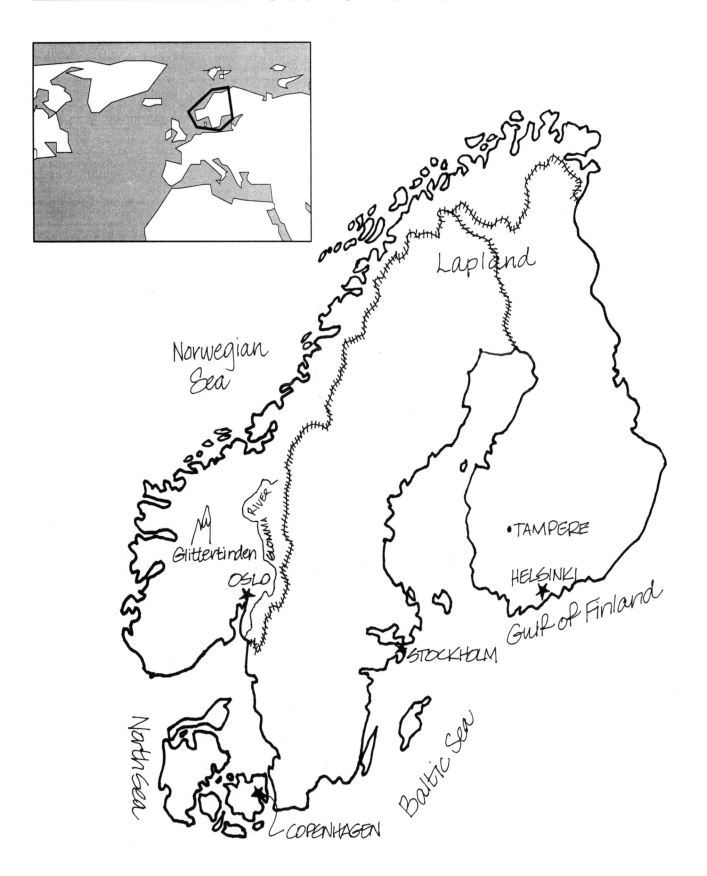

Norwegian Sea

Lapland

Glittertinden

GLOMMA RIVER

OSLO

TAMPERE

HELSINKI

Gulf of Finland

STOCKHOLM

North Sea

Baltic Sea

COPENHAGEN

The largest city of Denmark and the capital is **COPENHAGEN**. Copenhagen has almost 1/4 of the Danish population and almost 1/2 of the countries industries. The population is 5,130,000. Denmark is a constitutional monarchy, with a king or queen. The monarch, however, has little power.

LAND

Denmark is 16,600 square miles. Denmark consists of a peninsula and 482 nearby islands. One of Denmark's provinces, however, lies off the northeastern coast of Canada. The peninsula, Jutland, shares a border with West Germany.

CULTURE

Danish is the official language. Denmark offers religious freedom but almost the entire population belongs to the Evangelical Lutheran church. The Danes have the one of the world's highest living standards.

RESOURCES

Although the country is poor in natural resources, the Danes are very prosperous through their shipping and fishing. Denmark is famous for their dairy products, furniture, and silverware.

VOCABULARY

man – *manden*
oxygen – *ilt*

RECIPES

Danish Krumkakes
2 eggs
2/3 cup sugar
1/2 cup butter
1 3/4 cup flour
1 teaspoon vanilla

Combine ingredients to form dough. Cook 1 tablespoon of dough about 2 minutes on each side in a small amount of butter. As soon as you remove it, roll it on a wooden spoon handle. These wafers may be filled with ice cream or jelly.

ACTIVITIES

Robin's Alive

This game is based on an old Danish tale. Long ago, there was a Danish nobleman who possessed a pet bird, whom he loved very much. The nobleman had to go to battle, so he left the bird in the care of a peasant in his village. The nobleman warned the peasant to take good care of the bird. Unfortunately, the bird died and the peasant was severely punished on the nobleman's return.

The players stand in a circle and pass from hand to hand a beanbag or small rubber ball, saying, "*Lad Ikke min herre fugl doee!*" (Let not my Lord's bird die). The player with the "bird" in his hand at the end of the sentence becomes the "peasant" and is out. The game continues until there are only two players. The player left not holding the bird, wins!

KINGDOM OF DENMARK

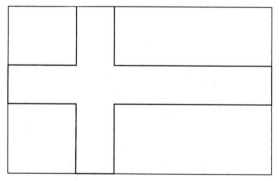

The red background represents blood. The white cross is called the Scandinavian Cross.

Sweden

Sweden is the fourth largest country in Europe. The population is 8 million. The capital is Stockholm. The government is a constitutional monarchy.

LAND

Sweden is 173,732 square miles. It has 96,000 lakes. It is a land of many forests, lowlands, and mountains.

CLIMATE

The cold winter in the north lasts more than seven months. You can see the midnight sun in Lapland, the northernmost province of Norrland. For six weeks in mid-summer, the sun never sets.

CULTURE

The predominant religion is Evangelical Lutheran. The official language is Swedish. English, German, Finnish, Norwegian, and Danish are also spoken. It has one of the highest standards of living in the world and on the average its people enjoy the longest life expectancy of the citizens of any country in the world.

Dala painting is an example of Swedish folk art. Many wooden pieces are painted in Dala. Dala painting is a style of bright colors with heavy black outlines. Lace making is also a popular folk art still practiced.

Swedes enjoy and excel at winter sports – skiing, ice skating, and hockey.

RESOURCES

The logging industry is principal to north Sweden's economy. The logging industry produces paper products, wood, and wood products. Dairy products such as cheese and butter are produced. The manufacturing industry produces automobiles, metals, and chemicals.

VOCABULARY

Welcome – *Valkommen!*
man – *mannen*
you – *du*
house – *huse*

RECIPES

Swedish Meatballs
1 pound ground beef
1 onion, minced
garlic, salt, pepper
1 beaten egg
crushed corn flakes or cracker crumbs

Mix all ingredients together. Shape into balls and cook slowly in a sauce made of lemon juice and one jar of grape jelly.

Fruit Soup (Fruktsoppa)***
1 1/2 cups mixed dried fruit
1 quart water
1 1/2 tablespoons sugar
2 tablespoons cornstarch

Simmer the fruit in the water until it is tender (about 20 minutes). Add the sugar. Mix the cornstarch with a little cold water, add it to the fruit mixture, and simmer 2 or 3 minutes more, until thick.

KINGDOM OF SWEDEN

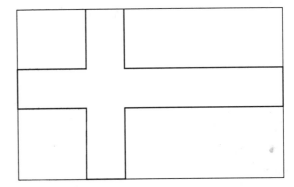

The flag's original design was originally designed in 1520. The background is blue, and the Scandinavian Cross is yellow.

Norway

Norway is the land of the Vikings. The capital is **OSLO**. The population is over 4 million. Norway is a constitutional monarchy. Norway borders Sweden to the east, and the Arctic Ocean to the west.

LAND

The country is 125,182 square miles (not including the 24,208 square miles of archipelago called Sualbard). The longest river in Norway is the **GLAMMA RIVER**. The highest mountain in Norway is Glittertinden, part of the Jotunheimen range. Norway has hundreds of glacier fields.

CLIMATE

The climate of Norway is actually quite mild. The average winter temperature in Norway is 24° F. The average summer temperature is 65° F. In the north, there is sunshine 24 hours a day from May to July. There is no sunshine from the end of November to January, but the aurora borealis can be seen.

CULTURE

The Norwegian language has two forms: Bokmaal, which is more prominently used; and Nynorsk. The only minority people in Norway are the Lapps (the Samis) who live in Finnmark, the most northern area. Norway offers religious freedom. The official church is the Evangelical Lutheran Church.

One of the most famous painters to come from Norway was Edvard Munch. Much of his work is gloomy and sad, but he is still celebrated among Norwegians.

Norway has a mythology handed down from their viking ancestors. The mythology is similar to Greek mythology in that it deals with gods and goddesses. Odin is the most powerful god in the Norse mythology. Thor, the god of thunder is the most popular, even today.

Norwegians love to ski. Children learn to ski at a very early age. Ice skating, soccer, and hockey are also popular sports.

Children must attend school from ages 7 to 14. In some areas, the age limit is extended to 16. The literacy rate in Norway is very high.

RESOURCES

Major mineral resources are iron ore, pyrites, lead, zinc, and petroleum. Norway produces dairy products, wheat, oats, rye, potatoes, barley, and fruit. Fishing yields more of the cold-water fish such as herring, cod, and capelin.

RECIPES

Norwegian Flarn
1 tablespoon flour
1/2 cup sugar
1/2 cup butter
2 tablespoons butter
2 tablespoons milk
2/3 cup blanched almonds

Mix ingredients in skillet and stir over low heat until butter melts. Drop spoonfuls onto cookie sheet and bake in 375-degree oven until brown.

KINGDOM OF NORWAY

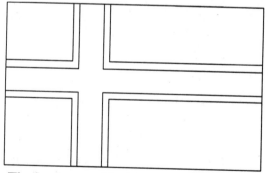

The flag has a red background with a blue cross outlined in white.

Finland

Finland is a beautiful country of lakes and forests. Finland is one of the most northern countries in the world. The capital of Finland is **HELSINKI**. The population is under 5 million, with over half living in the cities. The next largest city is Tampere.

LAND

Finland is 130,094 square miles. In the north of Finland, lies Lapland, where the Lapps (or Samis) raise reindeer. There are more than 60,000 lakes in Finland.

CLIMATE

Finland has cold, damp winters and warm summers. The lowest winter temperature can reach -22° F. Summer temperatures average 60° F. In Lapland, the northern lights can be seen during the long, sunless winters.

CULTURE

The official language is Finnish and Swedish. The Lapps speak their own language. The majority of the population belong to the Evangelical Lutheran Church.

Children must attend school from ages 7 to 16. Two languages are required for everyone. Finland has a very high literacy rate.

Finns are outstanding winter athletes. They have won many medals at the winter Olympic games in skiing and speed skating. During the warmer season, Finns enjoy rowing, archery, and Finnish baseball (**PESAPALLO**).

RESOURCES

Many Finns work in the fishing industry. The lumber industry is a major export of Finland. Much of the agriculture depends on the raising of livestock. Dairy products include chocolate, refined sugar, and butter. Liqueurs and vodka are also produced.

VOCABULARY

Good day – *Hyvaa paivaa*
Thank you – *Kiitos*
Please – *Olkaa hyva*
Pardon, excuse me – *Anteeksi*
Good bye – *Hyvasti*
So long – *Nakemiin*

RECIPES

Finns eat a lot of soup and drink great amounts of coffee. Reindeer sausage and stuffed cabbage are common to the Finn diet.

Finnish Pancakes (Ohukaiset) ****
1 tablespoon flour
1 egg
1/3 cup milk
butter for frying

Sift the flour. Beat the egg and mix with the flour. Add a little of milk, mix well. Add the rest of the milk and blend until smooth.

Heat a small skillet. Grease lightly with butter. Pour about 2 tablespoons of the batter into the skillet. Tip the skillet, spreading the batter evenly. Cook over medium heat until the batter is golden-brown. Turn over with a spatula and cook the other way.

Can be served with fruit as a breakfast food or as a dessert.

REPUBLIC OF FINLAND

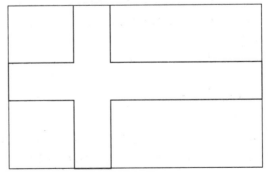

The flag has a blue cross on a white background. The blue represents the waters and the white the snows of Finland.

ACTIVITIES

Make a Scandinavian Rock Troll

Smooth stones for head, body, arms, feet, and/or nose
colored yarn
enamel, tempura, or acrylic paint or markers
heavy industrial glue
goggly eyes

1. Decorate the troll's body and face (remember to make the troll's face scary!)
2. Attach yarn for the troll's hair and tail.
3. Watch out for the troll. He can be tricky!

ACTIVITIES

Celebrate St. Lucia Day

On December 13, Saint Lucia's Day is celebrated. At dawn, a daughter wakes the family with a tray of coffee and saffron buns. She is dressed as Lucia, in a white robe tied with a red sash, a crown of candles on her head. Choose a girl (by luck of the draw) in the class to be Lucia.

St. Lucia Buns

2 1/2 cups Bisquick	1 egg
1/2 cup milk	raisins
4 tablespoons cooking oil	
1 cup of flour	

Mix and shape the dough into thick coils and cut 5" long strips. For each bun, either cross two strips into an X shape and curl the ends or shape into an S shape and curl the ends. Place a raisin in each of the curls and bake at 375-degrees for 12 minutes. Ice with 1 cup confectioner's sugar mixed with 3 teaspoons milk and a few drops of yellow food coloring. Brush onto warm buns.

St. Lucia Crown

white and green drawing paper
glue, stapler
orange marker or crayon

1. Cut out five candles (2"x 5"strips of white paper). Roll the tubes and glue. Cut out a flame in the front and color orange.
2. Cut out the headband to fit the girl's head (with room to spare). Staple the candles to the front of the crown.
3. Fasten the back of the crown with staples. Attach real leaves or cut out leaves around the candles.

Greece

REPUBLIC OF GREECE

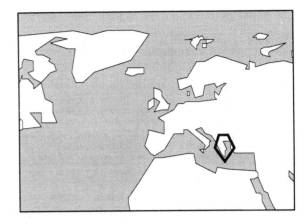

The white cross on the blue square can be taken to represent Christian values. The five blue stripes represent the sky and the sea. The four white stripes represent the purity of the people.

Mt. Olympus

Aegean Sea

ATHENS

Ionian Sea

CRETE

Mediterranean Sea

Greece

Greece is a small country located in Southern Europe. The capital is **ATHENS**, a city steeped in history. The population is over 10 million. The next largest city is Thessaloniki.

LAND

Greece is 51,000 square miles. A total of 1,425 islands make up Greece, which include the **IONIAN ISLANDS**, the island of **CRETE**, and most of the Aegean Islands. Only 166 of these islands are populated. Much of the land is mountainous with deep valleys and a rocky coastline. The **PINDOS MOUNTAINS** extend north/southeast towards Athens. The highest point of mainland Greece is **MT. OLYMPUS**.

CLIMATE

Greece has a Mediterranean climate. There are long hot summers with an average temperature of 75° F. The winters are mild and short.

CULTURE

We owe much of our modern knowledge to the ancient Greeks. In fact, ancient Greece can be called the birthplace of modern western civilization. They reached high levels of achievements in art, literature, mathematics, astronomy, and philosophy. Contributions were made by Pythagoras and Euclid in mathematics; Socrates, Plato, and Aristotle in philosophy; and Ptolemy in astronomy.

In addition to these achievements, we owe our form of government to the Greeks. Ancient Greece was the first democracy.

The original Olympic Games were held in ancient Greece to honor their gods. The name "Olympic" comes from the ancient Greek beliefs. They believed in many gods and goddesses, the most powerful being Zeus. From these beliefs, come many of the classical myths (such as Hercules, the Amazons, and Cupid).

The official language is Greek. The predominant religion is the Greek Orthodox Church. The church is a very powerful force in Greek society. Greeks must be members of the church in order to advance in Greek society.

Festivals are important in Greek society. Many of the festivals are to celebrate the feast day of their patron saint. Greek folk dancing is enjoyed at these festivals. A common dance danced alone, is called the **ZEIBEKIKO**.

Greeks enjoy volleyball and swimming. Soccer is a national past time. Greek children learn to play almost at the same time they learn to walk.

RESOURCES

Tourism is an important part of the national economy. Many tourists visit Athens to see the Acropolis, a hill where ancient Athens was centered; and the Parthenon, a temple of the Goddess Athena.

Greece is the least industrialized and most rural of all the European countries. A great majority of the economy is based on agriculture.

RECIPES

Greek food contains a lot of lamb and seafood. Most dishes are flavored with olive oil, fresh tomatoes, and lemon. Greek breakfasts are small and generally consist of coffee, but lunch is a large meal. Most take naps after lunch. Some popular Greek foods:

Moussaka – layers of eggplant and ground beef
Feta cheese – made from sheep or goat milk
Ouzo – a licorice flavored wine
Baklava – honey and almond pastry
Retsina – white wine
Soupa avgolemono – lemon flavored chicken soup
Dolmades – stuffed grape leaves

Crema Karamela

1 3/4 cup sugar
5 eggs
1 quart warmed milk
1 teaspoon vanilla
1 1/2 quart mold or 12 custard cups

Melt 1 cup of sugar over medium heat, stirring constantly until caramel consistency. Pour into bottom of mold or custard cups. Warm milk. Beat eggs with 3/4 cup sugar. Add milk gradually to eggs. Add vanilla. Pour into mold or custard cups and place in a pan of hot water. Then bake at 350-degrees until firm. Cool at room temperature and place in refrigerator until ready to serve.

VOCABULARY

one – *en*
two – *dio*
three – *tria*
four – *tessara*
five – *pente*
six – *x*
seven – *efta*
eight – *okto*
nine – *ennea*
ten – *deka*

English words borrowed form the Greeks

monarch	physical	architect
pharmacy	character	syllable
rhyme	synonym	rhythm
antonym	rheumatism	homonym
alphabet	pseudonym	apostrophe
ptomaine	atmosphere	pneumonia
cellophane	xylophone	

ACTIVITIES

Make a Karagos Puppet
The hero of the Greek children is Karagos, similar to Punch and Judy.

thin cardboard or posterboard
1/4" thick dowel stick
2 double-pronged brads
crayons or paints
glue
hole punch

1. Glue the cardboard to the following page.
2. Color and cut out on the lines.
3. Connect the pieces with the brads (A to A, B to B).
4. Place the dowel through the hole on the shoulder. Wind two pieces of tape on the stick behind the puppet to act as a stopper, so that the dowel will remain stationary. Traditionally the Karagos was a shadow puppet, so using a light in front of a white background might be more fun.

Karagos Puppet Pieces

Poland

POLAND

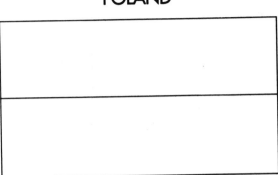

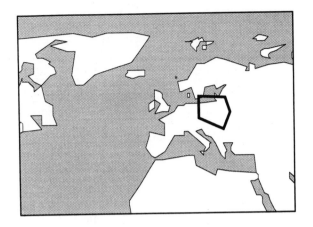

Red and white are the adopted colors of Poland since 1831. Before the communist government collapsed it was popular to say the white stripe on top and the red stripe on the bottom meant both peace and socialism.

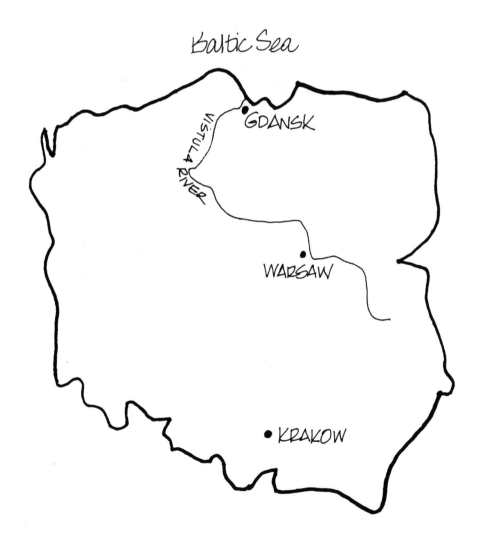

Baltic Sea

GDANSK

VISTULA RIVER

WARSAW

KRAKOW

Poland

Poland lies in central Europe. It is the largest country in central and eastern Europe except for Russia. The name Poland comes from the Polanie tribe, one of the earlier peoples of Poland. The capital of Poland is WARSAW. The population is 1,650,000. With the breakdown of Communism in the Soviet Union, Poland has gained her independence.

LAND

Poland is 37,900,000 square miles. The north of Poland lies on the Baltic Sea. To the south lies Czechoslovakia. To the west is eastern Germany, and to the east is Russia.

The northern part is the coastal lowlands, which form miles of beaches, one beach in particular called the Polish Riviera. South of the lowlands lie nearly over 7,700 lakes called the MAZURIAN LAKES. In central Poland lie flat, fertile plainlands. The majority of the population live in the central plains. The SUDETEN MOUNTAINS lie on the southwestern border. The TATRA MOUNTAINS, part of the Carpathian Range lie on the southeastern border. The VISTULA and the ODER RIVERS flow through the Carpathians into the plains.

CLIMATE

The coastal regions has much milder weather than inland. Average temperatures for summer are 75° F and during the winter are 25° F. Average annual precipitation is 24 inches.

CULTURE

Slavic tribes who peopled Poland were divided into sub-tribes. The biggest tribe were the Polanie. Others were the Kashubs, and Poueranians, all different in language and customs.

For thousands of years, Poland has been involved in wars between the Germans, the Ottoman Empire, and Russia. Poland lost a great deal of its original land and came under power of Russia. The Poles tried to get help from France, who was led by Napoleon Bonaparte. However, the French fought Russia and lost. Poland was again left in Russian control.

During World War II, Poland was pitted between Russia/Germany. Poland lost over 20% of the population during the war. In 1948, Russia urged the crippled government towards Communism. However, only a small minority of the population belonged to the Communist party.

Polish folk art is done in the more rural areas, including tapestry weaving, wood carving, pottery, embroidery, and painting on glass.

Famous Poles include Nicolaus Copernicus, who is called the Father of Astronomy; Frederic Chopin, a composer whose music involves traditional Polish folk music; Marie Curie, a woman scientist; and Pope John Paul II, the present head of the Roman Catholic Church.

Since 1966, the people have been Roman Catholic (over 90%). The Polish language which is similar to Russian (both are of the Slavic branch) uses Roman numerals and letters.

Education is free from preschool to university level. School is compulsory for ages 7 to 15. Polish school children go to school for 240 days. About 95% of the population are literate.

Poles enjoy hiking, camping, hunting, fishing, sailing, and horseback riding and in the winter, skiing. Hitchhiking is legal in Poland.

RESOURCES

There are large coal deposits in Poland, as well as copper, lead, salt, sulfur, zinc, natural gas, and petroleum. After World War II, the

Communist leaders insisted Poland become more industrialized. They produce iron and steel, machinery, chemicals, and ships. Agriculture, although not as strong as in the past, accounts for 1/3 of the industry. Major crops are rye, potatoes, barley, sugar beets, wheat, oats, alfalfa, and clover.

RECIPES

Chrusciki

4 egg yolks
1 tablespoon vinegar
1 tablespoon sugar
dash of salt
1 cup flour

Combine the ingredients. Knead dough and roll it out. Cut into strips 1" x 3", then slit in the middle of each strip. Pull one end of the strip through the slit. Deep fry until lightly browned. Top with powdered sugar.

Measure ze Smietana
(Cucumbers in Sour Cream)

3 cups sliced cucumbers
1 cup sour cream
dash of salt
2 tablespoons dill weed or chopped dill

Sprinkle cucumbers with salt and let stand a few minutes. Pat dry. Stir dill and cucumbers into sour cream and serve.

Zupa Jablkowa (Apple Soup)

6-7 apples
pot of water
3/4 cup sugar
dash cinnamon
1/2 cup lemon juice
1 cup whipping cream

Peel and core apples and cook in water until soft. Put into blender and blend into applesauce. Mix in sugar and cinnamon. Chill. Just before serving, mix cream into mixture. If desired, shred one apple, soak in lemon juice and add to the mixture. One 16 ounce jar of applesauce and 1 cup water may be substituted for fresh apples.

ACTIVITIES

Chant a Polish Lullaby

This is a popular Polish lullaby that is sung in a chant without music.

Ahh, Ahh
Kotki dwa
Czarny bude obid dwa
Nic nie bede az robili
Tylko Steven (add name of child) z bawili

Translation

Ah, Ah
Two kittens,
One is black, the other tan
With nothing else to do
But play with Steven.

ACTIVITIES

Make a Traditional Polish Paper Cut

In Poland, folk art is everywhere. One of the most popular is the Polish paper cut. The idea of the paper cut is to create a design with scissors without interrupting the cut.

1. In the following sample is a simple cut. Trace the rooster's body onto tracing paper. Turn the tracing paper over, and retrace the design onto colored paper.
2. Cut the main design of the rooster's body using only one cut.
3. Trace the wings on different pieces of colored paper, following the above directions.
4. Glue the wings onto the body and you have a traditional Polish paper cut!

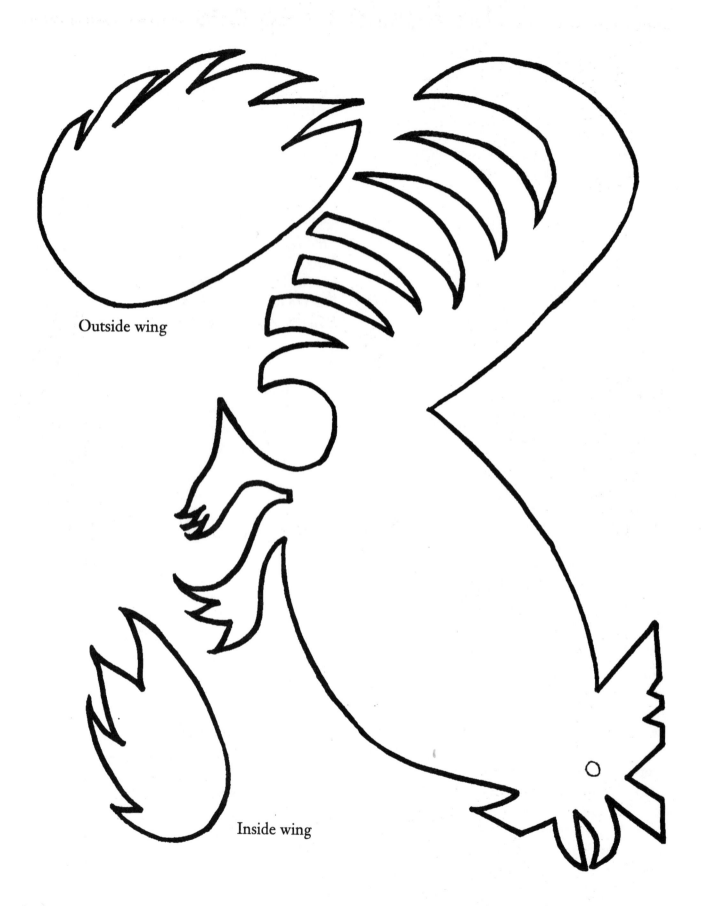

Outside wing

Inside wing

The Russian Regions

IDENTIFY

1. _____
2. _____
3. _____
4. _____
5. _____

The Russian Federation

THE RUSSIAN FEDERATION

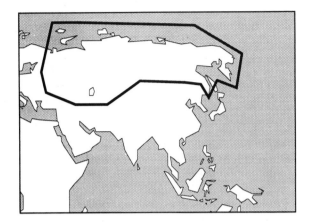

The flag was created in 1991 when the Russian Federation was formed from the breakup of the Union of Soviet Socialists Republics.

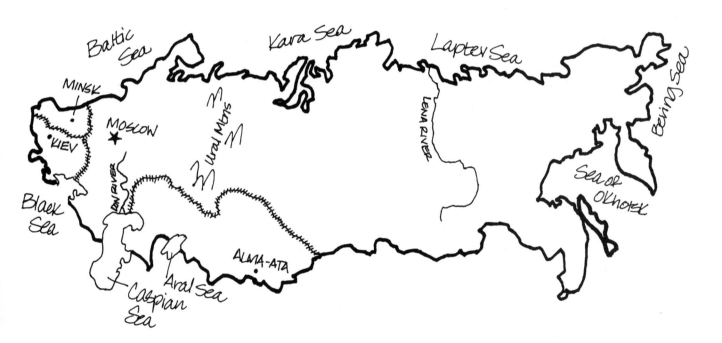

Baltic Sea

Kara Sea

Laptev Sea

Bering Sea

MINSK

MOSCOW

Ural Mtns

Lena River

Sea of Okhotsk

KIEV

Don River

Black Sea

Aral Sea

ALMA-ATA

Caspian Sea

The Russian Regions

The former Union of Soviet Socialist Republics (USSR), otherwise known as the Soviet Union, was the largest country in the world, encompassing one-sixth of the Earth's land surface. Before 1917, the land was known as Russia, ruled by a monarch called a **CZAR**. The USSR was formed on Dec. 22, 1922, and originally consisted of four member republics. It was a Communist state which was supposed to be a classless society in which production of any kind would be for the equal benefit of all the people. Through subdivision and annexation, the number of republics increased to 15 by the end of World War II. Within most Soviet republics smaller ethnic groups received representation. Thus, in addition to the 15 union republics, there were 20 autonomous republics, 8 autonomous regions, 10 autonomous districts, 6 territories, and 123 regions. Its 8,582,338 square miles made up the eastern half of Europe and the northern third of Asia.

As it existed from 1922 to 1990, the Soviet Union was a tightly-controlled Communist state, the largest union republic being the **RUSSIAN REPUBLIC**. The Soviet Union was more or less coextensive with the Russian Empire, which was overthrown by the **RUSSIAN REVOLUTIONS** of 1917. A civil war followed and the Communists, led by **LENIN**, prevailed.

After Lenin's death in 1924, **JOSEPH STALIN** seized power, and launched campaigns to collectivize agriculture and develop heavy industry; he provided the country with a modern industrial base., but at the cost of massive social dislocation, violence, and loss of life. In the Great Purge of 1936-38 millions perished. This was followed by World War II, remembered with pride because of the Soviet victory over the German invaders. The death of Stalin in 1953 was followed by a "thaw" in cultural policy and a period of economic and political reform under **NIKITA S. KHRUSHCHEV**. In October 1964,

Khrushchev was forced to resign because of the failure of his policies, and a series of diplomatic defeats. **LEONID BREZHNEV** presided over a period of political stability, economic prosperity, and **DETENTE** which led to improved relations with the West. Yuri Andropov (1982-84) and Konstantin Chernenko (1984-85), were followed by **MIKHAIL GORBACHEV**.

Gorbachev ("Gorby") inaugurated a period of reform and innovation unprecedented in Soviet history. Under the watchwords of **GLASNOST** ("openness") and **PERESTROIKA** ("restructuring"), Gorbachev encouraged free discussion of issues, reorganized the government on a more democratic basis, and relaxed the system of strict government on a more democratic basis, and relaxed the system of strict censorship and political repression that had prevailed under his predecessors. He also renewed friendly relations with the West. However, the different nationalities of the USSR began to demand greater autonomy, and the republics challenged the central government. Gorbachev resigned as president of the USSR on Dec. 25, 1991. Most of the republics then declared their independence, and at the end of the year eleven of them formed a new Commonwealth of Independent States to replace the old union. Virtually from the October Revolution of 1917, the soviets were dominated by the Communist party. In 1991, after Communist hard-liners attempted a coup and failed, the various republics disbanded the party and seized its property.

LAND

The land can be divided into seven regions. The most characteristic feature of the landscape is its flatness. This is called the Russian Plain. This broad plain, covering most of the European part of the country, extends from the

Baltic Sea to the Ural Mountains and from the shores of Arctic Ocean to the northern coast of the Black Sea. The result of extensive ice age glaciation in the north and water erosion in the south, the plain has an average altitude of 560 feet above sea level. Hills with an elevation of about 1000-1300 feet separate a series of lowland depressions. The plain is bordered in the extreme northwest by the uplands of KARELIA and the mountains of the Kola Peninsula; in the southwest and south by the moderately high Carpathian and Crimean mountain ranges.

The **CAUCASUS MOUNTAINS** are located in the southeast. They rise to a maximum height of 18,510 feet at Mount Elbrus.

The **URAL MOUNTAINS** which extend north/south for 1240 miles, are the traditional boundary between Europe and Asia.

To the east of the Urals lies the enormous expanse of **SIBERIA**. This is divided into a flat and largely swampy West Siberian Plain, which is connected in the south to the Turan Lowland; the Central Siberian Plateau, which is bounded by the Yenisei River on the west and the **LENA RIVER** on the east; and a series of mountain ranges running in an arc between the Lena and the Pacific Ocean.

The Southern Mountains are the highest ranges, lying along the country's southern border. In addition to the Caucasus, they include the Pamirs on the border with Afghanistan, the Tien Shan on the Chinese frontier, and further to the east, the Altai Mountains on the border of Mongolia. The highest elevation is Communism Peak (Garmo Mountain) with an elevation of 24,590 feet located in the Pamirs of Tajikistan.

Jutting out from eastern Siberia for nearly 800 miles is the Kamchtka Peninsula, which along with the Kuril Islands lying to its south forms part of the East Asian volcanic arc.

CULTURE

The large cities have many beautiful buildings. One of the most famous being Moscow's Saint Basil's Cathedral, built in the 16th century. There remain a number of palaces which were once the homes of the ruling czars. The people enjoy a wide variety of cultural activities, such as the ballet (among the world's finest), opera, and the circus. Sometimes the children might watch an ice hockey game played by trained bears!

RESOURCES

The land is rich in raw materials like gold, diamonds, hard coal, oil, natural gas, and uranium. Half the land area is covered by forests where animals like the sable, fox, lynx, and bear live. There is also an area of tundra which is frozen in winter and water-logged in summer. It is here that the reindeer live, being well-adapted for these conditions. The steppe is a treeless grassland of rich, black earth, not unlike the fertile farmlands of the Midwestern United States. The raw materials base of the USSR has shifted eastward. All substantial industrial enterprises were previously state-owned, but now private ownership and joint ownership of industrial enterprises with foreign firms is widespread. In agriculture the USSR was one of the world's largest producer of wheat, potatoes, cotton, and sugar. These and other crops were produced primarily on state farms (sovkhozy) and collective farms (kolkhozy). Private garden plots accounted for a much larger proportion of certain vegetable and dairy products.

Russia

The Russian republic is the largest and most populous of the republics that formerly comprised the Soviet Union. Since the end of 1991, it has been associated with th Commonwealth of Independent States. The population is 147,386,000. The capital of Russia is **MOSCOW**. The Russian republic is the homeland of the ethnic Russians and is the dominant political and economic entity of the commonwealth.

The Russian republic became known as a federation because it includes many smaller entities for ethnic minorities – 16 autonomous republics, 5 autonomous regions, and 10 autonomous areas. Under its president, Boris Yeltsin, the Russian republic played a leading role in the process of democratization and in defining the relationships among the union republics. On Dec. 8, 1991, the Russian republic became one of the founding members of the Commonwealth of Independent States.

LAND

The area of the Russian republic is 6,591,015 square miles. The topography is composed of four clearly defined regions: the Russian Plain, extending form the Arctic Ocean in the north to Caucasus Mountains in the south; the Ural Mountains; West Siberian Plain; and the uplands of East Siberia and the Soviet Far East extending to the Pacific.

CLIMATE

The climate is continental, with cold winters and warm summers. The annual temperature range increase from west to east, with the coldest spot in the Northern Hemisphere in northeast Siberia. Annual rainfall varies from 24 inches in the west to 15 inches in the southeast. Precipitation is abundant along the Pacific coast.

CULTURE

Ethnic Russians account for 83% of the republic's population. They are a Slavic people of the Eastern Orthodox religion. In addition to Moscow, the largest cities are Nizhni Novgorod (formerly Gorky), Samara (formerly Kuibyshev), and Saint Petersburg (formerly Leningrad), and Omsk.

RESOURCES

The republic has important mineral resources, including coal, petroleum, natural gas, iron ore, and other metals. Large manufacturing complexes are centered in its major cities. Agriculture – primarily wheat and cattle raising, is concentrated in the steppes. Transportation is oriented toward railroads. Water transport during the warm season takes place on the Amur, Lena, Ob, Volga, and Yenisei Rivers.

Belarus

Belarus, formerly called Belorussia was until late 1991, one of the republics of the Soviet Union. It borders on Poland on the west, Lithuania and Latvia on the northwest, the Russian republic on the east, and Ukraine on the south. The population is 10,25,000. The capital is **MENSK**.

Belarussians were a distinctive ethnic community under the control of Lithuania, which seized the region in the 14th century. It passed to Poland in 1569 and to Russia in the late 18th century. After World War I, the region was divided between Poland and the new Soviet

Union, where a Belorussian Soviet republic was proclaimed in 1919. In 1939, the Soviet republic annexed the Polish portion, only to have it occupied by the Germans. Belarus has a seat in the United Nations.

LAND

The republic's area is 80,134 square miles The topography of Belarus is a gently rolling plain, with the Pripet Marshes in the south. The land is swampy and requires drainage before it can be cultivated.

CLIMATE

The climate is continental, with cold winters and warm summers.

CULTURE

Belorussians are Slavic and traditionally practice Russian Orthodox Christianity. Their language is similar to Russian and Ukrainian.

RESOURCES

Mineral industries are limited to a modest potash and oil production. Peat is also produced. An important manufacturing industry produces heavy trucks, farm tractors, computers, radio and television sets, motorcycles, and bicycles. Oil refineries at Novopolotsk and Mozyr process oil and natural gas brought in by pipelines. Beef and dairy cattle, flax, grain, sugar beets, and potatoes are the primary agricultural products.

BELARUS

The flag has a bottom and top stripe of white. The middle stripe is red. The majority of white on the flag might have something to do with another name for Belorussia – White Russia.

Ukraine

Ukraine occupies the north shore of the Black Sea and the Sea of Azov; it borders the Russian republic, Moldova, Romania, Hungary, Czechoslovakia, Poland, and Belarus. The area is 233,030 square miles and its population is 51,704,000. The capital is **KIEV**. The name Ukraine means *"border territory"* reflecting its position on the Polish frontier.

By the beginning of the 15th century, most of Ukraine had been absorbed by the Kingdom of Poland-Lithuania. Eastern Ukraine became independent in 1654 but quickly fell under Russian control, becoming known as "Little Russia". Western Ukraine remained Polish until the partitions of Poland 1772-95, when most of it was annexed by Russia. After the 1917 Russian Revolutions, a portion of the western area was restored to Poland. The remainder formed the Ukrainian Soviet Socialist Republic, which became part of the Soviet Union in 1922. Ukrainian separatism was suppressed during the Stalin era, and millions of Ukrainians died of famine during the agricultural collectivization of the early 1930s. During World War II some Ukrainians sided with Germany against the Soviet Union, and in Polish-Ukraine, nationalist guerrillas resisted Soviet rule until the early 1950s. The territory of the Ukrainian SSR was enlarged by the addition of Carpathian-Ukraine taken from Hungary in 1945.

After the failed coup by Communist hardliners in the Moscow government in August 1991, Ukraine declared its independence. Ukraine then joined with Russia, Belarus, Moldova, Armenia, Azerbaijan, and the five Central Asian republics in the Commonwealth of Independent States.

LAND

Most of Ukraine is physically part of the Russian plain; the only uplands are the segment of the Carpathian Mountains in the southwest; and the Crimean Mountains along the southern coast of the Crimea. The Dnepr, the Dnestr, and the Donets Rivers all flow from northwest to southeast. Most of the region is covered with fertile soil.

CLIMATE

The climate is continental, with winter temperatures hitting 19° F. Precipitation ranges from about 28 inches in the northwest to about 12 inches in the southeast.

CULTURE

The Ukrainian people are a Slavic group, whose language is related to Russian and Polish. Russians represent 21% of the population. The Ukrainians are mostly of the Orthodox faith. The principal cities in addition to Kiev are Donetsk, Lviv, and Odessa.

RESOURCES

Rich in mineral resources, Ukraine produces large amounts of coal and iron-ore. The republic has a substantial output of steel, manganese, and titanium ores. Manufacturing is highly developed, producing a wide range of machinery and industrial equipment and chemicals. Ukraine is also an important agricultural region (known as the "breadbasket"), producing large grain and sugar beet crops. Irrigation is being expanded to increase yields. In 1986, an accident at the **CHERENOBYL** nuclear power plant north of Kiev spread harmful radiation across Ukraine and into neighboring countries, forcing the evacuation of 135,000 people from the area.

Kazakhstan

Kazakhstan extends from Siberia in the north to Central Asia in the south, and from the Caspian Sea in the west to the Chinese border in the east. The population is 16,690,300. The republic's capital is **ALMA-ATA**.

Kazakhstan was a sparsely populated region of nomadic herdsman until the Russians gained control in the mid-19th century. After the Bolshevik Revolution, the region was constituted in 1920 as the Kirghiz ASSR, the name Kirghiz having been mistakenly applied to the Kazakh in the past. It was renamed Kazak (the original spelling) in 1925, and in 1936, its status was raised to that of a full Soviet republic.

In 1991, Kazakhstan adopted an economic reform plan calling for the privatization of government-owned housing, shops, and small industrial enterprise and encouraged investment by foreign companies. In August 1991, the Kazakh declared the independence of the republic. On Dec. 13, 1991, Kazakhstan associated herself with the newly formed Commonwealth of Independent States.

LAND

Kazakhstan is 1,048,840 square miles. The topography of Kazakhstan is varied, largely lowland and upland plains and rolling hill country. In the northeast the republic reaches the Altai Mountains, and in the southeast it extends to the Tien Shan. The region is drained by the Irtysh, Syr Darya, Ural, Tobol, and the Ishim Rivers. Kazakhstan includes part of the Caspian and Aral Seas and all of Lake Balkhash.

CLIMATE

The climate becomes drier from north to south changing into desert with irrigated oases in the south. Annual precipitation varies from 9 to 20 inches.

CULTURE

The Kazakh constitute only 42% of the population. The Kazakh are a nomadic stock-herding group of Muslim religion and Turkic language, only 25% reside in the cities. Ethnic Russians and Ukrainians provide most of the industrial labor force.

RESOURCES

Kazakhstan is rich in mineral resources and raw materials. These have given rise to a highly diversified mineral industry. The region has large coal basins which provide fuel for an important electric-power industry. Kazakhstan is a major producer of iron ore, chromite, copper, lead, zinc, bauxite, and other metals. Petroleum is now being produced. The republic has extensive agricultural land, and produces significant amounts of grain. The Baikonur space-launching center is in Kazakhstan.

RECIPES

Borscht

8 beef bouillon cubes
6 cups water
2 tablespoons butter
1/2 large onion, chopped
1 bayleaf
1 clove garlic
1 1/2 cup tomato juice
1/2 can sauerkraut and juice
1 cup beets, cut up
1 cup potatoes, cut up
1 cup carrots or celery, cut up
6 peppercorns

Combine bouillon cubes, water, butter, onion, bayleaf, garlic, and peppercorns to make a broth. Simmer about 2 hours. Add carrots, tomato juice, and sauerkraut. Then add beets, potatoes, and more water if needed. Cook until potatoes are done. Serve with large spoonfuls of sour cream in each bowl. For a complete Russian meal, serve with black bread and cream cheese.

Ukrainian Noodle Kigel

1/2 pound medium noodles (4 cups)
6 tablespoons butter
3 eggs, beaten
1 1/4 teaspoons salt
1 cup cottage cheese

Cook the noodles in 8 cups of boiling water (add one 1 teaspoon salt to the water) for ten minutes until tender. Remove from heat, and drain. Add a little water, and stir in 4 tablespoons butter, eggs, salt, and cottage cheese.

Preheat oven to 375-degrees. Melt the remaining butter in a greased 8" x 8" baking dish. Heat the dish for 30 seconds over low heat. Pour in the noodle mixture, filling the entire dish. Bake for 50 minutes until golden brown on top.

Russian Sugar Cookies***

1/4 pound unsalted whipped butter
1/4 cup powdered sugar
1 1/4 cups flour
1 tablespoon orange juice
powdered sugar for dusting cookies

Allow the butter to soften in a deep bowl at room temperature. Whip with a fork. Add the sugar and flour. Blend well. Add the orange juice and mix, making a firm dough. Roll bits of dough into coils 3 1/2 inches long. On a cookie sheet, shape the sticks into S-shapes. Bake in a 350-degree oven for 15 minutes until lightly browned. When completely cool, dust generously with powdered sugar.

VOCABULARY

Russian airline – *Aeroflot*
guitar-like musical instrument – *balalaika*
Communist group led by Lenin – *Bolsheviks*
famous ballet company – *Bolshoi*
vegetable soup (beets and cabbage) – *borscho*
eggs of the sturgeon fish – *caviar*
Soviet astronaut – *cosmonaut*
traditional drink (rye beer) – *Kvass*
series of wooden dolls which fit inside each other – *matryoshka*
organization for young people – *Pioneers*
truth, newspaper published by the Communist Party – *Pravda*
babushka – *kerchief worn on the head of the grandmother*
artificial satellite – *Sputnik*
three-horse sled – *troika*
title of emperor in Old Russian – *Tsar or Czar*
fur hat with ear flaps – *ushanka*
national drink, distilled from rye – *vodka*

ACTIVITIES

Make a Matroyshka (Russian Doll)

All around Russia, children enjoy playing with their Matroyshka. They are different-size wooden dolls which fit into each other. Most have five to six dolls. The name is taken from the word meaning *grandmother*. Each matroyshka has a *babushka* (a kerchief on the head).

toilet paper roll
paint, markers or crayons
glue
stapler

1. Cut a white piece of paper 1 1/2"x 1 1/2" and glue or tape to the bottom of the toilet paper roll. Cut the big matroyshka out (shown on bottom) and color. Glue around the roll.

2. Cut and color the other two and make into a tube by a staple or tape. The small matroyshka will fit into the medium matroyshka and the medium one will fit into the big one.

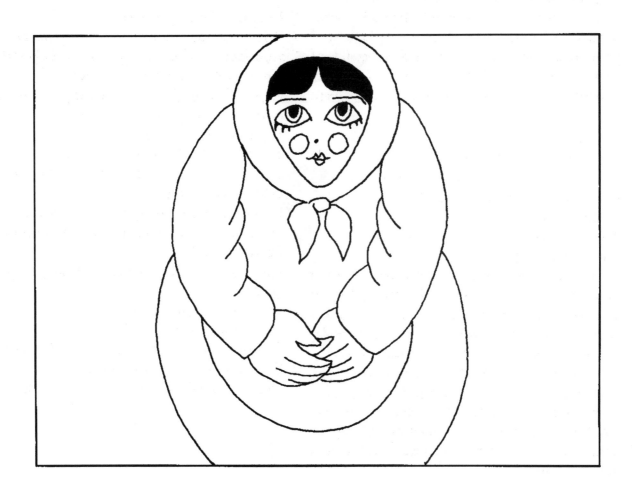

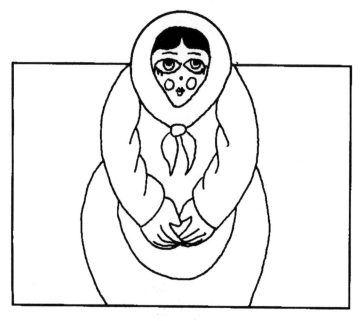

Bibliography

NORTH AMERICA
Stein, Conrad R. *Enchantment of the World – Mexico*. Chicago: Children's Press, 1984.
Shepherd, Jenifer. *Enchantment of the World – Canada*. Chicago: Children's Press, 1987.

THE CARIBBEAN AND CENTRAL AMERICA
————. *Haiti in Pictures*. Minneapolis, MN: Lerner Publications Company, 1987.
Hubley, John and Penny. *A Family in Jamaica*. Minneapolis, MN: Lerner Publications Company, 1985.
Anthony, Suzanne. *Places and Peoples of the World – West Indies*. New York: Chelsea House Publishers, 1989.
Vazquez, Ana B. *Enchantment of the World – Panama*. Chicago: Children's Press, 1991.

SOUTH AMERICA
Cross, Wilbur and Susanna. *Enchantment of the World – Brazil*. Chicago: Children's Press, 1984.
Hintz, Martin. *Enchantment of the World – Argentina*. Chicago: Children's Press, 1985.
————. *Columbia in Pictures*. Minneapolis, MN: Lerner Publications Company, 1987.
————. *Peru in Pictures*. Minneapolis, MN: Lerner Publications Company, 1987.
Hintz, Martin. *Enchantment of the World – Chile*. Chicago: Children's Press, 1985.

EAST ASIA
————. *The World and Southeast Asia*. Sidney, Australia. Oswald L. Ziegler Enterprises Pty., 1972.
Knowlton, Marylee and Sachner, Mark J. *Children of the World – Malaysia*. Milwaukee: Gareth Stevens Publishing, 1987.

AUSTRALIA AND THE SOUTH PACIFIC
Lepthien, Emilie U. *Enchantment of the World – Australia*. Chicago: Children's Press, 1982
Jacobs, Judy. *Indonesia, A Nation of Islands*. Minneapolis, MN: Dillon Press, Inc., 1990.

THE INDIAN SUB-CONTINENT
Sarin, Amita. Vohra. *India – An Ancient Land, A New Nation*. Minneapolis, MN: Dillon Press Inc., 1984.
Lye, Keith. *Take a Trip to India*. London: Franklin Watts, 1982.
Lye, Keith. *Take a Trip to Pakistan*. London: Franklin Watts, 1984.

THE MIDDLE EAST
Fox, Mary Virginia. *Enchantment of the World – Iran*. Chicago: Children's Press, 1991.
Foster, Leila Merrell. *Enchantment of the World – Iraq*. Chicago: Children's Press, 1991.
Mulloy, Martin. *Kuwait*. New York: Chelsea House Publishers, 1988.
Jones, Helen Hinckley. *Enchantment of the World – Israel*. Chicago: Children's Press, 1986.
Feinstein, Steve. *Turkey in Pictures*. Minneapolis, MN: Lerner Publications Company, 1988.

AFRICA
Allen, William D. and Jennings, Jerry E. *Africa*. Grand Rapids, MI: The Fideler Company, 1981.
Murphy, E. Jefferson. *Understanding Africa*. New York: Thomas Y. Crowell, 1978.
Cross, Wilbur. *Enchantment of the World – Egypt*. Chicago: Children's Press, 1982.
Brill, Marlene Targ. *Enchantment of the World – Libya*. Chicago: Children's Press, 1987.
Stein, R. Conrad. *Enchantment of the World – South Africa*. Chicago: Children's Press, 1986.
Laure, Jason. *Enchantment of the World – Angola*. Chicago: Children's Press, 1990.

EUROPE
Cross, Esther and Wilbur. *Enchantment of the World – Spain*. Chicago: Children's Press, 1985.
Stein, R. Conrad. *Enchantment of the World – Italy*. Chicago: Children's Press, 1987.
Hintz, Martin. *Enchantment of the World – Switzerland*. Chicago: Children's Press, 1986.
Moss, Peter and Palmer, Thelma. *Enchantment of the World – France*. Chicago: Children's Press, 1986.
Bruzzone, Catherine. *German for Children*. Lincolnwood, IL: Passport Books, 1993.
Hargrove, Jim. *Enchantment of the World – Germany*. Chicago: Children's Press, 1991.
Greene, Carol. *Enchantment of the World – England*. Chicago: Children's Press, 1982.
Sutherland, Dorothy B. *Enchantment of the World – Scotland*. Chicago: Children's Press, 1985.

Sutherland, Dorothy B. *Enchantment of the World – Wales*. Chicago: Children's Press, 1987.
Fradin, Dennis B. *Enchantment of the World – The Republic of Ireland*. Chicago: Children's Press, 1984.
Hintz, Martin. *Enchantment of the World – Norway*. Chicago: Children's Press, 1982.
Hintz, Martin. *Enchantment of the World – Finland*. Chicago: Children's Press, 1983.
Elliot, Drossoula Vassiliou and Sloan. *We Live in Greece*. New York: The Bookwright Press, 1984.
Stein, R. Conrad. *Enchantment of the World – Greece*. Chicago: Children's Press, 1987.
Greene, Carol. *Enchantment of the World – Poland*. Chicago: Children's Press, 1983.

THE RUSSIAN REGIONS

Clark, Mary Jane Behrends. *The Commonwealth of Independent States*. Brookfield, CT: The Millbrook Press, 1992.

ILLUSTRATIONS

Huber, Richard. *Treasury of Fantastic and Mythological Creatures*. New York: Dover Publications, Inc., 1981.
Petrie, Flinders. *Decorative Symbols and Motifs for Artists and Craftspeople*. New York: Dover Publications, Inc., 1986.
Boas, Franz. *Primitive Art*. New York: Dover Publications, Inc., 1986.
Devereux, Eve. *Flags of the World*. New York, Crescent Books, 1992.

RECIPES

Shapiro, Rebecca. *Wide World Cookbook for Girls and Boys*. Boston: Little, Brown & Company, 1962.***
Shapiro, Rebecca. *A Whole World of Cooking*. Boston: Little, Brown & Company, 1972.****
Note: Where a recipe included in the text of any particular section was adapted from a written source, that source has been marked with an asterisk (*).

ACTIVITIES

Boni, Margaret Bradford. *Fireside Book of Folk Songs*. New York: Simon and Schuster, 1947.
Caballero, Jane. *Art Projects for Young Children*. Atlanta, GA: Humanics Limited, 1990.
Comins, Jeremy. *Latin American Crafts and Their Cultural Backgrounds*. New York: Lothrop, Lee & Shepard Co, 1974.
Colgin, Mary Lou. *Chants for Children*. New York: Colgin Publishing Co., 1982. A collection of rhymes and ditties; animals, abc's, nursery rhymes, holidays, and seasons.*
D'Amato, Alex and Janet. *African Crafts for You to Make*. New York: Julie Messner, 1969.
Fichter, George S. *American Indian Music and Musical Instruments*. New York: David McKay Company, Inc., 19878.
Hunt, Sarah E. *Games and Sports The World Around*. New York: The Ronald Press Company, 1964.
Harbin, E.O. *Games of Many Nations*. Nashville: Abingdon Press, 1965.
Keene, Frances W. *Fun Around the World*. New York: The Seashore Press, 1955.
Lofgren, Ulf. *Swedish Toys, Dolls, and Gifts You Can Make Yourself*. New York: Collins + World, 1978.
McCarty, Janet R. and Peterson, Betty J. *Craft Fun Easy-to-Do Projects with Simple Materials*. Racine, WI: Western Publishing Company, Inc. 1973.
Parish, Peggy. *Let's Be Indians*. New York: Harper & Row, 1962.
Pflug, Betsy. *Funny Bags*. Princeton, NJ: D. Van Ndstrand Company, 1968.
Purdy, Susan and Sandak, Cass R. *A Civilization Project Book Eskimos*. New York: Franklin Watts, 1982.
Robinson, Adjai. *Singing Tales of Africa*. New York: Charles Scribner's Sons, 1974.
Soleillant, Claude. *Activities and Projects. India in Color*. New York: Sterling Publishing Co., 1977.
St. Tamara. *Asian Crafts*. New York: The Lion Press, 1970.
Temko, Florence. *Folk Crafts for World Friendship*. Garden City, NY: Doubleday & Company, Inc., 1976.
Winn, Marie. *The Fireside Book of Children's Songs*. New York: Simon and Schuster, 1966.

— Suggested Resources —

LITERATURE

A Story, A Story. An African tale retold and illustrated by Haley, Gail E. Hartford: Connecticut Printers, Inc., 1970. The 'spider story' tells how small defenseless men or animals outwit others and succeed against great odds.

Big Blue Marble Atlas. Brown, Paula S. and Garrison, Robert L. New York: Ideals Publishing Corp., 1980. An atlas of the earth including information about outer space.*

Children's Art. Goldin, Rafael and Alla. The Foundation of Children's History, Art and Culture, SOS Villages, 1981. Children's art from around the world.

Children Around the World. Troop. Miriam, New York: Grosset and Dunlap, Inc., 1964. Sketches include children in various countries illustrated in water color.

Children of the North Pole (Greenland). Herrmanns, Ralph. NY: Harcourt, Brace & World, 1963. Unexpected help comes to little Serkok who has lost his father's kayak while hunting for seals.

Children of Viet-nam. Tran-Khanh-Tuyet. Washington, D.C: Indochina Resource Center. A picture storybook.

The Five Chinese Brothers. Bishop, Clair Huchet and Wise, Kurt. Coward-McCann, Inc., 1938. A folktale, rich in wit and humor.

It's a Small World. Walt Disney Productions, USA: Western Publishing Co., Inc., 1968. The story of an orphan boy's journey through Disneyland.

Johnny-Cake. Jacobs, Joseph. New York: G.P. Putnam's Sons, 1933. An English fairy tale.

Josephine's Imagination. Dobrin, Arnold. New York: Scholastic Book Services, 1975. A young Haitian girl uses her imagination while walking to the market with her mother.

Little Toot on the Mississippi. Gramotky, Hardie. New York: G.P. Putnam's Sons, 1973. When the Mississippi River goes into flood, adventure-loving Little Toot sets out on a daring rescue mission.

Madeline's Rescue. Bemelman, Ludwig. New York: The Viking Press, 1953. Rhymed text about the story of Madeline's rescue and her rescuer, Genevive (French).

Saint George and the Dragon. Hodge, Margaret. Boston: Little, Brown and Co., 1984. A segment from Spencer's "The Fairie Queen" is told.

Nine Days to Christmas. Ets, Marie Hall and Labastida, Aurora. New York: The Viking Press, 1959. Ceci, a little Mexican girl is excited because she is old enough to buy a pinata for her first Christmas pasada.

The Story of Ping. Flack, Marjorie and Wises, Kurt. New York: The Viking Press, 1933. Ping runs away from his houseboat of the Yangtze River (Chinese).

RECORDS

Aloha Oe. Masaaki Hirao and the Waikiki Hawaiians. Honolulu: Waikiki Records.

A Child's Introduction to Spanish. Montalban, Carlos. Hudson Productions, Inc. Distributed by: New York: Affiliated Publishers, 1961.

Classical Indian Music. Yahudi Menuhin. New York: London Records Inc.

The Guru (sitar). Ustad Khan. New York: R.C.A., 1969.

It's a Small World. Walt Disney Productions, U.S.A.: Western Publishing Co., 1968.

Missa Luba. Congonese Boy's Choir. Baudouin.

The Religious Sounds of Tibet (Buddhist hymns recorded in Tibetan monasteries in Northern India). West Germany: Teldec Telefunken Decca Schallplatten, Ges. mbH.

Russian Folk Songs. V. Andreyev Russian Folk Orchestra. U.S.S.R.

Travellin' with Ella Jenkins. New York: Folkways Records and Service Corp., 1979.

Yellow Bird. Jamaica Duke and the Mento Swingers. Jamaica, West Indies: Dynamic Sounds Recording Co. Ltd.

Self-Esteem Activities

Giving Children From Birth to Six the Freedom to Grow

An gie Rose, Ph.D.　　　　　　**Lynn Weiss, Ph.D.**

Self-Esteem Activities
Giving Children From Birth to Six the Freedom to Grow
By Angie Rose, Ph.D. and Lynn Weiss, Ph.D.
Developed by two of the nation's foremost child development experts, these nurturing activities are arranged to parallel the five steps of a child's emotional development: trust, self-awareness, self-esteem, power, and self-control. An invaluable handbook of activities for parents and children (ages birth to six years).

046-4　　　　　　pp176　　　　　　$16.95

Can Piaget Cook?

Science Activities

By Mary Anne Christenberry, Ph.D. and Barbara C. Stevens, Ed.D.

This delightful book emphasizes the importance of food and the steps involved in the cooking process. These activities incorporate math and science skills that teach lessons about measurement and following directions.

078-2   **pp160**   **$15.95**

Science
AIR AND SPACE
Folder Games for the Classroom

Adapted for preschool by Leah M. Hughes
based on AVIATION AND SPACE by Jane Caballero-Hodges, Ph.D.

Science Air & Activities
Folder Games for the Classroom
By Jane A. Caballero, Ph.D.
Adapted for preschool by Leah M. Hughes

"What do you wear on the moon? what do you eat in space?" These are but two of the intriguing questions addressed in this book, a "First of its kind" manual, that provides teachers, students and space enthusiasts with a unique overview of aerospace education. Students will follow aerospace history from kites and balloons to helicopters, gliders, and airplanes and through to today's satellied and the Space Shuttle.

158-4   **pp168**   **$16.95**

Reading Resource Book

Mary Jett-Simpson, Ph.D.

Parents & Beginning Reading

Reading Resorce Book
Parents & Beginning Reading
By Mary Jett-Simpson, Ph.D.

How to introduce children to reading, virtually from birth. Includes an overview of development, reading skills games, lists of resources, and an excellent section of books evaluatins for young readers. Invaluable for teachers, parents, and other child-care providers.

044-8   **pp240**   **$16.95**

ORDER TODAY! 1-800-874-8844

ORDER
to insure that you receive your order promptly, please follow these guidelines:
1. Please make check payable to Humanics Learning and enclose it with your order.
2. Any order for less than $100.00 must be accompanied by payment in full.
3. Any order over $100.00 must be accompanied by payment, your credit card information or an institutional purchase order.
4, Postage is predetermined by the Shipping and Handling Schedule on the order form. Please include proper postage with your order.
5. Special Same Day Telephone Service!
Just call Humanics Learning telephone sales operator toll free at (800) 874-8844 and we will ship your order in 48 hours.

REVIEW
Administrative review prior to adopting for textbook use:
1. If the publication or publications are adopted and an order is placed with Humanics within-forty-five days, there will be no charge for the particular book in question.
2. Those books which are not adopted and for which no order is placed must be returned in suitable condition for resale within forty-five days of the date of shipment, or you will be billed for them.

RETURN
Satisfaction guaranteed or your money back! Enjoy and read any of our books for 30 days. If you do not enjoy our material, return it for credit. You pay only shipping charges and a 15% restocking fee. Returned

material must be accompanied by the original invoice number and have been purchased within 30 days. Books must be in re-salable condition or Humanics will return the books to you.

Shipping and Handling

Up to $100.00 net add $3.00
$10.01 to $20.00 net add $4.00
$20.01 to $40.00 net add $5.00
$40.01 to $70.00 net add $7.00
$70.01 to $100.00 net add $10.00
$100.01 to $125.00 net add $12.00
$125.01 to $150.00 net add $15.00
$150.01 to $175.00 net add $18.00
$175.01 to $200.00 net add $21.00

Orders over $200.00 vary depending on Method of shipment.

Minimum shipping charge is $3.00.
Prices subject to change without notice

ORDER FORM

QUANTITY ORDERED	ORDER NO.	BOOKTITLE	UNIT PRICE	TOTAL PRICE
		SUBTOTAL		
		GEORGIA RESIDENTS 8% SALES TAX		
		ADD SHIPPING AND HANDLING		
		TOTAL ORDER		

IN GA (404) 874-2176
OR FAX 1-404-874-1976

☐ Payment Enclosed
☐ Institutional Purchase
order No. _____

☐ Bill my Credit Card
When using a credit card, please check proper box and give appropriate card and number information
☐ MasterCard ☐ Visa   Exp. date _____
Credit Card Number
☐☐☐☐☐☐☐☐☐☐☐☐☐☐☐☐

Master Card Interbank No. _____

X_____
(authorized signature order must be signed)

SEND TO:
HUMANICS LEARNING
P.O. BOX 7400
ATLANTA, GA 30357-0400
SHIP TO:

NAME _____
ADDRESS_____
_____
CITY/STATE _____
ZIP _____
PHONE (____) _____